A 5TH AVENUE CHRISTMAS

Tracy Cozzens

ZEBRA BOOKS
Kensington Publishing Corp.
http://www.kensingtonbooks.com

ZEBRA BOOKS are published by

Kensington Publishing Corp.
850 Third Avenue
New York, NY 10022

All Kensington titles, imprints and distributed lines are available at special quantity discounts for bulk purchases for sales promotion, premiums, fund-raising, educational or institutional use.

Special book excerpts or customized printings can also be created to fit specific needs. For details, write or phone the office of the Kensington Special Sales Manager: Kensington Publishing Corp., 850 Third Avenue, New York, NY 10022. Attn. Special Sales Department. Phone: 1-800-221-2647.

Zebra and the Z logo Reg. U.S. Pat. & TM Off.

First Printing: October 2003
10 9 8 7 6 5 4 3 2 1

Printed in the United States of America

To my agent, Barbara Collins Rozenberg,
for making this book possible

One

"You have to keep your eye on your quarry, Meryl."

"I am." Meryl watched as her father peered through his binoculars toward the grasses edging the meadow.

As far as Meryl was concerned, her quarry wasn't the kind with feathers, but the owner of a vast empire—the man standing right beside her, his cheeks ruddy from the morning cold. Eager for an opportunity to discuss her future, she had left the warmth of their country home to join her father on his traditional Thanksgiving morning shoot. Mr. McDougall and Mr. Whitney, guests who had joined them this weekend, had followed their setter to a small rise several yards away. That gave Meryl a precious few minutes to speak to him.

Mr. Carrington lowered his field glasses and studied her. "You certainly seem less than enthusiastic about today's shoot. You could have stayed behind. Your mother would have welcomed your help with the meal."

"She doesn't need me, even with the servants taking the day off. There are four married women in that house, each of them with opinions on trivial matters. Mrs. McDougall considers herself an expert on cooking turkeys, and Mrs. Whitney has definite opinions about place settings, and Clara is discussing baby food, and—"

He held up his hand. "Quiet now. I see movement. Look."

He pushed the field glasses at her and she reluctantly accepted them.

"Keep an eye on the flock just to the left of the berry bush." Lifting his rifle, he began to take aim.

"Now, Jasper." The wiry golden retriever galloped toward the bush, sending a flock of grouse skyward.

"All right, I confess," Meryl blurted out.

Mr. Carrington jerked, his shot going wide. He lowered his gun and glared at her. "Confess what? What is it this time?" He sighed. "Never mind. I already know."

"You know how much I love working at the company," she began, hoping she would choose the right words. "It's all I've dreamt about for years. But I never expected it to be so dull—"

His eyes sparkled over his handlebar mustache, now almost entirely gray. "I told you women don't have a head for business. You were silly to think you'd like it."

"You wouldn't like it either if you spent all day filing papers," she said dryly.

Giving up on tracking the grouse, he set the butt of his rifle on the ground, his gloved hands wrapped around the barrel. "It's important work, and not below my daughter."

"It's been a good place to start, of course. But I'm ready for something much more demanding. I already know my way around the business. I have a degree now, from a respected college—"

"Bryn Mawr. A girl's school."

"—where I took an exhaustive course of study in history, languages, and mathematics. I think I'm well-suited to handle the Westgate acquisition."

His eyes opened and he focused fully on her at last. "Westgate? You think you're capable of managing the purchase of a railroad?"

She nodded vigorously. "Definitely. I'm ready, Father. I have studied all the reports, even drafted a purchase proposal for Westgate's board of directors. Perhaps you could read it today."

"Meryl—"

"Father, please." She laid her hand on the sleeve of his heavy shooting jacket. "You don't have a son. I'm the best you have. I promise I won't let you down."

He patted her hand, his eyes growing distant. "You are right about that. I had dreamed of grooming a son to take my place. Not that I haven't enjoyed every one of my daughters, including you, Pumpkin."

"Your 'Pumpkin' can be just like a son. Do the same things."

He sighed deeply, then patted her shoulder. "Meryl, you needn't worry about becoming a businesswoman. A pretty lass like you should only be concerned with finding a nice fellow and settling down. Then your mother can finally stop fretting," he added wryly. "You don't know how lucky you are to be the youngest of my five girls. Hannah and Lily—your mother would be satisfied with nothing less than titles for those two. Lily's fellow lacked the title, but Pauline made up for that with her marquess."

"Yes, but the company—" Meryl interrupted, trying to get the conversation back on track.

"The company is a fine place for you to meet a man of good quality. Hard-working, clever. A man who will treat you properly. Why, he could even be the boy next door. Speaking of which, guess who's coming this way." He looked past her with a smile of triumph.

Dread filled Meryl's chest. The matchmaking had begun. Now that she had graduated, she could no longer avoid it. Whomever her parents had set their sights on for her, she would have none of it. She hadn't struggled through mathematics simply to put her mind on a shelf and raise baby after baby.

The newcomer's voice rang through the clear morning air. "Richard, good morning. Olympia told me I'd find you here."

Mr. Carrington looked genuinely happy. "Joseph. You're back from Mexico."

Joe. Meryl heaved a sigh of relief. It was just Joe. Nothing to worry about. She had known him since they were children—when he had yanked on her pigtails and tormented her mercilessly.

The son of her father's business partner, Joe Hammond could be a royal pain, but at least he was a known quantity. Even if she hadn't seen him for four years while he had been managing the Atlantic-Southern Railroad's construction contract in Mexico.

Still, her nerves tensed as she braced herself to engage in the verbal sparring that was sure to begin. She turned around.

And found herself gazing at a stranger.

Don't be silly. It's Joe. He's just . . . older. And he seemed taller and broader, too. His face, always familiar to her, remained the same—almost. Except for a subtle roughness that had never been there before. He had the same square-jawed face she remembered, the same sandy hair that waved slightly despite pomade designed to tame it. Yet small crinkles lurked at the corners of his eyes as he smiled, and the shadow of a beard peppered his cheeks.

His sharp green eyes gazed at her in open curiosity. "Meryl? Is that you under all those layers and that red nose?"

"Don't be silly," she shot back, wishing her voice didn't sound so breathless. "I'm dressed appropriately for a November morning." Still, she rather wished she wore something more becoming than her heavy woolen cape and a scarf that covered her chin and hid her one vanity—her long, golden hair. "What else would I wear, a frilly dance-hall dress so my limbs would freeze?"

"Meryl," her father reprimanded, but Joe just smiled.

"As sassy and bratty as always," Joe said with irritating good humor. "And still speaking of things you ought to know nothing about."

"What is that supposed to mean?" Meryl planted herself in front of him and glared up at him.

"You've never even seen a dance-hall girl. What could you possibly know about them?"

"Oh, right," she said derisively. "While in Mexico you frequented saloons filled with them, no doubt."

He arched a sandy-hued eyebrow. "No doubt."

He turned back to her father, effectively putting her in her place and cutting her from the conversation at the same time. He began telling her father how the construction project had gone. The new line was in operation, taking passengers from the Baja Peninsula to Mexico City, through San Diego and lower California via another railroad, Westgate.

Meryl stewed, annoyed by Joe's composure and easy ability to discuss important business with her father. Had he really spent a lot of time in saloons, with dance-hall girls? How—*bohemian* of him. How rude and classless. How lucky of him to be on his own doing whatever he damn well pleased!

Oh, how she hated him at that moment. Almost as much as she longed to *be* him.

"We have plenty of time to discuss business," her father said. "It's good to see you again, Joe. Very good. I didn't think your family would make it this weekend."

"It's only me, sorry to say. Mother is still visiting friends in Italy. I hope you don't mind my sharing Thanksgiving dinner with you before I return to the city. I knew you would want a full report as soon as possible, now that the line is completed."

Her father gave Joe a companionable slap on the back. "That's my boy. Always thinking of work."

"Just like your girl," Meryl muttered, annoyed beyond bearing that her father valued traits in his former partner's son that he dismissed in her.

Mr. Carrington's voice dropped conspiratorially. "But, Joe. My baby daughter's silly comments notwithstanding, let's have no talk of dance-hall girls around Olympia. She still thinks you're the little boy who used to borrow books from my library and forget to return them."

"I did that?" Joe looked at him with wide-eyed innocence.

"You know you did," Meryl cut in. "You were always underfoot, running in and out of our house as if you lived there. I certainly hope you're not planning to move into our home now that you're back in New York."

He stared at her. "To be honest, dearest Meryl, I hadn't considered that possibility. I would certainly never impose myself—"

"We would be overjoyed to have you," her father said.

Meryl groaned, why had she suggested such a thing? Her father already thought of him as the son he never had. It was so unfair!

"Let's just get through this weekend," Joe said, his eyes narrowed on Meryl. "See if I survive your daughter's gracious hospitality."

"You have to excuse her," Mr. Carrington said with a weary air. "She's not exactly pleased with her role at the company—or with me."

"She's working for you? You're jesting."

Her father lowered his voice, as if he thought she wouldn't be able to hear him. "I gave her a small clerical position in contracts and accounts. She's doing well, according to her manager."

"Smithson, is it?"

"That's right. Talk is she has a tendency to pester him with questions and suggestions. But Smithson never complains."

"About the boss's daughter? Not too surprising."

"I'm not just the boss's daughter," Meryl protested, indignant at the thought that Smithson—that any of them—would view her differently because of her relationship to the company's owner. If she had been any other woman, she probably would have an easier time trying to succeed in a workplace run by men. There were, after all, a few dedicated ladies—considered spinsters by the men—who loved their careers as much as any man.

"Remarkable." Joe studied her as if she were a bug under glass. "I knew she had aspirations, but I'm a little surprised it's been carried this far. I'm not sure, if I were you, I would allow my tender daughter into such a . . . *frenetic* atmosphere." His eyes twinkled with silent amusement.

Nevertheless, Mr. Carrington's brow creased. He was actually giving Joe's blather due consideration! Yet she was certain Joe himself only half believed his words.

She shot Joe a withering look. He was nothing but a fly in the ointment of her plan. Turning her back to him, she directed her comments to her father. "I can do anything *he* can. I could have managed the Mexico contract, if I hadn't still been in school."

Joe barked out a laugh. "Oh, really?"

"Really."

"By God, you have nerve." Joe shook his head, wry amusement etched on his bold features. "I can't believe I'm hearing this. I shouldn't be surprised. You've never been very sensible. I remember when you hid in the coal bin to prove you could tolerate the dark—and got stuck. Took three grown men to free you."

Her father chuckled. "She looked like a native when we finally pulled her out, covered with soot from head to toe."

"Didn't you have to wash her off outside?" Joe asked.

"Olympia wouldn't hear of her coming inside like that." Both men laughed at the memory.

Meryl wanted to scream. She glared at her tormentor. Oh, how she hated Joe! He was the one who had bet her she couldn't stand the dark—a point he conveniently forgot to mention. "I was only seven! That incident has nothing to do with what I'm capable of now, Father."

"Yet Joe has a point," her father said. He cupped her chin in his gloved hand. "Business isn't a young lady's purview. You should be enjoying your youth dreaming of marriage to the right young gentleman, not listening to stuffy old fellows discuss railroad mergers and steel supplies."

Meryl took a step back, breaking the contact. How she wanted her father to pay attention, to see with his own eyes that she was just as capable as

Joe. Besides, Joe was so ridiculously confident, she longed to take him down a peg or two. Or more. All the way to the bottom.

Inspiration struck, a way to prove herself right here, right now. "I can prove to you, Father—to you both," she amended, glaring at Joe. "I can compete against men like Joe."

"How do you propose accomplishing such a wonder?" Joe asked.

"I can take down more grouse than he can. Send Jasper to flush that copse. Whoever bags the most grouse, wins."

At her proposal, Joe resumed his maddening chuckle, a sound as smooth as honey.

Mr. Carrington frowned. "Are you certain, Meryl? Joe is an excellent shot."

"So am I. *You* taught me, remember?" she patted his arm. "And I'm a fast learner, capable of learning anything you care to teach me, especially about the company."

He sighed. "Everything needn't be a contest, Pumpkin."

Meryl turned to Joe. "Are you up for it, or do you lack the courage to take me on?"

"A man would need mountains of courage to take you on," Joe said dryly. "But, lucky for me, I know you, and you don't intimidate me in the least, Pest."

Pest! He remembered his childhood name for her—and had actually used it! "Then prepare to be trounced, Dodo Bird," she shot back, using her own name for him. The name sounded silly now, and she fought back a smile.

He narrowed his eyes at her, but she caught a flicker of amusement in their emerald depths. She hadn't remembered his eyes being quite so green. They stared at each other in silence while her father reloaded his Winchester and handed it to Joe.

As he checked the barrel and heft of the rifle, Joe gave her another chance to back out—as if she would. "Are you sure about this? I spent a lot of time hunting fowl in Mexico."

"Time you should have spent working, no doubt." Settling her own rifle on her shoulder, she took aim. She was considered quite a good shot, even though the only shooting team she had done in college had been on the archery. He had no idea how good she was.

Joe sighed. "If you insist." He prepared to take aim.

With a sharp bark, Jasper again sent the grouse scuttling from the bushes where they had sought refuge. A dozen fat birds burst forth, their furious flapping sending them skyward en masse.

Before they scattered out of reach, Meryl picked off two with clean shots. She lowered her gun. "Not one, but two. What do you think of that?" she asked triumphantly, grinning at Joe.

He lowered his own rifle and nodded. "Impressive. Not bad, for a girl."

Girl. He still saw her as a girl. "Better than you."

He tucked his rifle under his arm and began to pick his way through the brush toward the fallen birds. Jasper already returned with one in his jaw which he deposited at her father's feet, while Meryl went to claim her own game.

When she returned to her father and Joe, she saw that five fowl had been taken down.

"Five! Father, did you shoot, too?" Meryl asked.

"Not me. Joe. Sorry, Pumpkin, but he took down three."

A sick feeling filled her stomach. No matter how well she did, she could never measure up. She would never convince the men she could contribute.

Gathering her composure, she turned to Joe. "Well, I suppose I ought to congratulate you, then." She thrust out her gloved hand.

He took it and squeezed gently. "No hard feelings. You have the right instincts. You need to learn caution—and not be so emotional. You were thinking more about beating me than shooting fowl."

"Telling a female not to be emotional. Good luck on that score, Joe," her father said ruefully.

Joe nodded, that annoying smile of victory still on his face. "That's the problem with women in business. I haven't met a single one that doesn't let her heart lead her—to the company's detriment."

Her father frowned. But to Meryl's surprise, he took her side. "My Meryl is a real firecracker. You have to admit she did very well in your little contest. Two birds down. A lot of men could do no better." He clapped his hand on Meryl's shoulder. Meryl flushed with joy at the blatant pride in his eyes. He addressed his next remark to her, filling her with excitement. "Perhaps we can find you a more responsible place in the company."

Meryl threw her arms around him and gave him

a fierce hug. "Oh, yes, father!" Over his shoulder, she gave Joe a smug smile. *Let him stew on this. I belong to this man in a way he never could.* She turned her back on Joe and smiled up at her father. "Thank you so much. Perhaps once you read the proposal I've been drafting—"

Before he could answer, Joe interrupted. "And in ten years, you'll be fat and unhappy, like most businesswomen. Tsk, tsk. You had such promise, too."

Meryl stiffened. How dare he douse her happiness with cold cynicism? "Why would you say that?"

"The world of men is draining on women. They have to become like men themselves if they're to survive."

"Do you think so?" Mr. Carrington looked almost swayed by his silly argument.

"Of course not," Meryl said.

Joe shrugged. "You have to admit, Mr. Carrington. Men are better equipped for certain things, and hunting is only one of them. It's God's law. So, you see, Meryl. You should never have bet against me. The law of nature stacked the deck against you. But don't fret. Some man will be foolish enough to marry you someday, and you can keep your femininity *and* your figure." He followed up his horrendous comments with an audacious wink.

Meryl gritted her teeth. Her father seemed to be considering Joe's words, for he spoke no more to her about what her new position in the company might entail. He focused instead on his hunting, until it was time to gather the rifles and game and return to the house with his guests.

On the mile-long walk back to the house, Meryl trailed behind her father, his two guests, and Joe. All of them continued to discuss business as if she wasn't there. Meryl realized she had to do something to earn his respect. *Their* respect. Only by achieving something spectacular could she prove her worth.

The Westgate contract provided the answer. She had taken the opportunity to study reports on Westgate when given them to file. She probably knew more about Westgate than anyone else at Atlantic-Southern. In fact, she had even prepared a purchase proposal, though she had yet to show it to anyone.

With her rifle balanced on her shoulder, Meryl stepped gingerly over a puddle with her mud-caked boots. Her father *had* to select her for the Westgate negotiation. He had to. By being away from his direct sphere of influence, out in California, she could prove her abilities to him—and the rest of the company men like Joe, who saw her only as the boss's daughter.

They crested the rise that overlooked the Carrington family country home. Only two miles from the village of Wallingford, the house dominated the neighborhood, the grandest edifice within thirty miles. The manor had been designed to reflect a rustic hunting lodge, framed in heavy wooden beams. Its numerous mullioned windows shone in the mellow light of the autumn morning. The exterior belied the elegant interior, complete with all the modern conveniences such as indoor plumbing and electricity.

Her father had commissioned the house ten years ago, to provide a retreat from the bustling city. Not that they had ever lacked for comfort in their Fifth Avenue mansion.

Meryl often reminded herself of her family's situation when she felt frustrated, knowing how hard life could be for others. She truly had been born blessed. Yet she lacked the natural inclination to dedicate herself to good works as her kind-hearted sister Clara did. She wanted to make her mark on the world in quite a different way, bringing progress to the world and honoring her family's heritage—if her father would stop thwarting her efforts to be the son he never had.

She trailed her father and Joe down the last slope leading to the rear porch. Mr. Whitney and Mr. McDougall had already reached the south lawn, where they had begun cleaning their guns and comparing the grouse they had bagged.

Their wives appeared, and took the birds inside for plucking, a task relegated to a local girl hired for the day while the main staff took the day off. Yet nothing happened in the kitchen today of all days without the full involvement of the women. They would ensure that Thanksgiving dinner would be perfect.

Meryl sighed. Why couldn't she be happy staying with the women, doing as they did? Why did she grow restless sitting at home, tending the kitchen and hearth fires?

Twenty feet from the rear porch, Mr. Carrington left Joe—who had no rifle to clean—to join Mr. McDougall and Mr. Whitney on the south lawn.

Before joining the men, Meryl grabbed the opportunity to put Joe in his place. She rounded on him at the base of the porch steps. "You certainly seem intent on impressing my father. It's obvious you're desperate for his good opinion."

"I don't have to be desperate. I already have it, and it's well-earned, thank you very much." He grinned, a dimple flashing in his stubbled cheek.

She shook her head and gave a theatrical sigh. "I don't know what you're thinking, Joe, but you have to realize that I have a natural advantage where my father is concerned."

His eyes narrowed and he focused his attention on her. "What do you mean by that?"

She shrugged. "It ought to be obvious. Already Father is considering the role I can play."

"Oh, that's right. You'll be promoted from file clerk to . . . what? Stenographer?"

She shrugged. "Everyone has to start somewhere. I'll be doing much more than that before long. Much, much more."

"Oh, I'm sure. Until you find some poor sod to marry and start making a family." He gave her a patronizing gaze. His eyes flicked up and down her body, making her feel uncomfortable even though she wore several layers of clothing. "God knows who that will be."

"You are the rudest, most despicable creature," she said, annoyed to discover that she actually cared about his opinion of her. "You're just as boorish as when you were a boy."

"Only toward you." His green gaze turned speculative, and his voice softened. "You bring it out in me, Meryl. You always have. And this nonsense about the business—I was sure you'd grow out of it eventually."

She lifted her chin. "Just one of your many misconceptions."

"What is that supposed to mean?"

"You simply can't understand my place in the family business, for one thing. Yet it's obvious to anyone with half a brain. Father has five daughters, and not a single son. Of all of them, I'm the only one interested in the company. Now that I've earned my degree, Father will be grooming me to be his successor. Someday I'll be running Atlantic-Southern Railroad." There. She'd said it. She had played her trump card. Nothing could top family ties, and Joe had to acknowledge that.

His expression froze into one of shock. "Don't tell me you actually think—" He gave her a long, hard stare. Then his eyes widened, sparkling with amazement and humor. "You *do!* You think you're going to take your father's place as president. Did he— Did he tell you that?"

She shrugged, and flat out lied. "He has hinted at it."

He relaxed with a sigh. Thrusting his hands in the pockets of his overcoat, he continued up the steps onto the porch. "Hints. Interpreted by a daft female mind."

Meryl glared daggers into his back. She pursued him up the steps, her winter boots clacking loudly on the wood. "Oh, right. I suppose you think you're going to be running it?"

"Honestly, Meryl, I haven't thought that far

ahead." He turned toward her, then glanced away, across the gray-brown autumn landscape. Overhead, a V of geese flew, crying into the wind, on their way to warmer climes. "I need to get used to being home before I do anything else."

His words hung in the silent morning chill, sparking a longing in Meryl to understand the mind and heart of this man, once her childhood antagonist and now little more than a stranger. He seemed about to confide in her, and to her surprise, she welcomed his confidence. "You mean—"

He held up his hand. "Don't say it. This isn't my home. I heard you the first time, loud and clear." Turning, he pushed through the back door into the house, leaving her alone, and feeling strangely bereft.

Two

Joe Hammond paused in the hall outside the parlor where the family was gathering before dinner. He smoothed a hand down his dove gray suit. He hoped he had dressed appropriately. He hadn't needed much business attire while working on the Mexico project, when he had slept in tents along the line being constructed. As soon as he returned to New York, he would have to become reacclimated to city living. He was looking forward to it, truth to tell. Looking forward to the bustle of working at Atlantic-Southern's headquarters.

His own family had been in Society, before his father's foolish mistake. Even in their heyday, the Hammonds were small fish compared to the Carringtons, one of the nation's leading industrial families. Yet their families had lived close by and had even summered together. Hoping to achieve the status of the Carringtons, Joe's father had joined Richard Carrington in several business ventures over the years, before the folly that ended it all.

Joe had been pursuing his degree at M.I.T. when his father grew ill from a "heart condition." Despite the embarrassing situation, Mr. Carrington had taken Joe into the company and under his wing, a situation which cushioned the blow when Joe's father succumbed to his illness two years ago.

Joe owed his future to Mr. Carrington. He vowed not to let his mentor down—even if his daughter got in his way.

Meryl's voice reached him through the closed parlor door. "Mother, did you appreciate all the game?"

"Well, we have a turkey for now, but we'll be enjoying grouse for the rest of the week, thanks to the men."

"I brought down two of them," Meryl said stiffly.

She's as petulant and spoiled as ever, Joe thought with only a minor trace of annoyance. He had always enjoyed tweaking her. As the baby of the Carrington clan, she had always been underfoot— trailing him down the hallway, challenging him, embarrassing him when he had a too-visible crush on her gorgeous older sister Lily. He'd been a sixteen-year-old schoolboy, besotted with a grown woman who turned the heads of every man in New York. Who could blame him?

Boys that age could be boors, and he'd been no exception. He had countered her volleys by detailing her physical and mental deficiencies.

Thinking back now, he acknowledged that Meryl hadn't been a homely child. True, her abundance of golden hair had accentuated her slight frame, making her appear rail thin. Freckles had peppered the bridge of her nose, and her blue eyes were too big for her narrow face. Even so, she might have at least been considered cute.

Unfortunately, whatever charms she may have possessed had been masked by her blunt tongue and aggressive nature. Her boundless energy exhausted everyone around her. For as long as he could recall, she had directed those energies toward him, first by following him about like an unwanted kid sister, and later by purposely antagonizing him every chance she got.

A tradition she had resumed just this morning.

He sighed. Perhaps he was being too harsh. Perhaps Meryl truly had grown up, in some way he had yet to see.

Pulling in a breath, he straightened his shoulders and pushed open the door.

He eyes immediately focused on a gorgeous woman he scarcely recognized. She stood beside her father next to a fireplace of natural stone. A shiver of surprise swept through him. He had once teased Meryl about never measuring up to her sister. Now he couldn't even recall her sister's face.

Where was the girl he'd known? A curious warmth curled in his stomach. He had never thought of Meryl as a woman—until now.

He had been around Latin ladies for so long, he had forgotten that skin could be so pale, yet glow with life, that hair could shine with that particular golden hue. Her generous crown of curls was topped by a jaunty blue feather, which teased the air when she moved.

Pale pink lips, a slender nose with slightly flaring nostrils, and large eyes—cornflower blue, shining

as she smiled at her father. An angel's counte-
nance.

His gaze drifted lower, to her figure. By God,
she'd filled out. Still slender, yes, but the form-fit-
ting powder-blue gown hugged a woman's gentle
curves. Soft lace insets along her neckline mod-
estly hid the swell of her bosom while hinting at
her true shape.

Entranced, he forgot for a moment who he was
admiring. Like any man enjoying the sight of a desirable woman, he found himself wondering how
soft her skin would feel, how her hair would smell,
how her lips would taste . . .

Until she opened those rosy lips and addressed
him.

"Why, Joe. You've shaved. Nice to know you
haven't completely lost touch with polite society in
the wilds of Mexico."

Joe's palm darted to his smooth cheek. He
caught himself and lowered his hand. Annoyance
flooded through him, and he welcomed it. Regardless of her appearance, she was the same
annoying girl underneath. It was important to remember that. No doubt she would continue to
provide him with plenty of reminders.

He needed those reminders. Thinking of her
as a desirable woman felt incredibly dangerous,
like treading the edge of a canyon during a gale. If
he didn't keep his head, he would fall, never to re-
cover.

Dragging his attention from Meryl, he focused
instead on her father. While he had been out of
the country, he had worried that Mr. Carrington

might have forgotten him, that his advancement in the company might have been jeopardized. Those fears had been immediately put to rest. Mr. Carrington continued to welcome him like the son he never had.

Mr. Carrington introduced him to the wives of the men who had been out shooting with him. Besides himself, the holiday guests included Meryl's sister Clara and her husband Stone, and their newborn daughter Amelia, as well as the McDougalls and the Whitneys.

His arrival in the parlor completed the gathering, so they all moved to the dining room to enjoy a delicious Thanksgiving dinner: roast turkey, cranberry sauce, chicken salad, sweet potatoes, wine, and cider. A crackling fire behind a screen warmed Joe's back, making the room feel cozy despite its considerable size and lofty exposed-beam ceiling.

The meal would have been perfect—if the lady opposite him had kept her mouth shut.

Meryl stabbed at her sweet potatoes with her fork. "So, Mr. Hammond. You enjoyed your time in Mexico?" she asked him. Her voice sounded innocent, but he knew better than to trust that.

"I found it fascinating," he said, addressing the gathering more than Meryl. "I confess I'm glad to be home. Not that I won't be happy to go wherever you send me," he quickly added, with a nod toward Mr. Carrington.

"Father, don't we have a new construction contract for a line in the Yukon?" Meryl said, her voice filled with sly innocence. "Joe would love it there,

I'm sure. I hear the Canadian dance-hall girls are the loveliest maidens."

"Women who can't find a lumberjack to marry, you mean," Joe countered.

"Arnold Bigsby is handling the Yukon contract," Mr. Carrington said. "Please pass the wine, Meryl. I'm quite unused to serving myself, sad to say."

"Oh, yes," Mrs. McDougall said. "Thanksgiving is such a hardship without the servants." A handful had remained in their quarters at the house, but they had still been given the day off. Those few were enjoying a similar meal in the kitchen. Joe was used to serving himself, and was just glad the conversation had been taken from Meryl's control.

As Meryl's sister Clara served the mincemeat pie, Joe edged into the topic uppermost on his mind. "Expansion into the Western states will give us control of the line from Mexico City to the Canadian border. Have you made any headway with Westgate Railroad?" he asked his employer. The financially strapped San Francisco-based company had expressed passing interest in being purchased by Atlantic-Southern Railroad—or one of its competitors.

"We're still considering how to make the purchase a viable move," Mr. Carrington said. "I'll be needing to send someone to San Francisco to propose a deal, once one is hammered out."

"I thought you might," Joe nodded.

"How do you know about the Westgate deal?" Meryl asked, her eyes narrowing over a forkful of pie.

Joe tried to ignore the sensuous way her lips

moved as she took a bite. Some girls should never be allowed to become women, with a full complement of feminine wiles. "I keep up with company correspondence."

"Westgate isn't something you need to worry about," she said coolly. "Father has already decided how he's going to proceed."

"Now, Meryl, I haven't yet agreed." Mr. Carrington seemed more interested in his pie than in discussing business.

Joe looked from him to his daughter, who wore a concerned expression. "Agreed? Don't tell me you're giving such an important negotiation to—" Joe caught himself. It wasn't his place to criticize his boss. "Never mind."

"Oh, no," Meryl said, her eyes shooting fire at him despite her cool tone. "Please continue. I'm sure we would all like to hear what you have to say."

"I was only going to point out that business negotiations can be extremely tricky. They require patience, a cool head, and experience—all things Mr. Carrington is aware of, I'm sure."

The man being discussed wouldn't meet his eyes.

Meryl wouldn't let it go. "Meaning?"

"Meaning someone like me." There. He'd said it. He'd thrown his hat in the ring.

"Oh, I'm sure," Meryl said dryly. "Father intends that whoever negotiates the deal will have a shot at running the division. Are you aware of that?"

"I have heard that, yes. I could see myself living in San Francisco."

"No doubt," she said derisively. "There are plenty of dance halls out West for you to frequent."

"Meryl, that's enough. Joe is our guest," Mrs. Carrington interrupted, her strong voice indicating she would brook no argument. "Besides, I find this talk of business tiring, especially over Thanksgiving dinner. Let's talk of more pleasant things. Mr. Whitney, Mrs. Whitney. I hear you are purchasing a house in South Carolina. Is that true? Aren't the insects atrocious down there?"

"Only in the summer. It will be our winter home," Mrs. Whitney said. Conversation moved on to houses and architects, communities and servants, none of which interested Joe, who personally owned very little. He polished off his pie and drank his coffee, all the while eyeing the lady across the table, whose own eyes kept flicking toward him. He glanced away, only to return his gaze to her when she wasn't looking—until she sneaked a peak toward him again, her blue eyes like cold steel.

My God, she hates me now, he thought, unnerved by the thought. He hadn't given Meryl much thought in the past four years, but to see her as a grown woman—to earn her distrust as such— made him feel remarkably bad.

It's her own fault, he reminded himself. *She's not qualified. I was right to emphasize that point. Her own father was probably looking for an excuse to deny her the Westgate negotiation.*

Not that he had, exactly. When Mrs. Carrington rose and announced it was time for the women to retire to the parlor, leaving the men with their brandy and cigars, Joe sighed in relief. Being left alone with his boss would give him the chance to press his case without Meryl's interference.

She left the room last, giving her father a pointed look before she exited.

"I apologize for causing dissension," Joe said, accepting a cigar from his host.

"You hardly caused it. As soon as Meryl learned I was seeking someone to work that contract, she's been pestering me to give it to her."

Joe laughed dryly, hoping to impress on Mr. Carrington how silly such a prospect would be. "She's completely unqualified."

"Not completely." Mr. Carrington sat back and toyed with his own cigar. "She's been negotiating with me hard enough since graduating. And she did graduate top of her class."

"Still, a college education isn't the same as experience in the real world."

Mr. Carrington sighed. "She's my daughter, Joe. My own flesh and blood. Other men in my position give their offspring every chance to succeed."

"Their *male* offspring."

"Be that as it may, she's the only one of my children who has expressed interest in the company my father, grandfather, and I built with our sweat and smarts. The only one. My last chance to leave a family legacy." He stared off into space, the smoke curling toward the beams.

Joe shifted in his chair. "I understand the sentiment, truly I do. But the Westgate deal— It's critical for Atlantic-Southern to gain a foothold west of the Mississippi."

"You don't have to tell me that. I'll make a decision soon enough." Mr. Carrington mashed out his cigar in an ashtray, then began to discuss President McKinley's policy on Cuba with Mr. Whitney and Mr. McDougall.

After another half hour, Mr. Carrington rose to his feet. "Gentlemen, the ladies are waiting for us." Leaving behind their talk of politics and business, the men headed toward the parlor.

In the hallway outside the parlor, Meryl waylaid Joe. She grasped his arm and tugged him away from the open parlor doors.

Twenty feet down the hall, she stopped and rounded on him. "So, you want my job, is that it?"

He laughed. "Don't be silly. I'm not interested in filing."

"Don't make a joke of this." Her serious expression deflated his humor.

"Very well. I didn't know you had your eye on Westgate. Not that it should matter. Being your father's daughter doesn't mean you're qualified, Meryl. What will the president of Westgate think when you flit into the room in your frippery and feathers?" He flicked the feather in her hair. "Do you really think they'll take you seriously?"

"I'll make them take me seriously, and I won't be wearing any feathers!"

"Your clothes are not the issue. It's your sex, something they'll hardly be able to ignore." Despite himself, his eyes flicked down her figure. He was certainly finding it hard to ignore.

"This is my chance, Joe. Don't you see that? My chance to make father take me seriously. If I have to spend one more day doing nothing but filing papers, I swear I'll be fit for Bedlam."

"Some would say you already are."

"I ought to slap you for that." She lifted her hand as if to do just that.

He caught it and squeezed, marveling at the softness of her tapered fingers. "Listen to me, Meryl. Millions of dollars are riding on this deal. Do you really think you can handle it? What if you fail? Have you considered that? The profits the company—your family—will lose . . ."

For the briefest instant, doubt flickered in her eyes. Despite himself, Joe felt a touch of shame for his blunt remark. But he wasn't talking with her as a man would a lady. He was trying to make the silly girl see sense for her own good. And his, he ruefully admitted.

The instant passed. She snatched her hand from his grip. "I can do as good a job as you can, Joseph Hammond. Better."

"You wouldn't know where to begin."

Her trim eyebrows arched. "Are you willing to bet on that?"

"Bet you? Any time, Pest. Just name it. You know I'll win, as I won that silly shooting contest of yours this morning."

"Then accept this one." She stepped even closer, her delicate rose scent surrounding him, teasing him. "Whichever of us succeeds in securing the Westgate deal, the other will step aside. If I succeed, I will take over presidency of the new division. If you succeed, the same."

Her audacious proposal stunned him. "Are you serious?"

"More than you'll ever know."

A bet . . . Joe quickly analyzed the possibilities. Once he succeeded, Meryl would have only herself to blame. "What about your father?"

"We'll tell him that you and I have agreed to negotiate the deal together. He will be happy not to have to decide between us."

To put it mildly. Joe found himself nodding. This bet would essentially make the decision for Mr. Carrington. More than that, Atlantic-Southern Railroad needed to move on the Westgate deal soon or it could go sour. Another buyer could swoop in at any time.

"You do realize I have much more experience in business than you do," he said carefully, concerned despite himself that she had bitten off far more than her pearly teeth could chew. "What exactly are your credentials? A few courses in history, perhaps mathematics and science? Oh, yes, and a few months filing papers in Mr. Smithson's office. We can't forget that experience. That hardly prepares you to go head-to-head with the key players in a major financial deal."

"Just try me."

He gave her a careful look. Her pretty oval face was tense with a determination at odds with her ladylike breeding. But then, Meryl had always defied simple definition. "So, when I win this, you won't be hounding him to name you president of the new division, is that right?"

"That's right."

As much as the idea of putting her in her place appealed to him, a serious obstacle presented itself. "Wait a minute. If we actually do this, if we travel to San Francisco, your father is going to expect me to mind you."

Meryl's eyes narrowed. "You had better not try. I'm perfectly capable of taking care of myself. I'm almost spinster age."

"Spinster! You." He couldn't imagine a less spinsterlike female.

"You needn't worry about my father thinking less of you for not hovering over me. After all is said and done, I'll explain everything to him. You have my word, and I expect yours in return."

The situation was a winner for Joe, no matter how he looked at it. His last concern alleviated, he thrust out his hand and she grasped it firmly. "Very well. You have my word in return. Whoever succeeds in negotiating the purchase of Westgate Railroad Company, wins the presidency."

"As simple as that."

Joe nodded. Instead of releasing her hand, he tugged her closer and looked into her face, so filled with ridiculous determination. "Pest. You *do* realize I have the advantage, as a man."

Pulling her hand free, she placed her palm on his chest and shoved him back. "Frankly, Joe, I don't think of you as a man."

With a swish of her skirts, she turned back toward the parlor. "Let's go tell my father."

Damn, she annoyed him. Fine. He didn't think of her as a woman, either. Just a silly girl who had silly ideas, and would soon be put in her place.

Three

"When are you planning to leave?" Mr. Carrington smiled at Joe and Meryl, who stood before him together, pretending to be a united force.

Meryl was happy to see that her father no longer looked so troubled, but she hated having to deceive him. "Oh, not until after this weekend," she said coolly, feeling no compunction about lying to Joe. She intended to leave that very day—somehow.

"I can't tell you how glad it makes me to see you two working together," Mr. Carrington said. "With both of you involved in working out the details, we're sure to secure the purchase of Westgate in record time."

He grasped Joe's shoulder. "And you, my son. I trust you to take good care of my little girl on this journey. She's my little pumpkin." He chucked Meryl under the chin.

Meryl's smile fell a little. She loved her father and had always been close to him. But he certainly knew how to choose the wrong moment to express tenderness toward her. Joe would think he had nothing to worry about if he thought he was going up against "little pumpkin."

Then again, with the bet sealed on a shake, now was the time for Joe to think she presented no challenge. She gave her father a wide smile and turned on the girlish charm. "Oh, Father, you're so sweet to me. I promise we won't let you down."

"Don't worry, Mr. Carrington," Joe said. "I'll take good care of her—as much as she'll allow it." After adding that caveat, his eyes met hers in silent understanding. He knew better than to try to "care for her." He smiled down at her, his audacious dimple appearing. "Meryl's just like a sister to me."

Meryl narrowed her eyes. If a childhood spent tormenting and teasing her qualified him to express filial affection, he was certainly entitled. Still, she could barely stomach the sugary smile he was now directing toward her father.

The afternoon dragged on, the mantel clock ticking away both time and opportunity. Meryl engaged in small talk with her family and friends, all the while fighting a tremendous urge to dart from the room and jump on a train, leaving Joe in the dust. She would have to bide her time, find just the right moment to take her leave.

"Clara, won't you play for us?" her mother suggested.

"Mother, you know I'm barely an adequate player." She glanced at her handsome husband, a former British Army captain bearing the unusual name of Stone Hawke.

He gave her a warm smile. "You're far too modest. Play for us, dear. I love to hear you." His intimate tone reflected the deep love that they shared. With his encouragement, Clara rose and smoothed her skirt. As she crossed to the piano, Meryl joined the others in finding places to sit and listen.

Soon, a Mozart sonata filled the air. Meryl couldn't concentrate on her talented sister's playing. Instead, she was making mental plans—what to pack, what route to take, how she could convince Manfred, their coachman, to take her to the station as fast as possible—and without Joe being the wiser.

She was so engrossed in her planning, she nearly missed her opening when Clara's sonata ended. Before Clara could begin another piece, Meryl jumped to her feet. "Clara, that was lovely. Mother, if you will excuse me, I feel a headache coming on." She pressed her palm to her forehead. "Perhaps I indulged in too much wine."

She caught Joe's suspicious eyes on her, and gave a hearty groan of pain. She would have to hurry, take advantage of her lead before he had a chance to make his own move.

Amid a flurry of concerned remarks and good wishes, she walked slowly, so as to appear weak and indisposed, until she had secured the parlor door behind her. Clear of her family—and Joe—she grasped her skirts and pounded up the stairs straight to her room.

Her maid had been given the day off to spend the holiday with her family, but Manfred was about. He would need to prepare the carriage right away to take her the two miles into town. If she hurried, she could make the six-o'clock train back to the city. From there, she would be able to buy a ticket directly to San Francisco.

She yanked on the bell pull connected to the kitchen, then spun toward her writing desk. Picking up a sheet of letter paper and a pen, she began scribbling a note.

> *Dear Mother and Father,*
> *Please don't worry. I have left for San Francisco to negotiate the Westgate contract. Joe will be meeting me at the station. You needn't—*

A tap at the door interrupted her. She laid the pen down and hurried to the door to find the coachman, a napkin still tucked in his collar. "Manfred. I'm sorry I interrupted your Thanksgiving dinner, but I'm in quite a hurry. I need you to take my trunk downstairs and load it on the carriage. I'm going back to the city with all due haste."

"Yes'm," Manfred said.

She lowered her voice, to impress upon him the need to be circumspect. "And bring the carriage 'round to the servants' entrance. I don't want to . . . disturb the guests." He looked at her suspiciously. "Does your mum know you're leaving, miss?"

"Of course! But she gave strict instructions to me to leave quietly, so as not to distract the Whitneys and McDougalls."

He didn't seem to believe her, but he also seemed more interested in getting back to his meal than in pressing the matter. "Yes'm." He looked over her shoulder. "Where's your trunk?"

Her trunk! She had to pack as fast as possible. "Come back in ten minutes. No, five."

"You plannin' on bein' packed in five minutes?" He gave her a look filled with disbelief. Most ladies took half a day to prepare for a trip.

"That's what I said."

He shook his head. "If you say, miss."

"And Manfred?"

"Yes'm?"

"Remember. Don't interrupt the gathering with talk of my trip. Please."

He gave her another suspicious look, but nodded. "Very well." He headed down the hallway.

Meryl closed the door. She hurried over to the two large armoires against one wall and flung open all four doors. Grasping the handle of the small trunk at the bottom of one armoire, she dragged it out. She flinched at the harsh squeal of metal against the wooden floor. She hoped no one downstairs wondered about the scraping sound.

She opened the trunk and turned back to her wardrobe. She had to travel light, yet she would be gone for several weeks. She didn't need more than one or two dinner gowns. Or perhaps three. Traveling suits. She would take mostly traveling suits. Making quick decisions, she threw clothing into the trunk at a furious pace.

She soon saw that, despite placing such a limit on her wardrobe, her basic needs threatened to overflow her smallest trunk.

"You're leaving?"

Meryl spun around. Her sister Clara stood at the door, a look of alarm on her face. Meryl pulled her inside and shut the door firmly behind her. "I have to, Clara."

"You're eloping? You know Mother and Father would love to see you wed to Joe."

The sheer ridiculousness of her sister's assumption nearly floored Meryl. "I am *not* eloping, especially with *him*."

"Then?" Clara raised her brows.

Meryl sighed. Because she had been discovered, she might as well fill Clara in on her plans. Of her four sisters, Clara was closest to her age, and closest to her heart. Clara was more likely to help her than hinder her. "I have a bet to win, against Joe."

She recounted their agreement as she struggled to choose among her outfits and accessories, to keep her baggage to the single small trunk. "Don't tell Mother and Father. Not until I'm gone. If they realize I'm leaving now, they'll want to make arrangements for me and send a chaperone along. And Joe will be long gone by then."

Clara considered for a moment, her calm expression relieving Meryl greatly. "I suppose you'll be safe enough, with Joe looking out for you."

Joe was right. Everyone would assume he would take care of her, when nothing could be further from the truth. "Looking out for me? He can barely tolerate me."

"Why would you say that? You two were always together when you were children," she smiled. "You were my closest playmate, and sometimes I felt a little jealous."

Meryl paused, a dress over her arm, and looked at her sister in disbelief. "What a waste of a strong emotion. Joe disliked me then, and he dislikes me now. But that's neither here nor there. The point is, he's hardly going to look out for me. He's my competition! Besides, I don't need to be looked out for. I can take care of myself."

"Still—"

"Help me pack."

Clara took the dress from Meryl's arms and found a way to squeeze it into the trunk. After a few more minutes of frenetic packing, she asked, "Do you have enough money?"

Meryl paused, thinking about her handbag, and the coin purse inside. She wouldn't get far without enough money, and couldn't very well visit the bank on this holiday. She checked her little embroidered coin purse and found less than fifty dollars inside. Her stomach sank. "I don't have much."

"I have some. Wait here." Clara hurried from the room. In a few minutes she was back, with more than three hundred dollars. She pressed the bills into Meryl's palm. "Stone and I already have our return tickets to the city. We don't need it."

"Thank you, Clara."

"If you need more, wire me and I'll send it. If you're serious about this—"

"You know I am."

"I'll do what I can to make sure you succeed."

Despite herself, Meryl's eyes began to fill with moisture. "Thank you. Thank you so much, Clara." She pulled her sister toward her and gave her a swift hug.

Clara pulled back. "I'd better return downstairs and tell them you're resting quietly, before Mother

becomes alarmed and comes to check on you herself."

Meryl nodded and Clara let herself out. She
would miss Clara most of all. She had no one else
to talk to, and traveling so far from home . . .

*Don't think that way. Think of what you will be prov-
ing, to Father. To all of them. To Joe Hammond.*

With renewed purpose, she began pulling hatboxes from the second armoire and emptying
them on the bed. She had to pack hats that
matched her suits, as well as shoes and gloves. And
petticoats, and her corsets—

Like a mad woman she dashed about the room,
throwing things into the trunk, packing her small
traveling valise with essentials, scrawling more of
the note to her parents—all the while praying that
Joe really believed she was resting. Yet she had
never moved with more urgency.

Still, packing took time. The last item was a matter of pure business, her purchase proposal. This
is what she would present to Mr. Philbottom of
Westgate Railroad. Even if he hesitated to deal with
a woman, her carefully penned papers would
prove she was worth doing business with. While
her father hadn't seen the full report, she had discussed each item with him, and knew that both
sides would benefit from what she proposed.

When she finally slammed the lid on the over-
stuffed trunk and finished her note to her parents,
she rang for Manfred.

Carrying two hat boxes, her valise, and her
handbag, she maneuvered down two flights of nar-

row servants' stairs ahead of Manfred and a young groom hefting her trunk.

Her heart pounded and her palms dampened her silk-lined gloves. So close now. No one but Clara knew, especially not Joe. She was going to sneak out without his being the wiser, while he sipped sherry and talked politics and tried to impress her father. He would never catch up, once she boarded the last train to the city. She would close the deal before Joe even arrived in San Francisco.

A sense of victory filled her, even though her journey hadn't even begun. She would do this; she would win the bet and prove herself. At the foot of the stairs, she asked Manfred, "You brought the carriage around to this door?"

"Yes, Miss. Had to bring out the brougham, with your heavy trunk and all." He opened the door. Together, he and the groom carried the trunk to the rear of a large brougham hitched to a pair of horses.

For several minutes, Manfred and the groom worked to strap the trunk to the carriage's luggage rack, leaving Meryl to cool her heels in the gravel by the carriage door. An eternity later, Manfred came back to the side of the carriage. Before opening the door, he gave her a curious look. "Where are we going, miss?"

"I have to get to the train station as fast as possible."

"You mean to catch the six-o'clock to the city?" Manfred asked. He idled by the door, not making a move to open it.

"Yes. We need to hurry, Manfred." She gestured toward the door, resisting the urge to dive for the handle and open it herself. She didn't want to insult him, but his glacial pace strained her every nerve.

Manfred nodded. He swung open the door and lowered the step for her. Meryl was halfway up when Manfred asked, "Not to be too bold, Miss, but Mr. Hammond just left in his own carriage for the station. There woulda been room for you, too,"

Meryl froze with her foot on the step and her hand in Manfred's. She stared at him. "Mr. Hammond already left? When?"

"A half hour ago, I'd say, carrying only a satchel. He was aiming to take the train to the city, just like you. There ain't much time for makin' the six-o'-clock train. Not now. It's almost a quarter 'til."

Meryl's heart fell to her shoes like a grouse felled by a shot, her sense of victory snuffed like a candle. Joe had outplayed her, and so soon. How humiliating.

It was her own fault. She had moved as fast as possible, but lost track of how late it had grown. Time had slipped through her fingers. Now Joe had already taken the lead in their race. Damn him for being able to travel so much lighter than she. It was another inequity women experienced, that they weren't properly dressed without an extensive wardrobe. She had packed only the barest essentials as it was.

He would catch the train; she would miss it. Manfred was right. There was no way she could make the train on time.

Four

Comfortably ensconced in a plush first-class train seat, Joe extracted his pocket watch from his gray foulard vest and clicked it open. Each moment that ticked by added to his reassurance. He had done it. And so easily.

His watch read six o'clock sharp. He smiled. What a satisfying alignment of clock hands. Any moment the train to New York City would pull out of the station, leaving little Meryl Carrington behind. God, what a heady feeling. Still, he found himself disappointed that his victory had been so easy. He had thought Meryl would present at least a token challenge. He had always been impressed by her fiery determination. To have so easily gotten the upper hand . . . He had definitely expected a better showing from the strong-headed chit.

During his time in Mexico, he hadn't thought much about Meryl. When he did, he remembered the girl who pestered and embarrassed him in front of her gorgeous older sister. Then later, when he had gotten over his puppy love for Lily Carrington, Meryl had still managed to get under his skin at the handful of family gatherings where their paths had crossed.

He almost regretted that they had seen each other so briefly during this visit—almost. If anything, she kept him on his toes, which was never a bad thing for an up-and-coming company president like himself.

The minutes ticked by, and still the train idled in the station. Joe tried not to grow concerned. Trains usually ran on time, after all—but there could be exceptions. Still, he wouldn't feel safe until he left Meryl far behind.

When a porter passed his seat, Joe snagged him. "Excuse me."

The tall dark-skinned man wore a dapper navy-blue uniform, hallmark of the Atlantic-Southern line. He paused at Joe's seat. "Yes, sir?"

"It's twenty past six." He tapped the face of his pocket watch. "Why haven't we left the station?"

"I apologize for the delay, sir. The train is being held for an important personage. It shouldn't be much longer."

Joe nodded and sat back with a sigh. He knew it would make no sense to take out his annoyance on the porter.

Important personage . . . There weren't many people who could have a train held for them. He peered out the window at the Wallingford station, a quaint colonial building with a wooden platform. Fog swirled around glowing lampposts. He wondered how much longer it would be. And who.

Ten long, interminable minutes later, a carriage pulled up to the station platform. A sense of dread filled him. The door swung open and *she* emerged. He groaned in frustration. She stepped down, all golden polish and tailored clothing, her hat resting just so on her head. The footmen worked to unstrap and lower a five-foot-long trunk from the back of the carriage, taking their sweet time about it.

He glanced again at his watch, conscious that there was a good chance he would miss the connection for the westbound line at Grand Central Depot. Of course, if he missed the connection, so would she. Still, he had lost his advantage.

The conductor himself escorted Meryl to her seat, just two rows in front of his. As she came closer, she spotted him. Her lips turned up in a triumphant smirk.

He grimaced. As much a brat as ever, trying to bend the world to fit her will. And, sadly, this time succeeding.

Only minutes after she was seated, the engine started up, the wheels chugging faster and faster as the train left the terminal. About time. Joe stared at the back of Meryl's well-dressed head, his annoyance building until he found himself on his feet.

He strode over and laid his hand on the back of her seat. Leaning over her shoulder, he bent down and murmured into her ear. "So, you resorted to using your family connection to hold the train. Clever."

Her eyes flicked toward his and her rosy lips tightened a fraction. "I will do whatever I must. No matter what it takes."

He shook his head slowly. "You talk a good

game, but you wouldn't know where to begin—or where to end."

"It seems to me I've gotten a good start." She turned pointedly away from him, her eyes straight ahead.

Disgusted—both with her, and with how easily he was annoyed by her—he returned to his seat. He didn't talk with her for the rest of the ninety-minute journey to New York City.

Joe Hammond was the first off the train at Grand Central Depot, his satchel gripped in his hand. He broke into a sprint, heading for the nearest ticket counter. Inside the crowded concourse, he had to dodge travelers and baggage carts at every step, earning more than one annoyed glance.

With any luck, he could catch the 9:15 out of the city, while Meryl was still fooling about with her excessive lady's baggage.

To his dismay, the line at the ticket counter was a dozen deep. Exasperated, Joe tapped his foot, praying for them to hurry. The ticket clerk moved as slowly as the earth rotated.

Joe tapped the shoulder of the man in front of him. "Excuse me, I'm in a hurry. If you don't mind—"

"You're in a hurry, are ye?" the man said in a thick Irish brogue. "Good fer ye. So are we all." He turned back, ignoring further entreaties. The line began to move again. Joe glanced around the terminal, but didn't see Meryl, thank goodness. It took precious time to gather checked baggage, and porters weren't always available.

Finally, the man in front of him received his ticket and left. "I need a ticket to San Francisco. The Continental Express leaving tonight should suit."

"Leaving tonight? Not many seats left for that one. And not much time, either. It departs in twenty minutes."

"Yes, I'm well aware of that. I work for Atlantic-Southern." He shoved his money at the man. "I'll take whatever you have."

The man seemed less than impressed that he was an employee of the railroad. "It's a Pullman sleeper. I'll need a good deal more than that."

"Fine." Pulling out his billfold, he extracted the additional fee for the deluxe passage and gave it to the clerk.

"Why, darling! You did get two tickets, didn't you?"

Joe inwardly groaned as Meryl's crystal-clear voice carried from behind him straight to the clerk's ears. She elbowed her way to the window right beside him. Behind her waited a porter with a cart bearing her trunk, two hatboxes, and her small valise. She smiled at the clerk. "He keeps pretending he's going to leave me behind. That's ever so impolite, don't you think, sir? Here. This should cover my ticket." The wad of cash she shoved toward the clerk made his eyes grow round as saucers.

"She's not with me," Joe protested.

Meryl looped her arm in his and patted his

shoulder. "Don't be silly, darling." She addressed the clerk, "He keeps playing this little game, but it's growing old. Ever since he found out I was—" She whispered, but so loudly, it disguised nothing of what she said—*"expecting."*

The clerk began to color. He didn't look at her or Joe as he finished writing out both tickets. He counted out the proffered money and shoved both tickets toward Joe.

Meryl snatched hers before Joe could touch it. "Thank you ever so much." Turning, she hurried from the window and into the crowd, heading for Platform 9. Her porter followed, pushing the cart with her baggage.

Joe caught up with her in half a dozen strides. "That was extremely rude."

She didn't look at him. "It secured me what I needed."

He grasped her elbow and swung her to face him. "But to say you're my wife—and that you're . . . you're . . ." The word jammed in his throat. He had barely begun to think of little Meryl as a grown woman. To imagine her married to him—and carrying his child—boggled his mind.

She jerked her arm from his grasp. "I said what I needed to say. We women must use every natural advantage we have."

"Yes, but to discuss something of such an intimate nature with an utter stranger—"

"I doubt I shall ever see that ticket clerk again, as I shall soon be moving to San Francisco to head the new Westgate Division." She arched her trim dark-blond eyebrows. "Unless you were referring to yourself?"

"I'm hardly a stranger, but we really don't know each other that well, either. Not anymore." Of their own volition, his eyes skidded down her svelte, womanly figure.

What had she learned at college? Just how sophisticated was she? Worry filled him. "Tell me, Meryl. How much is too much? What would you do, or say?" His voice increased in intensity. "Just how far would you go?"

Her lips tightened, but not before he saw the blush staining her cheeks. "You are absolutely right. We don't know each other. The Joe I knew would never insinuate—" Her lips remained parted, but no more words came out. Without finishing her sentence, she spun away and hurried the rest of the way toward the platform, her heels clicking a rapid staccato.

On the tracks ahead, The iron giant idled, belching steam. Passengers said their final farewells to family and friends, while uniformed porters hurried to load the last of the baggage in the baggage car. Meryl ignored them all, her movements determined and sharp. She tipped the porter, snatched her valise, and hurried up the steps into the railcar.

Had he actually hurt her feelings? Joe stared after her, stunned to his core. He had never rattled Meryl's composure in all the years he'd known her. He had come to believe her incapable of such gentler sentiments. Who was this woman? He found himself intrigued, but knew it would be wise to resist the impulse to learn more about her.

He resolved to find some way to leave her behind. He could hardly continue dashing about train stations merely to have her appear on his tail at every moment. He needed to shake her off so thoroughly, she could never catch up.

A Negro porter escorted Meryl to her seat in the Pullman car, a plushly decorated parlor on wheels. The porter glanced at her ticket, then gestured to a bench in flame-stitched tapestry. "Here you go, ma'am. This is your seat through to Omaha, where you'll be changing trains."

Meryl gave him an absent smile. "Thank you." She took her seat as the porter stowed her powder-blue leather valise under her seat. Across from her on an identical facing bench, an old man slumped, his hat covering most of his face, his arms crossed, his breaths rattling in sleep. Beside him, a boy of about nine kicked his feet, whomping his heels with annoying irregularity against the wall.

"We'll begin setting up sleeping compartments an hour after we leave the station," the porter said. "Just let me know when you're ready."

She nodded again, and the porter moved back to the door to greet another passenger. The Pullman porter would be on duty in that car for the entire journey.

Meryl was relieved the Pullman car had been available. She had been to Europe, but she had never gone out west, and she had always traveled in comfort. From the walls paneled with inlaid black walnut to the oriental carpeting and brass fixtures, the car was designed to appeal to passengers willing to pay a premium.

Still, there were limits to the comforts a narrow train car could provide to two dozen passengers. Every seat was taken except, apparently, the one beside her. She didn't mind. Opening her valise, she removed her red leather-bound journal and began penning an account of her encounter with Joe and their wager.

The train pulled away from Grand Central Depot. Meryl watched the iron and steel trusses of the terminal pass by her window, then fall behind. Soon, they were out of the city, and darkness surrounded the train, turning the passenger car into an intimate cocoon of warmth, light, and comfort.

As the miles rolled out beneath the train's wheels, strangers soon became traveling acquaintances. Meryl learned that the little boy across from her wasn't traveling with the older gentleman beside him, but the young mother in the seat across the aisle, tending three younger children.

The isolated child looked terribly bored. "Would you like to draw your mother a picture?" she asked him. Meryl tore a page from the back of her journal.

He nodded with a shy smile and accepted the paper, along with a spare pencil she carried.

"Tommy, don't bother the lady," his mother cautioned.

"I don't mind." Meryl smiled at her.

The harried mother gave her a wan, grateful smile.

With the boy occupied—and the old man still asleep—Meryl had to entertain herself. She hadn't seen Joe since they boarded. Perhaps he had ended up in another car after all. She pulled her copy of the train's timetable from her valise, then tucked the case under the seat.

According to the printed schedule, the train should arrive in Fort Wayne by five the next day, when there would be a break for dinner in town. Some passengers would leave the train at that point to head northwest to Chicago. She planned to stay right there on the train until it left the station, continuing the journey to Omaha.

With any luck, Joe would miss the train, while she—

"Well, won't this be cozy."

Joe removed his derby and dropped his satchel at her feet. "My seat is right next to yours, *Mrs. Hammond.* For the entire journey. Hundreds upon hundreds of miles." He snatched the timetable from her gloved fingers and glanced at it. "Until next Wednesday at noon, to be exact."

Meryl rescued her timetable from his clutches. She pulled in a quiet breath, counseling herself not to succumb to his baiting. "As I said, whatever gets me there," she said blithely as he took his seat beside her.

The woodsy scent of his hair pomade tickled her nose. He smelled far too masculine for comfort. Worse, his shoulder touched hers as she wriggled, trying to make room between them and failing.

When had lanky Joe grown so broad-shouldered? "If I have to put up with your presence—"

"What did you expect after passing yourself off as my wife?"

She shrugged, alarmed when the simple gesture increased the contact between them. "You told my father you would treat me like your sister. There isn't so much difference," she lied.

"Isn't there?" His green eyes bore into hers, unsettling her deeply.

Pulling her gaze away, Meryl tried to find something to focus on. She snapped open her handbag, a solid affair suitable for traveling, not one of those silly feminine reticules that held almost nothing. She tucked the timetable inside, then opened her journal. Ignoring the man beside her, she began writing.

Several weeks ago, when she had first learned of the Westgate deal, she had culled the company files for everything she could find relating to Westgate. Everything she discovered, she wrote in her journal. She was certain she knew more about the company and Mr. Philbottom, its president, than Joe did. After all, Joe had been out of the country for four years.

"A girl and her diary. How adorable." Joe was leaning close, trying to glimpse the page she was reading. Just as he had when she was a girl.

Shooting him a look of pure annoyance, she turned her back to him to keep her notes out of his line of sight. "If you don't mind, this is private."

"Still waxing poetic about your male admirers? I hope you're over my friend Bradford by now."

"Bradford who?" she retorted, despite knowing perfectly well who the fellow was. She'd been only thirteen, and believed Bradford—a dreamy, melancholy fellow—to be the most perfect male specimen God could create. She had been certain they were destined for each other.

Naturally, Joe had learned of her infatuation—when he'd had the bad manners to steal her diary. Three months of relentless teasing had followed, ending only when she learned he had an infatuation of his own, for her curvaceous, beautiful sister Lily.

Remembering his own weakness, she pinned him with a glare. "I'm not pining for Bradford any more than you're pining for Lily. Unless, of course, you are."

His eyes narrowed. "Don't be daft. I was sixteen. Every boy in the neighborhood had his eyes on her, and you know it."

"Oh, I know it." She adored Lily, but part of her had always been jealous that Lily could command such devotion merely by existing. No man had ever looked at her the way men looked at Lily. "I certainly know it."

He shook his head in disbelief. "By God, Meryl, you're still suffering from feelings of inferiority, aren't you?"

She slammed her journal shut. "Thank you for your concern, but I'm not suffering at all. Frankly, I'm glad I haven't been pestered by suitors the way Lily was. Sadly, you men aren't attracted to a woman's fine mind. Though you should be, rather than to—to . . ." Her generous curves and gorgeous, picture-perfect features, she silently added. "You men make me ill. All of you."

"Right," he said dryly, his jaw tense. Standing, he placed his derby on his head. "You've grown in some ways," he said, his eyes flicking up and down her figure. "No denying that. But you still have a lot of growing up to do."

That stung. Hiding her hurt, she shot back, "So you insult me, then run away. How mature of you."

"Not that you care, but I'm going to the club car," he said. "I expect the company there to be a good deal less judgmental."

Meryl watched him leave, her stomach clenched in a knot. When had Joe grown so worldly and confident? What had happened to the freckle-faced boy who had played silly, childish pranks on her? Who was this man?

And had he really consorted with dance-hall girls?

She had never been in a dance hall, but, like most Easterners, she was well-versed in the lore of the West through colorful newspaper and magazine articles. She imagined Joe in a smoky dance hall, watching the girls on a worn wooden stage. Fallen women, with their short ruffled skirts and slinky movements and come-hither glances, directed at the sandy-haired gent with the open face and warm smile. Oh, he would appreciate them, all right, those women with their buxom figures. Their painted faces and pouting lips probably enticed him to all manner of carnal sin. The thought made her feel embarrassingly hot inside. She unbuttoned the jacket of her blue serge traveling suit.

Underneath, she wore a proper white cotton blouse with a ruffled neckline.

She told herself to think of something else, tried to study her journal, but she kept wondering about those girls and Joe. What would it feel like to entice a man? With her lack of experience, she had always relied on her suitors to make the overtures, and none of them had seemed particularly taken by her . . . attributes. She glanced down at her blouse. No, she was most definitely not equipped to seduce a man, or entice him to do anything but become extremely annoyed with her.

Well, she had no intention of marrying anyway, not for a long time. So she was destined to remain pure, maybe her entire life.

She sighed and laid her head back against the seat. Why did she think such inappropriate thoughts, feel such dangerous urges, when she knew they could lead nowhere?

"Ma'am, would you like me to prepare your bed for the evening?"

The porter smiled down at her, his teeth bright against his dark skin. She nodded and stepped into the corridor to allow him access to the benches. Joe must still be in the club car. The old gentleman across from her had left, while the child was already in his pajamas in a bunk with his brothers across the aisle.

She might as well go to bed. With all the excitement of the day, her energy had deserted her.

As the porter folded down the backs of the facing seats to form a bed, the truth sank in. She and

Joe were assigned to the same sleeping berth. A shiver of trepidation swept through her.

In a matter of minutes, the porter had made up the bed with fresh linens, blankets, and pillows. Reaching up, he pulled down the fold-out berth from the wall above.

He was adjusting a pair of curtains across the front of the compartment when the old man reappeared. He pushed his way down the corridor, past passengers standing in the aisle or heading for the lavatory at the end of the car. A sleeper car left precious little room for modesty, regardless of people's delicate sensibilities. The old man had changed into nightwear, his feet adorned with leather slippers, a striped robe about his narrow frame. Without giving her a second glance, he parted the curtain and crawled into the upper bunk.

That left the lower berth to her—and Joe.

"Um, excuse me," she said, drawing the porter's attention. "Isn't there another berth available?" She glanced above the seats where fold-out berths were built into the walls.

"No, ma'am. The train's full up. The holiday and all. Your ticket is for a double berth. It should be large enough for you and for your husband. Atlantic-Southern prides itself on making certain its travelers are comfortable."

"Oh, I'm sure," she said dryly, fighting the urge to tell him who she really was. The rail line believed her to be Joe's wife. She had made her bed by pretending to be Joe's wife. Now she would—quite literally—have to lie in it. With him.

The porter turned away to make up a berth farther down the narrow corridor. Meryl chewed her lip, nerves in her stomach building into a tight knot. She could make a scene, throw her father's name about. If her identity were known, the conductor and porters would bend over backward to make her comfortable.

She had always prided herself on being able to succeed based on her own merits, not the family she had been born into. She had already broken that tenet once, by having the Wallingford train held for her. How Joe would disparage her should she do it again, and merely out of a sense of maidenly modesty! Making a scene wouldn't help her to arrive at her destination sooner. Besides, she hated the idea of tossing someone out of his bed.

She could handle the situation, she resolved. After all, as Joe constantly reminded her, he thought of her as nothing more than a sister.

A sense of urgency overtook her. She had to get ready as quickly as possible—put on her nightdress and hide under the blankets. Then, when Joe came in, she would pretend to be asleep.

Grabbing her valise, she headed to the ladies lavatory at the end of the car. The lavatory door was partly open. Inside, a full-figured lady with coal-black hair was studying her face in the mirror. She glanced toward Meryl. "Come on in, honey. I'm just checking the state of my skin. Looking for any new wrinkles."

Meryl slid into the tiny room and closed the door behind her. "Thank you. I'm in a bit of a hurry."

She laughed, deep and throaty. The woman seemed to breathe sensuality, from the sound of her laugh to the smile on her face. "In a hurry for bed? You must be a newlywed. I saw your husband. He's *delicious.*"

Joe? Delicious? Meryl's nose wrinkled, but she turned away so the lady couldn't see. She began yanking out hairpins to release her coiffure. "Oh, he's a regular marzipan."

The woman laughed. "You seem like a bright young thing. Not nearly as stuffy as some of the ladies on board. May I make your acquaintance? I am Mrs. Alphonse Yves-Kendall."

"Miss Meryl Carr—Mrs. Joe Hammond." Shaking out her hair, she dug in her valise for her washcloth.

Mrs. Yves-Kendall smiled. "You *are* a newlywed. You're still getting accustomed to your new name. It's nice to meet you, Mrs. Hammond." She turned back to studying herself in the mirror. "Have you yet to experience conjugal bliss on a train?"

Meryl nearly dropped her soap and washcloth. She looked up from her valise and found Mrs. Yves-Kendall's eyes studying hers in the mirror. What exactly did she mean?

"I've slept on a train dozens of times," she said slowly.

"I'm not talking about sleep, hon."

"I was afraid not," Meryl said in a small, tight voice.

"It's all about rhythm, after all. A train has a particular rhythm that can be quite beneficial for one's sex life. At least I've found it enjoyable." She winked.

Meryl pasted a smile on her face. She struggled not to imagine what the lady was referring to, but couldn't help it. At college, she had learned the basics of how men and women made love, that he had a certain part that went into the woman's special place, and—like a bee pollinating a flower—that's how babies began to grow. But the talk of rhythms meant little to her.

The woman's suggestive tone, however, was enough to make her blush to the roots of her hair. Throwing thoughts of Joe into the mix merely confused her further.

Had Joe given any thought to their sleeping arrangements? Did it bother him at all? Her gaze strayed to the other woman's full-busted figure and knowing eyes. Probably not. She was hardly a dance-hall girl, after all, or even a wise socialite like Mrs. Yves-Kendall. She hated that he understood these matters, when she had been left almost entirely in the dark. Perhaps . . . She glanced at the closed door. She knew that to succeed in life, it was essential that she grasp opportunity whenever she could, make use of every resource at hand. "Mrs. Yves-Kendall."

"Call me Annabelle."

"Annabelle. You're absolutely right. I *am* a newlywed. So new, I've never . . . We haven't . . ."

"Oh, really? My goodness, I didn't mean to offend you with my earthy talk."

"It's not that. But tonight—" In the mirror, she saw her cheeks turning pink.

Annabelle nodded. "I know what you're asking. Goodness knows, my first husband surprised me badly enough. Now that I'm on my third, I have things well in hand." She gestured to a wicker chair in the corner. "Sit down. I'll tell you everything you should know."

Five

Behind the curtain of her sleeping compartment, Meryl struggled to undo buttons and laces that her maid had fastened that morning, before leaving to spend the day with her family.

She wriggled about, trying to manage her toilet in the tiny space between the mattress and the upper bunk. More than once, she banged her head, causing the old man to grunt in annoyance. Up and down the compartment came muted voices engaged in intimate conversation. Two compartments over, a man with a scratchy throat rumbled instructions to his wife. Across the aisle, the young mother cajoled her children to sleep. And the old man—he was already snoring in the berth above her head.

The curtain gave her as much privacy as she could expect under such circumstances, considering strangers were sleeping all around her.

And she would have no privacy at all when Joe returned from the club car.

What a strange feeling. She had never felt so exposed, even though the other passengers couldn't see her. She had no experience with travel being so . . . public. When her family traveled south to North Carolina, they used the family's privately owned railcar. And in Europe, first-class passengers could expect closed compartments with doors, not flimsy curtains.

Yet she was determined to make the best of things. She wasn't about to let a situation faced by hundreds of travelers a day defeat her.

Her blouse partially unbuttoned, Meryl poked her nose out between the curtains and saw that other passengers had also vanished inside their little cocoons to undress. Apparently, this was a perfectly normal thing to do, even with complete strangers mere feet away.

Don't worry about it. Just hurry! a voice screamed inside her head. Joe could appear at any moment, and she couldn't bear the idea that he would catch her undressing. It was bad enough that she couldn't shake images from what Annabelle had told her. To her dismay, she imagined Joe—and only Joe—as the man moving inside a woman, enjoying the train's churning rhythm. She still felt hot—and a little naughty—for having discussed such a subject. She hadn't expected it would leave her so disturbed.

She wriggled out of her blouse and shirt. Left in her chemise, she climbed down to tuck her garments under the bed along with her shoes. Her corset also went under the bed.

Her heart pounded in her throat. Joe could return at any moment, and see her here, practically in her all-together, except for her knickers and chemise. As fast as she could, she scrambled into the berth, closed the curtain, and slid between the sheets. Her heart in her throat, she waited.

It was nearly midnight.

In the darkened, quiet sleeper car, Joe hesitated outside the closed curtain which marked where his seat had been. He slipped a finger around the edge of the curtain and peered inside. Muted moonlight from the curtained window edged the hills and valleys of a woman's body. She lay under the blanket, facing the wall, still and silent in sleep. Her golden mane lay spread over the second pillow—his pillow. He would have to brush it aside to lay his head down.

The blanket had slid down to expose her shoulder, clad only in a thin chemise. She couldn't be wearing much else except, perhaps, a pair of lacy knickers. And under that . . . Despite himself, the thought of Meryl's nakedness so near—so accessible—filled his body with torrid heat.

He had hoped she would make other arrangements, thought she might use her status to talk the porter into giving her another bed. Instead, she had left it up to him to find somewhere appropriate—somewhere *else*—to sleep.

He should have expected as much from a spoiled miss like her. Yet he had bought his ticket first. Posing as his wife was entirely her idea. The situation had been personally created by her. It would do her good to face a few consequences of her rash behavior.

Of course it would. Just the thought of her waking up and finding him lying in bed next to her—her shock alone would knock sense into her. If anything would make a woman face the truth of her female limitations, a dangerous indiscretion would do it. Even if it was entirely pretend. After all, he wouldn't dream of laying a hand on her.

He had promised her father he would take care of her. And he would—until he found some way to shake her.

His mind made up, he slipped off his coat. His movements slow and deliberate, he removed the rest of his clothing. He took unusual care to neatly fold each item he removed. He knew he was delaying. When he wore only his undershirt and drawers, he took the stack of clothing and tucked it under the bed—right on top of a frilly feminine petticoat.

He swore under his breath. There was no getting around it. He was about to share a bed with Meryl Carrington—his childhood nemesis, now grown, and with a woman's tempting body.

If he lay atop the sheet, at least, it would put a layer of cloth between them, thin as it was. Straightening, he carefully pulled back only the blanket, and slid beneath it.

Her hair . . . Even more carefully, he slid his palm under the tresses atop his pillow. She didn't stir, thank God.

He meant to release her hair, but the silken locks felt so good, he allowed the strands to remain in his hand where it rested on the pillow.

Hair this soft should be a crime, he thought to himself. And the scent—spring roses and a trace of lemon, probably what gave her hair its shine.

Lying back, he tried to relax, but his wide shoulders bumped her. He swore under his breath. He would have to lie on his side to even fit. Slowly, carefully, he rolled over, melding his shape to hers.

The deep-throated curse shivered down Meryl's spine. Her fist tightened on the sheet near her chin, her spine stiffening as the mattress shifted and Joe Hammond joined her in bed.

As he settled into place, curving around her, her memory flashed back more than a dozen years to a time when she had once before slept beside him. The Carringtons and Hammonds had gone on a picnic with friends at her family's country estate in Connecticut—the same place where she had so recently crossed paths with him again. That afternoon so many years ago, she hadn't felt well. She had spent most of the afternoon napping on a blanket in the shade of a tree.

At one point, she stirred from her drowsy sleep to find Joe lying on his side staring at her. Her eyes opened wide, and for a brief, silly moment, she imagined he was intending to kiss her.

"So you're *not* dead. Drat. She's not dead!" he called at the top of his lungs, his cry piercing her eardrums and making her head hurt.

He scrambled to his knees and muttered a curse she had never heard before. She knew if his mother heard it, she would wash his mouth out with soap.

He stared down at her, all gangly limbs and freckles. "Well, Pest, you made me lose a bet, not bein' underfoot and all. I've never seen you so pale and dead-looking."

Then he grinned. As usual, she had been the object of his amusement. He ran to rejoin two boys his age who were tossing a ball around, along with her tomboy sister Pauline. Joe probably never gave the moment a second thought.

Tonight, he was again cursing as he crawled into bed beside her. The bed was barely large enough for both of them. The heat of his body warmed her through. Or was that her blush of embarrassment? Or perhaps the heat was from a different source altogether.

She turned her head—and felt tension on her scalp. She slid her eyes toward him and saw his hand on the pillow by her head, her tresses lying across his palm. His eyes were closed, but his fingers fondled her stray locks, sending delicious tingles across her scalp and down her spine all the way to her toes.

He's stroking my hair. He must know he's doing it. He must feel something, too, this exciting heat under his skin . . .

She shifted her thighs, unable to hold completely still. Then she caught herself and froze. She couldn't let him know she was aware that he was lying beside her.

Too late. He jerked his hand from her hair and flipped all the way over, his back to her. The blanket slid halfway down his arm. In the tiny five-foot-wide bed, he was a massive presence.

Muted light from the moon, and the occasional station lights, slid along his body, revealing enough for her to see just how big he really was, now that he was grown. She hadn't realized how *wide* he was. His shoulders had to be three feet across, and his arms—they were packed tight with muscle. Her fingers tingled with the need to touch him, to learn what a young man's body felt like.

Embarrassed at her unexpected weakness where Joe was concerned, she turned to face the wall and tried her best to put him from her mind.

Her efforts failed miserably. When she managed to drift to sleep hours later, a curious sensation awakened her. Warm, she felt so warm. She floated in a blissful cloud, supported and comfortable.

Coming more awake, she realized that Joe's body enfolded hers, spoonlike, his front cradling her back, her bottom nestled against his abdomen.

Her eyes shot open as her situation sank in. Joe had secured her against him with one brawny arm. His palm burned where he cradled her lower abdomen, his fingers so close to her womanhood, they sparked an unfamiliar passion deep within her.

She closed her eyes, relaxing into the forbidden touch. Being held by him gave her a delicious feeling of comfort tinged with excitement. Who was this man who could tease her senses so? Had she ever really known him? Or, perhaps, she had always known him.

Unless he didn't feel the same.

He wasn't even aware of her inner turmoil. His deep, even breaths stirred the hair at the nape of her neck. If she pulled away from his grasp, she would wake him. He would turn his back to her, ignore her, say something cutting or rude.

Instead, she chose to stay where she was, and allow herself to pretend he liked her, just a little.

With a final look in the mirror, Meryl pulled in a deep breath. Morning had come, and she was finally ready to face the day. She was never one to run from confrontations.

Joe had left their bed—*their bed!*—at least an hour ago. The evening before, she had given the dining car steward a breakfast time an hour later than Joe's. Still, he hadn't yet returned to the passenger car. If he was still in the dining car, she'd simply ignore him, that's all.

She had waited for her turn at the women's lavatory. Now every hair was in place. Her hat perched neatly on her head, she grasped her gloves and handbag and headed for the end of the car. Sliding open a door, she entered the vestibule between the cars. The rattle of the wheels on the tracks was loud here, and the wind nipped at her neatly done coiffure. She hurried on, into the next passenger car. She wanted to look calm, and collected, not blowsy or windblown.

After passing through two other passenger cars, she arrived at the door to the dining car. She paused, feeling the car shudder beneath her boots.

If Joe was in there . . . *Don't run away, silly. He'll see your discomfort in your face!*

She couldn't hide her feelings from him. He

knew her far too well, unfortunately. Her idea of avoiding him was not only impractical on a closed train, it was silly and childish—exactly what Joe believed of her already. She would only be proving his point.

Instead of avoiding him, she realized, she had to face him head on. Even better, she shouldn't allow him to pretend he'd done nothing last night. He had to acknowledge the intimacy they had shared. That was the only sensible solution. She couldn't go through the tenseness of another sleepless night with Joe nearly naked beside her, *holding* her, without knowing how he felt about her.

She pushed through the door to the dining car. Tables covered in white linen packed the diners as tightly as possible—tables for two on the left; tables for four on the right. The sun shining through the windows softened the dark-wood paneling and deep blue carpet. Chandeliers hung overhead, and chrysanthemums in crystal vases decorated each table. Uniformed and attentive stewards did their utmost to foster the atmosphere of a fine dining experience.

In a matter of seconds, Meryl spotted Joe. He sat at the fifth table on the right, and he wasn't alone. Annabelle had joined him, and they seemed to be enjoying congenial conversation along with their breakfasts. At least there was room at the table for her—should she decide to join them.

Meryl wasn't at all sure she ought to. Joe had found the loveliest woman traveling alone to dine with. It certainly hadn't taken him long. *I hardly care, except that Annabelle thinks he's my husband.*

Yet that had been her idea alone. He had never agreed to the ruse.

She suddenly felt uncomfortable with the idea of confronting him, or even being with him in front of Annabelle's inquisitive, experienced eye. Without Joe's cooperation, Annabelle would know immediately that they were the furthest thing from newlyweds. Even if he played along, Annabelle would find it odd that Meryl showed no affection for her husband, particularly after what the married woman had described to Meryl the evening before. Meryl turned to leave, but Annabelle's clear voice derailed her escape plan.

"Mrs. Hammond? Meryl! Good morning."

Meryl forced a smile to her face and walked down the narrow aisle to their table. A steward appeared and pulled out a chair for her next to Joe. She pretended not to notice and took the chair beside Annabelle instead.

"I wondered when you would make an appearance," Annabelle said. "Your husband was kind enough to let me join him while he waited for you. We're almost finished." She gestured to their nearly empty plates.

"She's such a lazybones," Joe drawled, giving her a dimpled smile coupled with a flinty look. "I swear, if the porter hadn't needed to make up the berth, she'd still be lying there, snoozing."

"It's not entirely my fault I slept so poorly," Meryl countered.

"Ah," Annabelle said with a knowing glint in her eyes. "You've discovered train travel can be quite exhausting." She glanced from Meryl to Joe, clearly assuming they had enjoyed the train's "rhythm" during the night.

Embarrassed beyond bearing, Meryl was glad to turn her attention to the menu the steward placed in her hands. After a moment, she peeked over the top. Across from her, Joe was toying with his napkin and avoiding both women's gazes. Perhaps the intimate topic disturbed him as well. Good.

Meryl ordered the first breakfast listed—eggs Benedict, juice and coffee. While she waited for her meal to arrive, Joe and Annabelle resumed their conversation about Joe's life in Mexico.

"You lived in a tent, you were saying?" Annabelle asked Joe, her expression one of avid interest.

"Wherever my crews were laying down track."

"Oh, Meryl," Annabelle said. "You must have missed him terribly."

Meryl began, "I hadn't met him yet—"

"She wrote me every day—" Joe said, speaking on top of Meryl's words.

Joe grasped her hand where it rested beside her plate and gave it a hard squeeze. She forced herself not to snatch it back.

"My little eggplant. She gets confused sometimes." He gave her a patronizing look. "We were talking about my time *in* Mexico. You remember me going to Mexico, don't you? The big country south of here?"

Meryl gritted her teeth. He was making her sound like an idiot. "Of course I remember, dearest darling." She pried her hand free of his. "Remember how supportive I was? If you ever want to go back, feel free."

A single laugh burst from his tight lips. "I hardly think a second round is in my future. Unlike *some* employees of Atlantic-Southern, I paid my dues on the frontier."

Awkward silence strung out between them, finally broken by Annabelle. "Please tell me more about your experiences, Mr. Hammond. Didn't you mention desperados tried to raid your camp?"

"Actually, yes. More than once. We managed to scare them off, with a little ingenuity." Warming to his tale, Joe focused again on Annabelle, pointedly ignoring Meryl. She concentrated on the breakfast the steward brought her and pretended his stories didn't fascinate her.

At least her apparent lack of interest might be understandable for Annabelle. The lady must conclude that Joe had already told his wife all of these stories. In truth, Joe hadn't bothered to tell her much of anything about his life. They had been too occupied with arguing to engage in anything resembling a normal conversation.

A sad situation, considering they had known each other their entire lives.

She shoved away her barely touched meal, her appetite deserting her. Not wanting Joe to think she was listening to his stories, she extracted her timetable from her handbag and pretended to study it.

"It's not going to change."

Several seconds passed before Meryl realized Joe was addressing her. "My little eggplant. So excited by her very first train trip." Reaching across the table, he chucked he on the chin as if she were five years old. Meryl glared at him.

Annabelle looked from her to Joe. "Her first trip as a wife, at least," she said dryly. Meryl had told her earlier that she frequently traveled. "Why don't I leave you two to enjoy each other's company? A little time alone might relieve the *stress* of traveling."

"You're leaving?" Meryl stiffened, alarm coursing through her. With Annabelle gone, she would have no excuse not to confront Joe about last night.

Annabelle rose and dropped her napkin on the table. "I'm sure I'll see you two later. It's not as if one can leave this train."

The minute Annabelle was out of sight, Joe began to spar with her. "You certainly woke up on the wrong side of the bed this morning. Or I should say, 'berth'?"

Meryl set down her timetable and focused all her attention on Joe. "And you're certainly congenial. At least to ladies traveling alone."

He shrugged. "Mrs. Yves-Kendall was good enough to join me. You were too lazy to bother."

She tossed down her napkin. "I know exactly why you're interested in Mrs. Yves-Kendall. It's obvious."

"Meaning?"

"When you were sixteen, you couldn't take your eyes off my sister Lily, remember?"

He leaned back, a look of disbelief on his face. "You can't mean—"

"I certainly do mean. Men like women who are . . . you know."

He threw his head back and laughed. "Poor Meryl, still wishing she had more up top."

"Shut up, Joe." She fidgeted in her chair, desperate to keep some semblance of composure. "I have no intention of attracting a man in such a way."

"No danger of it, either."

His words, delivered with a smile, cut deeper than she ever would have imagined. So, he found her physically unattractive. She shouldn't care, but her pride certainly did.

The feelings he'd stirred in her the night before rushed back to her. He had touched her. Despite his words, he had *wanted* to touch her!

What she wouldn't do to hear him admit it! "Odd that you should say that," she slowly began, determined to gain the upper hand. "Considering your actions last night."

He avoided her gaze. "I haven't the faintest idea what you're prattling on about. Eat your breakfast like a good girl and leave me be."

Oh, how she hated his condescending attitude! She pressed her palms to the table and leaned forward, her voice carefully low, but filled with tension. "You crawled into bed with me last night. If my father knew—"

"I had every right. It's my berth, Mrs. Hammond," he said with derision. "Besides, you're like a sister to me, remember? Brothers and sisters in Mexico—or the American frontier, for that matter—share beds all the time, if their families are poor."

Meryl sat back, dismayed at his casual dismissal of something that had deeply affected her. "That's all you have to say about it? It didn't bother you in the least?"

He shrugged, a broad, self-assured smile growing on his face. "Not in the least. Obviously my presence bothered *you*. I had no idea you were soft for me."

Her mouth dropped open in shock. "I'm not—"

"You seem bound and determined to believe our sleeping arrangements meant something. Poor, disillusioned Meryl."

How dare he? She forced her next words through gritted teeth. "Then how do you explain that you were holding me?"

That made his cocky smile fade. "What?"

"Last night. You wrapped your arm around my waist and held me, right against you."

He shrugged nonchalantly, but didn't meet her eyes. "The bed was so small, it was the only comfortable way to sleep."

"That doesn't explain why you were stroking my hair."

"This is getting ridiculous." He pushed back from the table, preparing to leave her.

She whipped out her hand and pinned his to the table to keep him there. "You thrust your hand into my hair and—" She glanced around. The intensity of their conversation in the cramped quarters was drawing the notice of nearby diners.

She lowered her voice even further. "You played with it."

His lips tightened, and his smile seemed forced. "Hah! As if I could avoid it. There's rather a lot of it." His eyes focused on her chignon, under a pert hat.

Instinctively, her hand slipped toward her neck, her fingertips brushing the fullness at the nape of her neck. "That's not the point." She cleared her throat, determined not to let his assessment unnerve her, even if it bordered on being a compliment. "You were—you were—"

"What?" he demanded, his flinty eyes on hers.

Her voice slid into a harsh whisper. "*Enjoying* yourself."

He gave her a cool stare. Crossing his arms, he leaned back, continuing to study her with those cool, green eyes. "I pet dogs, **too,** because it's enjoyable. It means nothing."

She slapped the table, sloshing coffee from her cup onto the linen tablecloth. "Fine, Joe. Compare me to a beast. I always knew you would fail to grow into a gentleman." She lurched to her feet, prepared to stamp out of there—until she realized he would only laugh at such a childish display.

Changing her strategy, she took a deep breath to regain a semblance of composure. "You may compare me to a dog, or a . . . an *eggplant,* but as far as I'm concerned, you're the real beast," she said, her words hard. "From now on, keep your roaming paws to yourself."

He opened his mouth to reply, but no words emerged. Her eruption had drawn the notice of all the diners at their end of the car. After a few seconds of heavy silence, the other passengers began murmuring among themselves. Meryl ignored them. She took two steps toward the connecting door at the end of the car, then spun back to him. "And don't call me a vegetable!" Her parting shot delivered, she strode from the car.

"Is there anything else I can get you, sir?" An ebony hand slid the bill into his line of sight on the tabletop.

Joe pulled his thoughts off Meryl and looked at the steward. Laying his palm on the bill, he dragged it toward him and picked it up. The total included Meryl's breakfast. Again she interfered with his life. Yet that fact didn't bother him nearly as much as the puzzle of what to do about her.

He never doubted he would win this bet. But Meryl's interference disrupted his usually sharp thinking. He prided himself on being savvy and analytical, the most capable of businessmen. Meryl managed to confound his plans merely with her presence. It had always been like that. Even as a girl she had intruded on his games with other children, her sharp tongue cutting him down to size.

And as a woman— *As a woman* . . . By God, he couldn't stop thinking of her as a woman. Not after last night, when he had shared her bed, felt her shapeliness in his arms, the warmth of her body intensifying the heat in his blood.

Now, just a handful of hours later, the memory sent his pulse racing.

Shaking his head at his weakness, he extracted his billfold and placed the money on the table.

The steward appeared to retrieve it instantly. "Thank you, sir. It has been a pleasure serving you."

Joe barely heard him. He stared into his coffee cup, seeing only Meryl's victorious smile. He had to find a way to shake her, once and for all. Get so far ahead she would never catch up. Rather difficult to do when they were on the same train. Short of throwing her off the train, he was stuck with her, at least until they changed trains in Omaha.

After a moment, he realized the steward remained beside his chair. "Are you certain there is nothing else you need, sir?" he asked.

"No, I'm fine."

"Then, sir, may I suggest the club car for drinks and cigars? Or even a newspaper? We receive daily papers from every town we pass, if you are interested in the stock market or other news."

Joe finally looked around, and saw other passengers standing near the entrance, waiting for tables. Embarrassed by his lack of manners, he quickly rose. "Of course."

Damn that girl. She had him completely distracted.

The steward immediately began clearing the table. Joe was about to walk out when he spotted one item the steward had left behind—Meryl's timetable.

Joe picked it up. God knew what fascinated her about the thing. They would get there when they

got there, and none of the numerous stops in between made a whit of difference.

   He squinted at the rows of numbers lined up in
neat columns. Tonight they would arrive at Fort
Wayne for a dinner break, more than an hour and
a half for passengers to take dinner at a restaurant
off the train and stretch their legs. The train would
leave the Fort Wayne station at 6:47 P.M.

   6:47 P.M. A six didn't look that much different
from other numbers, say, an eight . . . A flash of inspiration filled him, possibly his ticket out of this
mess. He thrust the timetable into his jacket
pocket and headed for the club car.

Six

With wheels squealing and air brakes hissing, the train slowed, rolling to a stop in the Fort Wayne station.

Joe held his breath as Meryl pulled out her timetable. Apparently, she hadn't noticed that she had left it behind at breakfast. He had slipped it back into her handbag when she had visited the lavatory.

"Hmm." Her brow furrowed.

Trying to appear calm despite his racing heart, he stretched his arm along the back of her seat. "Is something wrong?"

She gave him a wary look, as if she expected every utterance from his mouth to be a lie. He couldn't blame her for that. "Of course not," she said. "It's only that I thought we'd be leaving Fort Wayne around seven. But it will be almost nine."

He flashed his dimple. "Giving us plenty of time for dinner."

"Us?"

"Since we'll be here for almost three hours, we might as well make the best of it."

Little frown lines gathered between her baby

blue eyes. "Meaning?" Good Lord, could she be any more suspicious of him?

"A temporary truce, as long as dinner lasts." He rose and settled his derby on his head. "The nicest place at this stop that serves travelers is just around the corner. What do you say?" He thrust out his hand.

"I suppose it wouldn't hurt. Just this once." With that ringing endorsement, Meryl accepted his hand and allowed him to pull her to her feet.

Her hand resting in his, he gazed down into her eyes. In the narrow space between the seats, she stood so close, her scent enfolded him.

As he studied her sweet face, guilt tingled in his gut. He had always looked out for Meryl as a kid sister. And she would be furious when she found out he had fooled her. She would never trust him again.

Yet she had to recognize that this was a competition. His entire future hinged on his success. On defeating her. On erasing his father's legacy.

Until then, he would allow himself to enjoy her company. He might never have another chance. Lifting her fur-lined cloak, he held it open for her. "Let's go."

After a long hesitation, she turned her back to him and allowed him to slip the cloak over her shoulders. She picked up her handbag, adjusted her hat and gloves, and followed the line of exiting passengers to the steps at the end of the car.

To Meryl's surprise, Joe linked his arm with hers as they left the station. They passed a few store windows decorated with tinsel and paper angels for the coming Christmas holiday. It seemed far too early to think about Christmas. Then again, she had been distracted.

She wondered where she would be on Christmas day. In San Francisco, completing the details of the purchase of Westgate Railroad? Or would she already have successfully negotiated the deal, and be back home to share the holidays with her family? She had always spent Christmas with her family, and found it difficult to imagine going through the holidays alone.

You're a businesswoman now, she counseled herself. For the first time, she realized there could be a price to pay for dedicating herself to her profession. Yet she wasn't a little girl anymore, dreaming of sugarplums and Father Christmas. It was time for her to make her way in the world. If she made her way alone, so be it.

She glanced at the tall, dapper man beside her. On his arm, she didn't feel at all alone, and it felt good. She noticed other women's eyes following them as they passed. She had to admit he was a handsome fellow, an escort any woman would be proud to display.

They passed several restaurants that catered to train travelers, yet Joe continued walking. At the end of the second block, he paused and glanced down the street, then turned the corner.

"I thought you said it was nearby," Meryl said. He seemed not to know where he was going.

He patted her hand reassuringly as he contin-

ued to peer down the street. "It's right around
here. I'm sure of it. There it is!"

He headed toward a run-down establishment
fronted by a sagging boardwalk. Honky-tonk music
spilled into the street from a partly open door.
Under the tinny piano, she caught snatches of conversation and the clink of glasses.

"You must be jesting," Meryl said, dragging her
feet.

Grasping her arm, Joe propelled her through
the door into the smoky interior.

"*This* is your fine establishment?" Meryl began to
wonder whether Joe's comprehension—or at least
his taste—had been damaged by the hot Mexican
sun.

"I didn't say fine. I said nice. Sit." He pulled out
a chair for her at a scarred round table near the
door. Along the entire length of one wall stretched
a bar, where several men who looked as if they had
just come from factories and farms sipped beers
and whiskey.

At the back, a man with slicked back hair and a
droopy mustache plunked half-heartedly at an upright piano, his narrow fingers drawing forth the
plaintive notes of "Bird in a Gilded Cage."

"Don't tell me you're so used to being pam-
pered that you can't dine where regular folk dine,"
Joe chided. Already seated, he signaled the waiter.

"Regular folk?" Only three other women pa-
tronized the place, two of whom appeared to be of
questionable virtue.

Joe heaved a sigh. "You can take the girl away

from Fifth Avenue, but you can't take Fifth Avenue away from the girl."

"Don't be snide. I've dined in plenty of places like this," she lied. She slowly lowered herself into the rickety pine chair. Despite her best intentions, she wondered if the furniture would stain her finely tailored traveling suit. *You have to get used to the world beyond what you know,* she told herself sternly, *or you'll never be able to compete with men like Joe.*

A man in a stained apron came from behind the bar. "What'll it be?"

"Your steak dinner special," Joe said, pointing to a blackboard at the end of the bar. "A whiskey for me and a tonic water for the lady."

"I would prefer a glass of red wine," Meryl said just to annoy him.

"Don't have wine. Beer and hard liquor only," the waiter said disinterestedly.

"A Coca-cola then."

The waiter turned to leave.

"And we have a train to catch," Meryl rushed to add. "We're on the Continental Limited, and we leave in . . ." She checked the watch pinned to her jacket. "Two hours and nineteen minutes."

"Yeah, yeah, everybody's in a hurry," the waiter muttered as he left.

As they waited for their meal, silence fell between Meryl and her dinner partner. What were they supposed to talk about? He disliked her, and she certainly couldn't stand being in his company for long. "I'm sure you wish Mrs. Yves-Kendall was your dining companion, rather than I."

He arched a brow. "Why do you say that? You're fairly charming, when you want to be."

Was that a compliment? She didn't know how to react to a Joseph Hammond who was polite to her. "Thank you," she muttered.

He cocked his head and studied her. "Is that a blush?" He leaned closer. "Did I make little Pest blush? By God, I did!"

"Shut up, Dodo Bird." Shaking out her napkin—or, rather, the worn linen square that passed for a napkin, she laid it on her lap and avoided his gaze.

He chuckled. "You seem awfully concerned with my good opinion."

"I couldn't care less what you think."

"I don't hate you, Meryl. You have to know that."

Her gaze flicked up and she caught him gazing at her with something approaching kindness. She wasn't sure she could deal with a Joseph Hammond who was kind to her. Before joining him for breakfast, she had penned an effusive entry in her journal about how Joe had held her while she slept, how she imagined growing closer to him. After his rude denials at breakfast, those silly, girlish thoughts had suffered a merciful death.

Now, his kindness began to stir them up again, putting her on edge. There was no question it would be easy for a woman to fall for his charms.

The steaks arrived. To her dismay, but not surprise, Meryl found hers as tough as shoe leather. Picking up her knife, she fruitlessly sawed at the slab of meat. "You consider this a good place to eat? Too bad your college education failed to transform you into a sophisticated fellow. It's not too late to go to another restaurant."

Joe shook his head and dug into his own steak with gusto. "The food here is fine. I would hate to insult the proprietor by walking out now."

Meryl glanced at the waiter behind the bar. He looked decidedly bored. "I don't think he cares."

"Still." He popped a chunk of meat into his mouth. After several moments of chewing, he swallowed hard, his Adam's apple bobbing with the strain. He downed several swallows of beer.

They ate in silence. Unable to stomach more than a few bites of the lumpy mashed potatoes, Meryl occupied herself watching Joe dine. He ate with the same gusto and determination he had exhibited during their shooting contest.

He took the last bite, washed it down with beer, then shoved his empty plate aside. Leaning back, he gazed at her assessingly. "Meryl, why is this business deal important to you? Why are you willing to race across the country just to talk railroads with some gent in San Francisco? You know the chances he'll listen to a woman are slim to none."

"I know nothing of the sort," she said stiffly. "You're doing exactly the same thing. So why is my ambition less worthy than yours?"

Instead of a sharp comeback, he paused a moment. When he spoke again, his words were slow and thoughtful. "That's a valid question. Mr. Carrington has been more of a father to me than my own, more concerned with me as a person. The opportunities he has provided me . . . I can't begin to express how greatly I appreciate it."

She hadn't imagined Joe feeling particularly grateful. "But why wouldn't he? Your father was one of his business partners. You're longtime friends of our family."

"Who went bankrupt, costing your own family millions."

His abrupt statement shocked Meryl beyond words. As the revelation sank in, she reflected on her family's relationship with the Hammonds. She had noticed they had socialized less in the year before Mr. Hammond succumbed to a heart ailment, but hadn't given it much thought until now.

She studied Joe across the rough pine table. His lips were pressed into a thin line, and the muscles outlining his strong jaw had tensed, creating hollows in his cheeks. "What happened?"

He looked genuinely surprised. "You don't know? I thought everyone on the East Coast knew what a fool my father was, bless his soul."

"Tell me," she said gently, anxious for him to share. The bet forgotten, she found herself wanting to understand what drove him. She sensed he was in pain, an emotion she had never associated with the happy-go-lucky Joseph Hammond.

He took a sip of his beer, then began. "It's an embarrassingly predictable story. A land dealer sold him mining rights to a worthless parcel in Nevada. Showed him engineering diagrams and prospectors' reports—enough false information to convince him that mining the land was worth the gamble. My father relished the idea of becoming as rich as Midas—or a Carrington," he said wryly.

Meryl grimaced. Another revelation she'd been

blind to. The Hammonds had felt beneath her family, and she'd never even suspected it.

Joe continued quietly, "The land failed to yield anything, except a few specks of fool's gold. But once my father started his foolhardy venture, he couldn't stop. He ended up sinking most of our family's capital into the mine, losing all the money he had earned in partnership with your father."

He smiled grimly and shook his head. "But that wasn't bad enough. He had to involve your family, too. Halfway through the project, even more capital was needed to keep the project afloat. My father convinced your father to invest in the mine, too. After more than a year of trying to find gold, the money ran out, and he had to face the truth. He owned mining rights to a worthless stretch of desert coughing up nothing but sand. That was when the Panic of '93 hit. It finished the job, leaving us virtually penniless except for a small trust set aside for me. The humiliation did Father in as much as his weak heart. That's the real reason why, in his last year of life, my family stopped visiting with yours."

"I didn't even notice," Meryl murmured, struck by how self-involved she had been. "I must have been blind, too wrapped up in my own dreams and plans to pay heed to anybody else."

He shrugged. "You had just left for college before the bottom fell out."

"Still, I spent school breaks at home. I should have seen . . ." She hated to think this of her parents, but she had to know. "Did my— Did my parents cut yours socially?" The cut was the worst punishment that could be meted out to anyone within their circle. If Mrs. Carrington had socially cut the Hammonds, who stood below them on the social scale, the Hammonds would no longer have been welcome in any home on New York's Fifth Avenue.

Joe shook his head. "No. Your mother continued to invite us to gatherings, but my father couldn't bring himself to accept. He was growing weaker, and that made for a convenient excuse. Eventually our families would have gone their separate ways, having no truck with each other—if it hadn't been for your father's generosity."

Meryl leaned forward intently. "What did he do?"

His long fingers stroked his beer glass, drawing her gaze to their restless, almost sensual, movements as the past pulled him in. "I was out of college with my engineering degree, but had very few employment prospects. The Hammond name was no longer respected in the railroading industry. I had always dreamed of following in my father's footsteps in railroading, and could think of only one possible way in. So, I girded my loins, so to speak, and paid a visit to your father, thoroughly expecting to be tossed out on my ear. To my pleasant surprise, he offered me a job."

Pride filled her at her father's action. "The job in Mexico?"

"That opportunity came after about six months assisting Mr. Bainbridge."

She nodded. "The head of engineering."

"Mexico was the first in a long road of accomplishments which might one day erase the shame of my father's poor business dealings."

"And you imagine Westgate Railroad is the second."

The challenge came back into his eyes. "That's right."

She had known he was determined, but hadn't realized why. Hadn't seen the pain of his father's actions steering his own. "But you could have any position in my father's company. Why this one?"

A smile traced his lips. "There aren't that many division presidencies, as you well know."

"Aren't you letting your ambition get the better of you? The same thing happened to your father."

He grimaced and pulled back, pain etched on his strong features. Meryl immediately regretted her hasty volley.

"Ouch," he muttered. "That was hardly pleasant, but not unexpected, coming from you. I see you don't understand me at all. I *care* about pleasing your father."

Fighting to cover her guilt for her rude observation, she said stiffly, "No more than I do."

He leaned toward her, placed his arms on the table, and gave her a penetrating look. "Then why are you chasing this dream, instead of finding some fellow to settle down with? Why not ask yourself which would please your father more?"

Meryl glared at him. "Now you're being unfair. My father wants me to be happy. And I happen to believe being the heir to his company—our company—will make me happy, as well as him."

Joe stared hard at her, his gaze probing her own.

After a tension-filled moment, he leaned back in his chair, his frame relaxing against the slender pine chair back. "Then we're at an impasse."

She lifted her chin. "You expected that to change? You don't know me at all, Joseph Hammond."

He rose to his feet. Placing his hand on the back of her chair, he smiled down at her, his dimple appearing like a crescent in his left cheek. "Perhaps, when we're back aboard, we can remedy that."

His smile did strange things to her insides, warming her more than his arms had the night before. "We're leaving?"

He shook his head and glanced at her barely touched meal. "Enjoy your . . . potatoes for a moment. I need to go out back. I'll only be a minute." He gave her an audacious wink, then disappeared out the door.

She stared after him. That wink had unnerved her worse than his smile. She thought again about his story of lost family honor, of devotion to her father. She hadn't known such passionate feelings drove him. Hadn't guessed such depths brewed inside him.

Now that she did know, she felt a little sad that they were at such cross purposes. *He'll have another opportunity,* she told herself. *Of course he will. He's a man. But I may not, not if I don't prove myself now, before I'm forever looked upon as a file clerk.*

She sighed and picked at her meal. Joe wasn't very good at selecting eating establishments, but he had been decent company. She had to admit that, at least. She had always found Joe easy to talk to, ever since they were children. She had always said what she thought, and, she believed, so had he. Now that they were adults, saying exactly what she thought had become much more difficult. She wasn't about to tell him she enjoyed his company. Whenever he chose to grace her with it again.

She glanced at her lapel watch, and saw that fifteen minutes had passed. No doubt the only facility for this place was an outhouse around back. Perhaps the steak hadn't agreed with him? Or was the outhouse difficult to find?

She tapped her fingers on the table and studied her plate. Picking up her fork, she pushed the potatoes around, now and then sampling a bit.

After awhile, she again checked her watch, and was stunned to see that almost thirty minutes had gone by. In the distance came a high-pitched, familiar whistle, and Meryl realized she had heard the train whistle a few minutes earlier. The final boarding call for a train leaving the station. Not hers, of course. The Continental Limited wasn't leaving for more than an hour yet.

She stared at Joe's empty plate and nearly empty beer glass. What was keeping him?

Another few minutes passed, and her niggling concern began to transform into worry. Had something terrible happened to him out on the street? She was dimly aware of the muted blast of a train funnel venting steam, followed by the echoey rumble of an engine chugging away from the station.

Unable to sit still a second longer, she jumped to her feet and headed for the door.

"Just you wait a minute, miss. You ain't paid up yet." The proprietor crossed toward the door, positioning himself there as an obstacle.

"I'm sorry." Yanking open her handbag, Meryl fished out five dollars. "Will this cover it?"

The waiter smiled and snatched the money as if afraid she would take it back.

Out on the boardwalk, Meryl tightened the fur collar of her cloak about her neck. A fine sleet had begun to fall, making the November night even more dreary and unwelcoming. She looked up and down the dark, icy street. Heading to the end of the building, she glanced into the alley and spotted the outhouse. The door hung crookedly open on squeaking hinges, swinging back and forth in the breeze. Either Joe was lacking in all modesty, or he wasn't in there.

A sick feeling churned in her stomach. In that instant, she knew the truth. The scoundrel had abandoned her, leaving her to pay for the meal. Fine. They were even.

Yes, in her anger she had deserted him that morning in the dining car, making him pay for breakfast. But to abandon her here, in this part of town . . . How could he do such a thing, merely over a few dollars?

Her angry strides carried her toward the corner. When she caught up with him on the train, she would chastise him so soundly, he would melt into a puddle and beg forgiveness. He would regret treating her like this. She vented her anger into the night air. "How dare you, Joe Hammond! My father told you to watch out for me. Leaving me in a saloon, of all things—"

She turned the corner, and froze. Two blocks down stood the train station. And behind it, on the tracks, was . . . nothing. No train idled there belching steam, waiting for passengers to load and unload. No passengers waited on the platform to board.

The Continental Limited had departed without her.

Seven

Joe sagged back in his seat as the train left the station, without Meryl Carrington.

He stared at his reflection in the window. Sleet spattered the glass in slender wet streaks like spider webs. Or a woman's tears.

He began to relax. He'd done it. About now, Meryl had dissolved into tears. Not much could make the stalwart, feisty girl cry, but he'd no doubt succeeded with his treachery.

His success satisfied him. Of course it did. Meryl must realize now that she couldn't begin to compete with men like him. He imagined her wiring her father, begging him to come rescue her. He imagined her back home in the warm embrace of her family and, eventually, in the embrace of a husband. Holding her, caressing her.

He squeezed his eyes shut and willed the image away, only to have it linger, and grow more detailed. Despite his best efforts, he imagined her future husband stroking her silken skin, breathing in the scent of her hair, exploring her curves with his hands. He would gaze into her eyes and she would gaze back, her blue eyes filled with tenderness and understanding. He pictured it with painful clarity, for she had gazed upon him at dinner in just such a heartfelt way. He had held her close and breathed in her scent. *He* had, no one else.

That man won't be you, he fiercely reminded himself. *Not after the wicked trick you just pulled.*

She would hate him now. A sick feeling swelled in his gut. Had he gone too far? Had he severed ties better left intact?

An even worse possibility, which had been nagging at the back of his mind, now pushed to the fore. He forced himself to consider the possibilities. Had he put Meryl in danger? He would never forgive himself if anything happened to her. Much as he tried to deny it, he *did* care for her, more than he wanted to admit.

She was so damned young and inexperienced. Too young to be playing a man's game. Worse, he had made a promise to her father. Even though Meryl had absolved him of responsibility for her, he still felt answerable to her father for her safety. If he had harmed Meryl by his actions, his future would be ruined, and deservedly so.

He began to have the dreadful feeling that he had just cut off his nose to spite his face.

Stranded at night in the snow-covered Fort Wayne street, Meryl threw back her head and screamed bloody murder.

A passing hobo glanced at her, then started running in the other direction. Ignoring him, Meryl picked up her skirts and sprinted toward the station. Joe had tricked her. He had fed her a sob story that was utterly false. He had lulled her into a feeling of companionship and encouraged her to let down her defenses, only to slap her in the face. He had played her for a fool.

That fact didn't sting her pride nearly as much as the realization that he had outsmarted her. Despite all her claims of being his equal, at his first opportunity, he had tricked her into staying off the train!

He'd been so amenable during dinner. She had actually begun to fall for his charms, actually believed that he enjoyed sharing his feelings with her. What a dupe she had been.

She should have used her brain, should have realized how silly such a notion was. She and Joe had spent hours together on the train, but he hadn't enjoyed being with her then. How foolish of her to believe they had actually started to grow closer!

He'd taken her in completely, with his smiling green eyes, dimpled grin, and tall tale filled with pain. Completely and utterly hoodwinked her.

How had he done it? The timetable—she had looked at it a dozen times, and been confused when she saw they would leave Fort Wayne at 8:47 instead of 6:47. Pulling the timetable from her handbag, she stepped under a sputtering gaslight and studied it closely. Sure enough, the surface of the card had been scratched. A few dots of ink from a fountain pen had transformed the number six into an eight. And she had fallen for the ruse.

A tiny kernel of admiration shone through her

anger. Very well, she admitted to herself, Joe was remarkably clever. A true competitor. She had never doubted it.

And if *she* had thought of such a ploy, she wouldn't have hesitated to do exactly the same to him.

Her anger at Joe gave way to anger at herself. She had no one but herself to blame, she admitted ruefully. He couldn't have gotten the better of her if she hadn't allowed it. Yes, she enjoyed being held by him. Yes, she found his smile attractive, his winks irresistible.

Yet she shouldn't allow her feelings for him to affect their competition. *He* certainly hadn't—assuming he felt anything for her. If she allowed her feelings to be an obstacle, she was nothing but the emotional female Joe had warned her father about.

Joe had won this battle. But he wouldn't win the war. She had no idea how she could possibly catch up with him. There was no mode of transportation faster than the steam engine, and no more direct route than the Continental Limited. Still, she had to try. She refused to admit defeat, not until the deal was done.

Meryl hurried to the ticket window at the station, only to find the small gate closed and locked. According to the posted schedule, the Continental Limited was the last train to leave Fort Wayne that evening. The next train west didn't come through until eight the next morning.

Her shoulders sagged. It was late, and she was growing colder by the second. She would have to find a hotel. That thought made her realize something else. All of her luggage, even her little traveling case, was on that train. All of her clothing and toiletries.

She had been stranded with nothing but a few dollars in her handbag, the doctored timetable, and the clothes on her back. She looked again in her handbag, hoping to find something more there, something that might help her hopeless situation. And another painful truth hit her.

Her journal, with her notes and observations about Westgate Railroad, was still on the train, tucked into a pocket of her small valise. She had left it there after writing in it that morning. After penning ridiculous female emotions about how Joe made her feel! And now Joe had access to her innermost thoughts.

Oh, Lord. A sick feeling filled her already tense stomach. By sheer force of will, she forced herself not to panic. He probably wouldn't think to look in it. He never believed she had written anything of value, and he wouldn't care a whit for her personal observations.

Or would he? *Don't worry about it now. Think only of catching up to him. Of winning.*

Looking down the street, she spotted a hotel sign swinging in the chill wind. The Kensington Arms probably catered to travelers by virtue of its location. It was hardly the Waldorf-Astoria, but it would be dry and warm. Besides, she had no choice. No choice at all. After a night's rest, she would think of something. Somehow, she would catch up to Joe. Not just catch up, but best him at his own game.

Revenge simmering within her, she yanked up her skirts and trudged through the churned up slush toward the modest inn.

What a waste of time. Cooling one's heels in an Omaha hotel could roughly be compared to having teeth pulled at the dentist's. Unfortunately, Joe had no choice. Changing trains in Omaha meant that he had to wait almost an entire day before he could continue his journey west. The Pacific Express, operated by Union Pacific, left for Sacramento once a day at 12:15. To his frustration, he had missed the connection by only a handful of hours.

Which meant a slim possibility that Meryl could catch up.

She won't make it, he assured himself. He had left her high and dry in Fort Wayne, with nothing but her handbag. It was now the weekend—she may not even be able to wire her family for money, should she need it.

God, he hoped she didn't need it. He would never forgive himself if she really lacked enough money to rent a room at an inn. Why hadn't he thought of that? What kind of gentleman was he? He should have slipped some bills into her handbag when she wasn't looking. It was the least he could have done, considering how easily he was going to win this wager.

He threw himself down on the plump mattress

and stared at the ceiling. Warmth from a small grille piped heat into a well-appointed room decorated with solid oak furniture, gold and blue wallpaper, and clean curtains and bedding. A throw rug had been spread across the hardwood floor.

Right then, he wished he were in a broken-down shack. Then he might feel less guilty. He was relaxing in a room for well-to-do travelers, while Meryl was somewhere out there . . . Visions of Meryl accosted by bandits, robbed by pickpockets, molested by strange men—

He squeezed his eyes shut. *Lord, no.* It wouldn't happen. It couldn't. She was a resourceful girl. She would be fine. Furious with him, but fine.

At least he'd thought to take care of her baggage. Silly chit, attempting to race him across the country with a trunk in tow. Of course, if she had managed to remain on the train, the trunk would have posed no problems. Even now, it sat in storage at the station, waiting to be claimed. Once he reached San Francisco, he would wire her back in New York and tell her where it was.

As for her small valise, he had carried that off the train along with his own bag. Swinging his legs off the bed, he lifted it off the floor and set it beside him on the bed. That journal of hers . . . While looking over her shoulder, he had briefly spied the name Mr. Philbottom, Westgate's president. Did she have information on him that he lacked? Something that might help him seal the purchase of Westgate Railroad? He ought to check, since he would be the company's representative. For the benefit of Atlantic-Southern Railroad.

Half convinced he was doing the right thing, he snapped the latch on the valise. He paused, his gaze playing over the sensuous, personal nature of the items within. He fingered a silky nightgown edged in Spanish lace. Beside it lay her hairbrush, which had captured a few strands of her golden hair. The intimacy of the items made him feel like a complete scoundrel, and he began to close the lid.

Until he spotted the corner of her red-leather journal. Lifting a satin corset—and struggling not to imagine Meryl wearing such a feminine item—he slid it out. Fighting back twinges of guilt, he flipped it open, determined to glance through it quickly for helpful information, and then put it firmly away.

The book fell open to the most recent entry. His own name jumped out at him, penned in her small, neat handwriting. *Damn, I shouldn't be reading this,* his conscience screamed. Too late. She had written about their night sleeping in the same bed, and he couldn't resist. His eyes flew over the lines.

> *I hardly know where to begin. I can scarcely believe the events of last night transpired. Yet I still feel the warmth of Joe's arms around me, the imprint of his body cradling mine in heavenly embrace. We slept side by side, so close, one could not slide a feather between us. I have known Joe for so long; in truth, the whole of my life. What, then, explains my passionate response to his touch?*
>
> *I can no longer claim to know this person, nor, I fear, myself. This Joe is a different being entirely, someone who engenders within me womanly feel-*

ings of a perilous and dangerous nature. Despite my common sense, despite the knowledge that this is Joe, I did not want our intimacy to end. I have never felt so alive, so right, comforted by the knowledge that I was not alone in the dark.

Joe, of all people, made me feel this way. I have always thought of him as an annoying boy. Now, however, that child has fled, leaving a confident man in his stead. I now wonder whether I ever truly knew Joe. Despite my common sense, despite our competition, I am filled with yearning to understand this man.

Now I must go to breakfast, where I intend to learn whether he feels the same.

Joe let the journal fall closed in his hands. Meryl had feelings for him. She had *feelings* for him? He certainly hadn't found it easy to sleep beside her. On the contrary, if Meryl had known about male anatomy, she would have felt his excitement as he pressed against her. Holding her had caused an ache in his groin so severe, he hadn't fallen asleep for hours. Unfortunately. spooning had been the only comfortable position in which to sleep.

Certainly, there was nothing unusual about his reaction to her. She was pretty. More than pretty. Positively arresting, with her pale skin, fine features, and golden mane.

The point being, she was female; he was male. Any man would have experienced the same heated physical response when lying beside her.

Which didn't quite explain why he couldn't put her out of his mind.

Meryl was an inexperienced woman. Only twenty-one years old, and unmarried. Naturally, she misconstrued her own physical response, believing it to be of a romantic nature. She didn't understand that any man with youth and vigor would probably cause her to feel the same.

Just as any attractive woman—

Stop fooling yourself. The truth struck him, and he finally allowed himself to acknowledge it. He had felt something for her, too, something hot and powerful and true. He could no longer deny the strength of his feelings for her. No woman would ever hold the place in his heart that Meryl had as a girl. Yet he felt anything but brotherly toward her. She interested him as a unique and lovely woman—clever, gorgeous, and brimming with life and sass. Perhaps someday . . .

"Don't be ridiculous," he chastised himself aloud in the silent room. "She drives you 'round the bend."

Besides, he had ruined their renewed acquaintance by accepting her bet, then playing her for a fool. He had already destroyed her feelings for him. He shouldn't think any further about it.

Yet he couldn't help himself.

An insistent tap on the door yanked him from his reverie. "Joe, it's Meryl. Please let me in."

Eight

Meryl? It couldn't be. Shock raced through Joe, along with the strange feeling that his own longings had conjured her out of thin air. How had she managed to catch up?

"Joseph Hammond, I know you're in there," she said, her voice muffled by the oak door. "Open up."

He felt like a boy caught with his hand in the cookie jar. Lurching to his feet he strode to the door, realized his folly, then raced back to the bed, where her journal lay open, damning evidence of his prying. He stuffed the journal back in the valise and latched it. On his way to the door, he set the case by the wall.

His hand was on the doorknob when he realized he wore nothing but his drawers and undershirt. He dug in his bag and pulled out his burgundy robe. He slipped it on and tied it around his waist.

Sucking in a breath, he swung open the door. Meryl looked much as he had left her—as neat as a pin in her tailored suit, though it showed a few additional wrinkles. The girl hadn't been able to change her clothing, because of him.

Her eyes sparked as they struck his. She laid her hand on his chest and pushed him back, maneuvering into the room. He easily gave way. He never once considered blocking her path, despite the storm he knew was about to come.

"How did you catch up? How could you possibly have—"

"You have no idea how happy I was to learn you couldn't continue west until tomorrow. I just came into town myself." Looking far more composed than he anticipated, Meryl shut the door behind her and faced him.

"Yes, that turn of events caught me by surprise," he admitted ruefully.

"Perhaps you should have read the timetable, instead of merely tinkering with it." A smile teased the corners of her soft rosy lips.

"Still, you caught up. You're . . . safe."

Her mouth turned down. "A situation that I cannot thank you for." She set her handbag on the bed and faced him, her blue eyes wide and earnest. "You left me, Joseph. All alone. In a strange city. In all our years together, despite all the silly pranks you pulled as a child at my expense, I never thought you capable of that magnitude of deceit."

He squeezed his eyes shut briefly, then forced himself to focus on her. She looked like an angel, a sad, weary angel, and he wanted desperately to hold her close and offer her comfort.

But it was too late for that. She detested him. "And you hate me for what I did."

"Hate? No, Joseph. I don't hate you."

She took a step closer to him, then another.

"You don't?" The hope that filled his chest surprised him. He had never felt such relief.

She stood right before him, her chin tilted, her eyes on his. "No, Joseph. Of course I was angry, and hurt." She pressed her hand to his chest once more and looked beseechingly into his eyes. "Deeply hurt."

She was calling him by his full name, as if they had just met. The formality gave him the sense she had changed, too. She was no longer Meryl the Pest, but a mature woman, eager to discuss intimate matters with an equally mature man. From out of nowhere came a feeling quite different from the longing to comfort. He had the sudden urge to pull her close and kiss her, to test her true feelings for him, feelings that had survived his betrayal. "I'm sorry," he whispered.

Sorry? What was he talking about? He wasn't sorry. He'd done what he had to do to earn his place as president of Westgate Railroad. And he had no intention of kissing her. Resolved, he stepped back, determined to break the spell she was weaving around him. "You must have realized I would do my best to win, even if that meant—"

"Stranding me with barely a penny to my name? In a saloon, of all places?"

"I couldn't take you to one of the nicer places, where other passengers would be. You would have seen them leaving to catch the train." He shuddered inwardly. His excuse sounded so crass.

"Thank goodness I had enough for a hotel room. I hate to think what may have happened to me if—" Her voice caught. She looked down, then her eyelids fluttered and she met his gaze once more.

Her uncharacteristic vulnerability struck him like a hammer blow. This was a Meryl he scarcely knew, yet had always suspected lay beneath her bravado. Unable to resist a moment longer, he pulled her against his chest. He wrapped his arms around her and held her tenderly. "I'm sorry, Meryl," he said low into her ear. "I was hasty. I have nothing to say in my defense except that I expected . . . That is, I thought you . . ."

She buried her face in his shoulder, her words muffled in the silk of his robe, her arms sliding around his waist in her desperation to cling to him. "Oh, Joe, I was so frightened."

He had done this to her. He had reduced a vibrant, self-confident female into this quivering, terrified mouse. What a cad he was! He should have seen her weakness, should have realized his own power.

He stroked her back, then allowed his fingers to drift to her hairline, just behind her ear. So soft . . . "Shhh, it's okay, darling. You're not alone. You're safe now, with me."

She leaned back and studied his face. "Am I, Joe? Can I trust you to keep me safe?"

"Yes," he breathed, completely entranced by her. "Oh, yes."

"Thank you!" She threw her arms around his neck and kissed his cheek.

The world tilted on its axis. *I want to kiss her. By God, I want to* bed *her.* When had this happened? When had his feelings for Meryl grown so strong?

Until now, he hadn't known, hadn't realized, the power she held over him. Thank goodness she didn't realize it herself. Didn't know that he longed, right this moment, to capture her mouth with his, to carry her to the bed and make love to her.

Meryl looked over his shoulder. "Is that my valise?" She shoved away from him as quickly as she'd fallen against him, her eyes on the case by the door. "It is!"

Joe felt bereft without her in his arms. "I took it with me, for safekeeping. Your trunk is at the depot."

"Is it?" she spun toward him, her blue skirt flaring around her legs. "Wonderful! Simply wonderful."

He opened his arms, certain she would move into them again, and that he could gently lead her where he longed to go. Instead, she picked up her case and moved toward the door. With sick certainty, Joe acknowledged that making love to this woman wasn't going to be quite that easy. Not that anything involving Meryl had ever been easy.

At the door, she turned back to him, her brow furrowed in concern. "Oh, Joe, you did respect my privacy, didn't you? I have some awfully personal things in here." She lifted the case and cradled it against her pert breasts.

He arched a brow. "I imagine any lady's overnight case would, what with underthings and such." His thoughts still on her body, so recently in his arms, he imagined her dressed in that satin corset he'd found—and nothing else, her breasts pushed up, swelling deliciously against the edges of the fabric.

"I meant my journal, frankly. I'm amazed you could resist looking inside it. Unless, of course you think it contains nothing of value, because of how little you value my thoughts," she said acerbically.

"Meryl . . ." He didn't want the angry Meryl to return. He wanted the woman who had willingly fallen into his arms.

With relief, he saw her brow ease and her smile return. "No matter. I'll leave you be. Oh, don't worry," she laughed brightly. "I have my own bed this time, in my own room, right down the hall."

"Right. Of course." Of course she had no intention of sleeping with him. Meryl was a lady.

"Well," she said, looking as if she didn't want to leave. "I'll see you tomorrow, then."

"You will?"

"Yes, on the Pacific Express." With a broad smile, she swept through the door, closing it firmly behind her.

She would be on his train. Of course she would. He hadn't won their bet at all. He'd lost all the ground he had gained through his treachery. Yet, despite his intellectual understanding of that fact, his thoughts dwelled on quite another matter regarding Meryl.

I want her. I want to bed her. I'm a fool. It's impossible. The first obstacle was their ever-present bet. One of them would win, one lose, and either ending meant nothing of an intimate nature would occur between them. On top of that, she was the boss's daughter. He could hardly steal her virtue without committing himself to her.

He should never have agreed. He should have worked on convincing her father he was right for the job. Then, he might feel free to consider Meryl as a woman, instead of a rival.

When another knock came at the door, Joe knew it couldn't be Meryl. The pounding sounded as if it might tear the door from its hinges. Joe quickly finished dressing before he answered it.

"Joseph Hammond?" Two men stood in the doorway. The first was a lanky, raw-boned man about his age with a black handlebar mustache and ten-gallon hat, who wore a shiny star-shaped badge on his jacket lapel. A lawman? The second was a broad fellow in overalls and mud-caked boots.

"Yes?" he asked, his stomach tensing.

The lawman gave him a stern look. "You're under arrest for thievery."

Nine

"Take him."

At the lawman's grim command, his burly companion advanced on Joe.

Joe instinctively stepped back in the room, questions tumbling through his mind. "Arrest? I haven't stolen anything. This is a mistake."

"Never heard that one before." The lawman pushed past him into the room. The second fellow grasped Joe and yanked his hands behind his back, then secured them with handcuffs.

"Hey, wait a minute! This isn't fair. I haven't done anything."

The lawman ignored him, his face impassive. He glanced toward a chair by the bed, where Joe had tossed his robe the night before. "She said he was wearing that." Crossing to it, the lawman dug his hands into the pockets.

"She?" Joe burst out, anger beginning to replace his confusion. *"She?"*

"Eureka." The lawman turned back, his face still impassive despite his exclamation. He confronted Joe and held up his hand. Dangling from between his fingers was an expensive diamond bracelet. He'd seen that bracelet before, on Meryl's wrist.

"The owner of this trinket told us you coerced her into your room last night on the pretense of needing help with your window. Then you accosted her and stole her bracelet. This is good enough proof for me." Whipping the bracelet into his palm, he slid it into his jacket and led the way out the door.

The lug pushed Joe along, forcing him to follow the lawman out the door, along the hall, and down the stairs to the first floor. Joe's shoulders ached from the handcuffs that twisted his arms into an unnatural position.

Every second of pain increased his fury. She would pay for this. This was beyond the pale. This was serious business! He could go to prison for such a theft. She must have slipped her bracelet into his pocket when he was holding her. He had fancied that she was as enamored of him as he with her, yet all along she had been plotting and planning, the little tart. "I'm going to kill her," he muttered.

"What's that? Contemplatin' murder?" the lawman asked.

Joe kept his mouth shut after that. Until he found himself a lawyer, he would be wise not to say anything.

Outside the hotel, that resolve vanished when the lawman approached a woman in a fur-lined cloak over a wrinkled blue suit. Meryl. His gaze caught hers, and he gave her the angriest glare he was capable of. She didn't even bat an eyelash.

"Hello again, ma'am. This the fella?" the lawman asked, shoving him forward.

"That's him. Did you find my bracelet?"

The lawman produced the bracelet and handed it back to her, no questions asked. He removed his Stetson. "I 'pologize for this, ma'am. Omaha is a good town, with kind folk. We cain't always keep track of drifters who come through on the train. He sure ain't a local boy I recognize."

"You may not recognize me, but she certainly does," Joe bit out. "Meryl, this isn't funny. These are serious charges! Tell them the truth. Tell them I didn't take your bracelet."

Meryl looked confused. "My goodness, I don't know what he's on about. Everything happened just as I told you, Sheriff." She laid her gloved hand on the lawman's arm, and a crimson glow appeared on the man's cheeks.

"I'm just a deputy, ma'am."

"I'm sure you'll be sheriff someday," she said, giving him a gamine smile. She cast her gaze toward Joe and sighed theatrically. "I was such a fool to believe him. He seemed so well-bred, and he sounded quite distressed."

"You cain't trust big-city fellas," the deputy said, ignoring the fact that Omaha was a sizable town in its own right. "Too slick for their own good. I'm just glad you're safe. Next time, pay no mind to strange fellas, you hear?"

"I promise, Sheriff." She smiled up at him, once more giving him a promotion.

The deputy doffed his hat again. "If you like, I kin escort you to the station."

"That's so kind of you, but it's not necessary. It's right over there." Meryl gestured with her gloved hand toward the brick building a block away. "I don't mind a little stroll. The autumn air is so invigorating."

"If you're sure . . . I don't got no place I gotta be, not right now."

Again she touched his arm. "You've done more than enough."

Her gaze slid to Joe's, and he scowled at her. What was with the flirtatious banter? She couldn't possibly be interested in encouraging the fellow. He may be young, and fairly decent looking, but he had straw stuck to his boots! It went well with his atrocious accent.

"Effen you say, ma´am. We'll take care of this fella. Make sure he gets what he deserves. G'day to you, now." He doffed his Stetson for a third time and began to turn away, and the lug shoving Joe after him.

"Oh, Sheriff?" Meryl called.

The deputy turned around, hope flaring in his eyes.

Meryl's eyes flicked to Joe. If he hadn't known it was impossible, he would say she looked concerned. "You won't . . . mistreat him, will you? I'm sure it's his first offense."

"What makes you say that?" the deputy asked.

She shrugged. "It's obvious. He was so easily apprehended."

The deputy nodded and eyed Joe. "You have a point, ma'am. A few days in jail ought to teach him a lesson."

Meryl clapped her hands and cast Joe a victorious smile over the deputy's shoulder. "That would be perfect. A perfect sentence, I mean. I would feel so awfully guilty if you should punish him too severely. Thank you, Sheriff." Standing on tiptoe, she gave the deputy a peck on the cheek, causing the man's blush to intensify to an unnatural degree.

Joe watched the exchange in disgust. She had bussed *him* the same way the night before. She had used her feminine wiles to play him, and he had fallen for it, hook, line and sinker.

Right then he made a vow to himself. Once he got out of this jam, he would never again allow Meryl to touch his heart.

Joe gripped the bars of his cell and spoke urgently to the man sitting at the desk ten feet away. "You have to listen to me. Please. It's a matter of life or death."

The deputy who had arrested him didn't even look toward his only prisoner, despite sitting only ten feet away at a worn pine desk. His Stetson pulled low on his forehead, he remained intent on cleaning his nails with his whittling knife.

"You don't understand. I'm not a thief," Joe said, determined to get the man's attention. "She slipped the bracelet in my pocket, then called you to arrest me. She needed me to miss my train."

The deputy thumbed back his hat. "Quit your squawkin'. We don't cotton hereabouts to drifters on the make. You should have stayed in the city, where the marks are easy and people are dagblamed fools."

"I'm not a drifter, I'm an engineer," he explained yet again, his patience straining. Still, he had no choice but to attempt to reason with the resident hayseed. "I work for Atlantic-Southern Railroad, the company owned by the lady's father. She planted the bracelet on me on purpose, so I would miss the train."

The deputy returned to cleaning his nails, as if Joe hadn't said a word.

Joe sighed. After twenty minutes of alternately pleading with the lawman and cooling his heels on the rusty bunk in this dreary cell, he was no closer to securing his freedom. And the longer he remained in here, the more difficult it would be to catch up to Meryl.

He let go of the bars and paced in a tight circle, all that the tiny cell allowed him. If he could find a way to prove what he said was true . . . If only there had been a witness to their wager . . .

Meryl's journal. She had been keeping a record of everything that happened between them in that red-leather book of hers.

With renewed hope, Joe gripped the bars again. "Sir, listen to me. If I can prove to you that she set me up, will you let me go?"

His intensity drew the deputy's attention. "How ya goin' to do that, stuck in there like y'are?" he asked, his eyes peering at him from under the brim of his hat: Joe could tell the lawman was humoring him. He probably heard similar tales from all of his captives.

But Joe had an ace in the hole, if he could get the deputy to cooperate. "My satchel. There's a book inside. It tells all about who I am, who she is, and how we're racing to San Francisco."

"You mean *that* bag?" The deputy gestured to his satchel, which rested against the wall beside him. The bag had been dropped off by hotel management, and Joe had watched as the lawman searched his personal effects for more evidence. Of course, the deputy had found no more women's jewelry, or anything of particular value except a pair of cufflinks which luckily had his initials engraved on them.

"Yes, that one," Joe said in annoyance. The deputy knew perfectly well that was his satchel. "Look inside it. There's a book, a journal—"

"Yours?"

"Hers."

"You stole her diary, too?" He shook his head in dismay. "You really are heartless."

"I didn't steal it—exactly," he corrected. "I can explain that, too. But it's not important why I have it. Just read it."

The deputy tilted his chair back. "I don't cotton to pokin' around in a lady's diary."

Joe's hands tightened on the bars, panic filling him. He was so close to convincing him, he could taste it. "You have to make an exception this time—"

"I don't *have* to do anything."

Joe gave his head a furious shake. Antagonizing

the fellow would get him nowhere. "I don't mean to say that. But if you want to know the truth, it's probably in there."

"Probably?" The deputy drawled, sarcasm heavy in his voice. "Don't you know?"

"Yes," he hazarded. "Yes, it's in there. Look at her entry for Thanksgiving. You'll read all about our wager. If you're serious about upholding the law, and not jailing an innocent man who has been framed by an unethical woman who would as soon see him dead—" He gripped the bars so hard, his knuckles paled. When he got his hands on Meryl, she would regret sticking him in here. By God, she would regret it.

"Settle down, there, fella. I don't need some city slicker tellin' me my business." He leaned forward, bringing the chair legs down with a loud thwack. Scraping the chair back, he stood up.

Joe took a step away from the bars, half expecting the lawman to head his way with some kind of medieval torture on his mind. To Joe's relief, he placed the satchel on his desk and popped open the latches. He lifted out the book and sat back down.

On tenterhooks, Joe watched him. His teeth gritted so hard his jaw hurt. Silently, he urged the man on, praying that he wouldn't be proven wrong. Meryl must have poured out her strong feelings about their bet. She certainly had time on the train to write.

Please let it be in there, he silently prayed. He stared hard at the deputy's face, looking for any indication that he was reading words that could set him free.

"Lessee here . . ." The deputy again leaned back in the chair and with slow, deliberate movements, opened the journal.

Joe could hardly breathe as he waited for the deputy to come across something that might free him.

"There's sure a lot of flowery talk in here, goin' on about a dodo bird. She's gonna rid herself of the dodo bird. What's that to do with the price of grain?"

Joe shifted his feet. "Uh, nothing. Keep reading. Please."

The deputy again turned his eyes to the book. After an endless interval, his brow furrowed. "This it?" he asked without taking his eyes from the journal. "This part about racing to San Francisco, making some deal with Westgate Railroad?"

Joe exhaled in a rush. Meryl's natural verbosity hadn't let him down. His excitement mounting, he pressed even closer to the bars. "That's it! See? I told you she knew me."

"You two do this often? Seems kinda strange to me. She sure has a lot to say about you." He shook his head. "Whew."

The very next entry dealt with their night in the train bunk. He wasn't keen on having that particular intimacy exposed.

"You don't need to keep reading. That is, the bet is what I wanted you to learn about. Do you see now? That's why she set me up."

"I suppose it's possible," he drawled. He looked

at Joe suspiciously. "How do I know you didn't write these words?"

Joe sighed. "Because I'm the dodo bird."

"Ah." The deputy's chair slammed on the floor again, making Joe jump. "She sure is right cross with you, mad as a wet hen. Why is that?"

"It's a long story. Very long. And not all that interesting." He didn't want to be sidetracked, not when he was so close to success. "Suffice it to say we're old family friends."

"Friends? More like enemies, effen you ask me. Course, knowin' women, she might have a hankerin' for you. Hard to tell sometimes. They don't always make a right bit o' sense."

"And liars. Don't forget she lied to you. About me. She framed me. She's the one who should be behind bars."

Removing his hat, the deputy smoothed back his thick black hair, then replaced it. "Yeah. Seems I was fed a load of bull, all right. That pretty little thing made a right fool out of me. Dayum." He ambled toward Joe's cell and began pulling out his keys. "T'ain't right to keep you."

Joe nearly collapsed in relief. "Thank God."

"'Course, there ain't no way you're gonna catch up with her. Ain't another train heading west until Tuesday."

Tuesday? "I have to catch up. After what she did to me, how she lied— This is your country, officer. Perhaps you can think of something. I surely would appreciate it."

The deputy paused in the act of inserting the key

in the lock. "Well, stopping a train ain't unheard of," he said slowly. "There are a few ways . . ."

"You mean like a train robbery?"

He scowled and glanced sharply at Joe, giving Joe the sense that the fellow was cleverer than his accent let on. "Not what I had in mind."

"But you have *something* in mind."

He turned the key and the lock squeaked. Joe shoved past him out the door. He was free. Free! He fought down an urge to hug the lawman in gratitude. The reserved fellow wouldn't "cotton" to that.

Joe crossed to the desk and retrieved the journal that had saved his life. He returned it to his satchel, then looked at the deputy. "I'm fairly desperate here. I have no time, but I have money. If there's anything you can do—"

The lawman frowned thoughtfully and scratched his forehead. Joe felt every passing second draining the life from him.

"Anything," he repeated. "Any idea at all."

"Well," the deputy finally said in his slow drawl. "I got a cousin lives down the line. He wouldn't say no to a little help, financially. I s'pose I could send him a wire . . ."

"Great. I'll pay it. Tell me what he can do."

Ten

I'm going to burn in hell.

Meryl stared unseeing out the train window as mile after mile of fallow, snow-covered prairie slid by. Mile after mile, taking her far away from Omaha, and from Joe.

She shifted on the thinly padded seat. After Omaha, the accommodations had declined in quality. She hadn't had the luxury of waiting until the next day to take a first-class train. Instead of the height of Pullman luxury, she was traveling in a day coach in a worn car with tightly packed seats. Squealing babies and ranchers with mud-covered boots squeezed beside traveling salesmen in tired overcoats, women in homespun and bonnets, even a collared reverend.

Meryl had never traveled this far west. At first, the wide-open spaces had amazed her. Now the never-changing landscape left her feeling lonely and melancholy.

How was he getting on? She shouldn't be worrying so much about him, yet she couldn't help it.

She glanced at her lapel watch. The train had left the station only a half hour ago, yet it seemed like hours. She wouldn't leave him there, of course. If he hadn't managed to bail himself out, in three days she would telegraph her father and ask him to help Joe. With her father's influence, he would be free in no time. And she would stop feeling so guilty.

In the meantime, she would have reached San Francisco, and Joe would have no possible way of catching up.

She leaned her head against the seatback. She had done the right thing. Well, not the *right* thing, perhaps, but Joe had left her little choice but to be devious. He had tricked her into missing her train. She had merely repaid the favor, with an added bonus of keeping him at bay for more than one day.

Yet no matter how she rationalized her actions, she couldn't rid herself of the guilt.

The train's tempo shifted, and Meryl realized they were slowing down. Yet the conductor hadn't passed by to call out the name of a station. They weren't due in North Platte for several hours.

The other passengers began talking among themselves as the train continued to decrease speed. After a moment, it came to a full, shuddering halt. Meryl looked out the window, but saw nothing that would explain the interruption. Field after fallow field stretched to the overcast horizon, broken only by a twisting, rutted wagon track. Far in the distance stood a weathered farmhouse and a ramshackle barn.

"Cattle," the man next to her said.

"Excuse me?" He hadn't said two words to her since they departed Omaha.

"Cows."

"I know what cattle is. Why would they stop the train? Isn't that what cow catchers are for, to nudge them off the tracks?"

"Not for this size herd."

He apparently intended to say no more, so she prodded him for an explanation. "They come this way, the cows?"

He looked at her as if she were the slowest person on Earth. "Cattle always have to be moved about in winter, or they'll starve. Sometimes they have to be driven across train tracks."

Meryl sighed. "How long will we be here?"

He shrugged. "Could be a few hours."

"Hours! That's ridiculous. How many cows are we talking about?"

"Couple hundred, maybe. Maybe thousands. Who knows?"

Thousands? Of cows? All in one place? She had never seen such a thing. Curious, Meryl rose and headed toward the front of the car, hoping to catch a better view from the vestibule.

It was slow going. With the train at a standstill, many of the passengers had risen to stretch or walk about. She maneuvered around them as best she could, until she reached the vestibule. She pushed open the door leading outside—and was instantly struck by a freezing wind. Unlike the deluxe car that had brought her to Omaha, this car's vestibule was open to the air. A narrow railing was all that kept passengers from tumbling off. Thank goodness they weren't moving.

Leaning over the left railing, Meryl looked down the side of the cars in front of hers. Sure enough, a mass of brown and white cattle shifted and pushed over the track. Though there seemed to be only a few hundred head instead of thousands, they were moving awfully slowly, churning up a good deal of mud along the way. They very well could be stopped for an hour or more.

She leaned on the railing and watched the herd, silently urging them to hurry. A pair of mounted cowboys in heavy coats, with hats pulled low over their eyes, drove the herd. What she glimpsed of their faces appeared ruddy and chapped. *Poor fellows*, she thought. *Such hard work in such awful weather.* She clutched her cloak at the neck and shivered.

With snapping bullwhips and fierce cries, the two cowboys kept the animals from straying. Oddly, their actions sometimes seemed to drive the cattle back the other way, making for a frustrating loss of progress. The train's whistle kept sounding, over and over again, as if the engineer thought that might help.

The train couldn't be much farther than thirty miles outside Omaha. Still, with the westbound track blocked, there was no way under heaven that Joe could catch her. The wind picked up and her face began to grow numb. Watching the cows mill about grew tedious, so she returned to her seat.

A long, slow hour later, the train brakes squealed as they released, and the wheels finally began to move. Meryl laid her head back and sighed. Of course Joe could never have caught up. It was impossible. He was in jail; she was on a train. Knowing her train was again on the move gave her a great sense of relief.

Around her, the voices of the passengers suddenly grew louder. She glanced about. Passengers seated on both sides of the aisle were straining toward the windows on the opposite side from where she sat. The taciturn man beside her rose and joined them.

"It's coming even with us," a woman said.

"Do you think it's trying to catch us?" a little boy asked his mother.

Her seatmate replied, "It better hurry. We're gaining speed."

Meryl scrambled to join them, a curious fear building in the pit of her stomach. Standing on tiptoe, she caught a glimpse of a stagecoach, pulled by a team of four, racing down the road that paralleled the tracks.

A tremor of concern wound up Meryl's spine. She told herself she was worrying needlessly. But she couldn't convince herself that Joe hadn't found some way to catch up with her.

Slipping under a taller man, she pressed against the glass, her eyes glued to the stagecoach as it raced toward the train. While the other passengers gamely urged the coach to catch up, Meryl silently urged the accelerating train to leave the stage in the cold prairie snow.

The horses strained in their harnesses, and soon the stagecoach had come alongside the train's rear car, two down from the one Meryl rode in. Then, it swung dangerously close.

Her breath cast a fog on the window, and she rubbed it clear with her hand, but the stagecoach had disappeared from her line of sight. She grasped the window latches and shoved the pane up. Sticking out her head, she caught sight of a man standing in the coach's open doorway, balancing precariously, his hands gripping the doorway. From this distance, she couldn't make out his face, but a dreaded sense of familiarity swept through her.

Other passengers had followed her lead, and soon half a dozen windows had been raised. Their voices rose in excitement. "What's he doing?"

"He can't be meaning to jump."

"Did he miss the train?"

"Maybe he's a robber."

"The coach is falling back. He's not going to make it."

"Please, please, please," Meryl whispered, unsure whether she wanted the man to succeed or fail. Above all, she didn't want him to get hurt— God forbid Joe should be hurt by all this. "Don't be an idiot!" Her words came out strained, louder than she intended.

"Too late," her seatmate said, his tone as laconic as ever. "We're past them."

The coach had fallen so far behind, she was certain there was no way he could reach the train. She exhaled in relief. A split second later, the man leapt from the coach toward the end of the caboose.

Meryl stared, aghast, certain he would miss, expecting to see him fall to the ground. For a moment, he vanished from sight, and she feared he'd done just that. Desperate to know his fate, she leaned even further out of the window, her waist over the sill. The chill wind tore at her hair and threatened to tear her cloak from her shoulders.

She ignored the wind. She spotted the man gripping a pole on the caboose railing, a tenuous hold at best. Her chest froze in fear as she watched him fumble about, seeking a firmer grip. The wind had snatched his hat away and tore at his clothing. His sandy hair lost its natural curl as the icy blasts whipped it away from his wind-burnished face.

Meryl gripped the window sill, her eyes riveted to the man. He could be Joe. He looked like Joe. Heaven knew, Joe had always been willing to take risks.

She watched the man readjust his position. He stepped onto the platform at the rear, then vanished from sight, presumably into the caboose.

Meryl pulled herself out of the window and announced, "He made it!"

Cheering and applause broke out in the train car.

"Why are you clapping? He could be a robber!" one man said.

"Then he'll have me to answer to." A man in a cowboy hat pulled his duster aside to reveal a six-shooter.

Outside, the stage had fallen away into the distance. As the train had reached full speed, excitement lingered in the passenger car for several minutes. People debated who the fellow was and why he might have tried such a dangerous stunt to catch the train.

A porter entered the car and was immediately deluged with questions. He held up his palm. "No, ma'am," he said to a lady in a bonnet. "He's not a robber. He's a payin' passenger who missed the train in Omaha."

"You're not serious," her seatmate said. "Risking his neck just to catch a train. He should have been organized, shown up earlier to the station."

"That's one determined fella," the cowboy said, shaking his head in admiration.

"Don't I know it," Meryl murmured, her stomach dropping to her feet. He had somehow managed the impossible. The sheer lunacy of his actions stunned her almost as much as they secretly impressed her. And her relief that he hadn't fallen to his death, partly on her account, brought tears to her eyes.

The door at the rear of the car opened and the man in question stepped through. His appearance stole Meryl's breath. He looked surprisingly rugged, his face windburned from the cold, his hair mussed. She almost ran to him—until she saw his expression.

He was scanning the passengers, his eyes predatory and hard. He held his body like a tightly coiled spring, his hands fisted at his sides, his jaw tense. The fierce look on his face—of passionate determination, of barely controlled fury—sent her blood racing. A tingling sensation filled her stomach, and she admitted to herself that he really was a handsome man.

Handsome, and dangerous.

Like a falcon finding its prey, his eyes locked on her. His lips hardened and he took a step toward her.

Feeling like a trapped animal, Meryl slowly came to her feet. How could she avoid him? The train offered few opportunities for concealment. Despite that truth, an instinct for self-preservation took hold of her. Never turning her back on him, she edged into the aisle.

He took a threatening step toward her, his emerald eyes glittering.

She took a counterstep back.

At his third step, she spun on the ball of her foot, hiked up her skirts, and fled down the aisle as fast as she could. His steps pounded behind her, twenty feet away.

Her skirt caught on a seatback and she yanked it free, tearing the fine gabardine of her tan and gray traveling suit. She didn't care. Not with Joe bearing down on her, his hands out as if he meant to wring her neck.

She rushed through the door at the end, then through another door into the next car. She raced past the startled passengers, marginally aware that they were shooting her annoyed glances and complaining about her. The door at the end was her only route of escape. When she reached it, she risked a glance over her shoulder. Joe was already halfway down the car and closing fast.

He could easily outrun her. She had no idea

what he intended once he caught her. Surely he wouldn't hurt her, here among all these people. But he certainly looked like he had murder on his mind. She wasn't about to wait around to find out.

She had to shake him. As soon as she entered the third car, she spotted the ladies' lavatory. She slipped inside and closed the door. Pressed against the door, she gasped for breath, her corset stays digging into her ribs.

Despite the loud voices her flight had stirred up, she could still hear Joe's pounding footsteps pass by her hiding place. She prayed no one would reveal her presence to him.

She waited several more minutes, giving him ample time to continue into the next car. Sucking in her breath, she unlatched the door and began to open the door when she again heard the sound of clomping steps coming back past the lavatory. He was like a hound trying to pick up her scent.

Then a child's high voice called out, "She went in there!"

Meryl groaned. The gig was up—unless she acted immediately. Praying surprise might give her a needed edge, she slammed back the door and bolted for the door at the end.

"Meryl!"

His booming voice didn't slow her one bit. She kept running through the train, all the way to the baggage car behind the engine. She knew he would eventually find her, but perhaps after running so hard, his fury would be spent. *At least a little,* she prayed. *Just a little. I don't want to be thrown off a moving train!*

To her relief, the door to the baggage car was unlocked. She stepped through and let it close behind her. She found herself in a simple wood-sided car. The noise of the train was much louder here, the clatter of the wheels on the tracks vibrating through her feet.

She had reached the end of the line; there was nowhere else to run. At a loss, she gazed upon the rows of neatly stacked baggage. The trunks and suitcases had been made as accessible as possible for the porters, positioned on pallets in the order the train's destinations would be reached.

She spotted her blue trunk resting on the pallet at the far end. The sight of the familiar piece of luggage drew her like an oasis in a desert, and she stumbled toward it.

Reaching the trunk, she sagged against it and fought to catch her breath. She had packed this trunk ages ago, or so it seemed. She had left so quickly, not giving herself time to say proper farewells to her family.

In the days following Thanksgiving, her family would return to their Fifth Avenue home and begin decorating it for Christmas. Clara loved decorating, and their mother loved planning the menu.

How she envied them their uncomplicated enjoyment of the coming holiday. Simple home pleasures seemed so appealing right now. Much better than being embroiled in trouble in the middle of an endless prairie, pursued by a madman with revenge on his mind.

She had never spent the holiday anywhere but with her family. This year, she would be alone in

San Francisco. Her closest tie to family was the man who now hated her, who was looking all over the train for her. God knew what he would do once he found her.

She ought to lock the door, in case he thought to look for her in here. Yet why delay the inevitable? Besides, she was too tired to move. Her ribs ached under her corset stays, her skin damp under her layers of clothing. She no longer wanted to run.

Joe. She had ruined things. She had forever destroyed whatever feelings he may have held for her as a longtime family acquaintance. She hesitated to call him a friend.

Tears sprang to her eyes. She had destroyed their relationship without a second thought, for purely selfish reasons.

The door squealed open, jerking her from her reverie. Joe stepped inside and closed it behind him. At the sight of his imposing presence, her heart began to beat furiously.

He glared at her, his voice filled with derision. "You thought you could run away from me? We're on a *train*, Meryl."

Meryl straightened, bracing herself for the storm about to be unleashed upon her.

He stepped toward her. "Thank goodness some nice passengers told me where you'd run off to."

"How—" Her voice caught, and she swallowed her tears. She didn't dare show him her weakness. "How did you manage to catch the train? How did you even imagine you could try?"

He took another step closer. "Surely you didn't think I would give up."

"But if the train hadn't been stopped by the cows—"

He arched an eyebrow. "Why do you think the drivers chose that moment to take the herd across the tracks?"

"I don't know! The drivers. They decided to, that's all. You couldn't have anything to do with that." Yet with sudden certainty, she knew that he had.

He pushed back his coat and braced his hands on his hips. "I have news for you. Remember the deputy you were flirting with? Turns out he has a cousin with a cattle ranch just off the track. Fancy that. All he had to do was wire him for a favor, and the cattle stopped the train."

"He did that for you?" This couldn't be true. It simply couldn't. She shook her head, trying to wrap her head around the miracle Joe had pulled off. "You were in jail. Why would he—"

"Jail. That's right, I was in *jail*. Damn it, Meryl." His icy cool snapped, anger burning in his eyes. "This wasn't like slipping castor oil into my lemonade or short-sheeting my bed. You had me thrown in jail!"

"I wasn't going to leave you there," she said, her voice high and thready.

He glared at her, his disbelief in her claim apparent in the grim set of his jaw.

She rushed to explain, "Once Mr. Philbottom signed the papers, I would have arranged for you to be freed."

"When? A month from now? Two months?" He stood a mere fifteen feet from her now.

She lifted her chin. "Your faith in my ability to seal a negotiation is woefully lacking!"

"You *left* me there." He again paced toward her, inescapable, relentless. "You framed me. You've gone too far this time, Meryl."

At his inexorable advance, Meryl retreated until her back hit the car's rear wall. The angry challenge in his eyes drowned her sentimental feeling for her childhood friend, replacing it with a desperation and passion she had never felt before. He had never seemed so masculine, so compelling and strong. Perversely, she knew she had to resist that attraction. She couldn't let him win. She *wouldn't* let him win.

Several seconds slid by. Underneath their feet, the train wheels churned rhythmically along the track, vibrating the entire car.

Another second passed. Suddenly, Joe lunged for her.

Meryl wasted no time making her escape. Leaping over a trunk, she dashed past him.

He was no more inclined to give up than she was. He began pursuing her around the pallets of luggage. Dodging the reach of his arms, she scrambled through a narrow gap between one pallet and the wall, a gap too small for him to squeeze through.

She came out the other side and glanced back. He had paused in the aisle, his feet spread, his posture showing he was ready to move to either side of the pile. Then he spotted her. She turned and clambered on top of the stack, seven feet in the air.

She lay flat, pressed almost against the ceiling of the car.

He stared up at her, then at the pile of luggage, probably considering whether a big man like him should risk such a precarious climb.

She could never win this race. Eventually he would catch her. She had to reason with him. "Stay away from me, Joe," Meryl called down, her voice quavering fiercely. "Leave me alone. I'm warning you."

"And let you try something else, something even more dangerous? You ought to be locked away. You're a danger to society, or at least to *me*." His fingers splayed on the side of a crate, he glared up at her. "You with your innocent act, coming to my hotel room."

"It's not my fault you fell for it," she shot back.

"Sobbing in my arms just so you could plant that bracelet on me." With a quick burst of energy, he scrambled up a few feet and snagged her ankles. With a tremendous yank, he pulled her right toward him. A moment later she was falling, right into his arms.

She let her whole weight land on him, which shoved him back against the crates behind him. Yet he kept his grip on her, his arms locked around her waist.

Leaning with her against the crates, he stared hard at her, his face mere inches away. "All the while, making me think—"

"Think what?" She fruitlessly shoved at his chest, her breath coming in short gasps. She was balanced on a single foot; he alone was keeping her upright.

"Think you cared," he spit out. "Think you wanted *this*." Then he claimed her mouth with his.

His kiss shocked her so thoroughly, she failed to resist. His lips swept over hers, pressing in all the right places, making it impossible for her to catch her breath. He shifted his hold on her, pressing her full body against his. Her breasts pressed against his chest, her hips against his. A hardness pressed into her belly and she recalled what Annabelle had said about aroused men.

That's when her sense returned, and a shiver of fear. She shoved back on his shoulders and tore her mouth away. "What do you think you're doing?"

"You know damn well what I'm doing."

She struggled to free herself from his hold and reclaim her feet. This time, he let her go. Standing back, she stared at him in shock and anger. He was experienced; he knew she wasn't. "You're using— I can't believe you would try to distract me with—You bastard!" Lifting her hand, she slapped him across the face.

Like a shot, the slap echoed around the enclosed car. His hand flew to his face, his eyes narrowing into twin beams of emerald heat. "That's what you think? That *I* was playing *you*?"

Doubt pressed against her anger. "You—You know what you're doing—"

"Not when I'm around you, sweetheart." He pulled in a ragged breath. "God knows I don't want you to have this power over me. Only a fool or an idiot would want you under his skin, in his blood."

Meryl listened to his tirade with only half an ear, her heart still pounding from the feel of his warm, firm lips on hers. *He desires me*, she realized. Her heart sang, shocked and delighted at the possibilities.

Joe continued to rant, "You think I enjoy feeling desire for you, *you*, the most aggravating female on Earth, the woman who had me locked up, the most spoiled, unpredictable—"

Before he could finish describing her many attributes, Meryl grasped his lapels and dragged his face down to meet hers. She had never been a girl who played it safe. "Shut up, Joe."

This time, she pressed her mouth to his.

Eleven

At Meryl's bold gesture, the last of Joe's common sense disintegrated. A drumbeat pounded in his head, drowning out everything but the feel of her lips on his, warm and willing and enthusiastic. He stumbled backward, clasping Meryl against him. His back hit the trunk, his legs gave way, and he carried her with him to the floor.

He slid her onto his lap to keep her from falling away from him. She seemed not to mind. She twined her arms around his neck and pressed her slender body to his. Her eager innocence sent a rush of desire through his blood and he pulled her tighter, slanting his lips on hers to drink deeply of her lush mouth.

She responded to his urging. Her lips opened under his, inviting him to explore the secret, warm recesses within. She moaned low in her throat. The pure sensuality of the sound sent a fresh jolt of desire through him. His groin ached so harshly, he knew he was on the verge of losing all control.

He broke the kiss. Grasping her waist, he began sliding her off his lap. Meryl would have none of it. She wrapped herself even tighter against him.

Her enthusiasm threw him off balance, and he fell back on the wooden floor with Meryl atop him.

"Oh, God," he groaned, as she pressed her mouth to his again. Their kiss muffled his words into an incomprehensible, throaty murmur. His hands swept up and down her narrow back, then lower, past her waist to her hips.

With gentle pressure, he urged her hips against his, desperate to assuage the burning need in his groin. His fingers delved into her voluminous skirt, finding satisfaction as his palms discovered the curve of her fanny.

You're going too far. She's a lady, and an unmarried one at that, his conscience reminded him. Far from being offended by his bold caress, Meryl shifted her lithe, slender body atop him, her urgent little movements letting him know she enjoyed his touches, and wanted more. She had taken command of his senses, pressed her attentions on him, and now she had him flat on his back.

He wasn't about to let her keep the upper hand. With one swift, decisive motion, he rolled over, sliding her beneath him.

A squeal erupted from her. He broke the kiss and braced himself for a backlash, for a torrent of recriminations that would no doubt cast him as the aggressor and guilty party.

"My hair," she said. She pressed her hand to her mussed chignon. A lock had caught under her shoulder. He freed it, then gazed down at her, his hands braced on either side of her shoulders. Her porcelain face was flushed, her lips swollen and ripe, her breath coming in delicate pants. She pre-

sented such an arousing picture, he shuddered
with passion.

"This is a very bad idea, you know that, don't
you?" he finally found the strength to say.

"I'm not an idiot, Joseph Hammond," she shot
back, just before digging her fingers into the hair
at back of his head and pulling his mouth against
hers once more.

He groaned, deep in his throat. She wanted
him; he certainly wanted her. Nothing would stop
the inevitable from happening. Nothing—

A loud bang echoed through the baggage car,
followed by an intruder's voice. "What do you
think— By God, this is no place for a tryst. Get out
of here!"

Joe felt as silly as a schoolboy called on the carpet. As quickly as humanly possible, he righted
himself, pulling Meryl to her feet beside him. He
slid behind her to hide his arousal and give him a
modicum of dignity.

The furious conductor stood just inside the
door, his crisp uniform a stark contrast to their
rumpled clothing. At his glare, Joe laid his hands
protectively on Meryl's shoulders.

"Yes, well, we weren't intending . . ." Joe began,
uncertain how he was going to respond, seeing as
Meryl and he were entirely in the wrong.

"You have no business being in here. "You—"
He narrowed his eyes at Joe. "You're the fellow
who hopped on board from the stage."

Joe nodded, silently praying his stunt might win
him some appreciation from the angry fellow.

He was wrong. "Well, that's enough blasted foolishness from you." His gaze shifted to Meryl. "From both of you. Running up and down my cars like misbehaving children, disrupting our passengers' relaxing trips. Hiding in here where you don't belong, doing Heaven knows what! I won't have it. I'm putting you both off at the next stop." He glanced at his pocket watch. "In twenty minutes we'll be at North Platte. That's as far as I'm taking you."

"You can't throw us off the train," Meryl said, taking a step forward. "We paid for our tickets."

"I reserve the right to rid our train of unsavory passengers. And that includes the both of you."

"Well, we refuse to go!" Meryl said, her chin high, fire in her eyes. She spoke like a queen, apparently unconcerned that her hair was a mess, half pinned up, half tumbling about her shoulders.

"Meryl," Joe murmured in her ear, knowing it was a losing battle.

She didn't appear to hear him. "What harm have we caused, really? Riding the train is deadly dull. The passengers loved watching Joe jump aboard. We've provided the only decent entertainment all day! We've given them something interesting to discuss."

"Our passengers don't need your hijinks, miss. You're getting off, and that's the last I'm going to say of it." He turned to leave.

"Oh, really?" Meryl pulled away from Joe and confronted him. "Do you know who my father is?"

The man frowned down at her. "I don't see—"

"*Do* you? He's Richard Carrington, that's who. Owner of half the railroads in this country." It was a slight exaggeration, but not by much.

The conductor shrugged. "He doesn't own Union Pacific." Again he turned to leave.

And again, Meryl stopped him. "Not yet. But he's in negotiations to purchase it." Another lie— as far as Joe knew. "And when he does, and I let him know how I was treated—"

"Supposing I let him know about what you were up to, eh?" His gaze swept her from head to toe. "I'm guessing your *daddy* wouldn't be too happy to hear about it."

Joe cringed. The conductor had thrown an excellent volley back at Meryl. No woman wanted her reputation sullied. If word of their indiscretion leaked out, she would be shamed among all who knew her. And he was entirely at fault for letting things get out of hand.

Yet Meryl didn't seem at all disturbed. "Go ahead. My father knows all about me and this gentleman here. After all, we *are* married." She slipped her hand into his.

That ruse again. "Meryl," Joe began, hoping that she would see the light before digging herself an even deeper hole filled with falsehoods.

"Then why is your ticket under the name Carrington, while his is Hammond?" the conductor asked, suspicion lacing his words. "I know his name, because I checked his ticket right after he came aboard—again."

Meryl gasped then, a deep, wet sob tearing through her. She pressed her hands to her mouth. "Because—because—I was going to leave him. We were having a rough time, you see, so I fled. But when he worked so hard to catch up with me, we—

Well, as you saw for yourself, we reconciled." Facing Joe, she pressed her hands to his chest and gazed up at him. Her expression was a remarkably good imitation of a besotted young wife's.

Joe gazed into her wide, adoring eyes. *False* adoration, he reminded himself. She had pulled the same teary-eyed act on him back in the Omaha hotel, while planting that bracelet on him. Nevertheless, he couldn't help but admire her audacity and quick thinking. She certainly had a gift for thinking on her feet.

At her maudlin story, the conductor's face finally softened. "Yeah, okay." He chewed his lip. "I suppose you may stay aboard, but no more antics, or I *will* throw you off my train." Turning, he stormed out of the car.

Meryl dropped her hands from Joe's chest. She released a heavy sigh, then looked up at him brightly. "Well, that was close."

"I'll say. If he had interrupted us much later . . ." He stared at her a moment, silence stretching out between them.

Her cheeks colored slightly and her eyes darted away. "It was a mistake. A silly, foolish mistake."

Disappointment stabbed at him. Yet he wasn't at all surprised she regretted their indiscretion. "That's putting it mildly," he replied, trying his damnedest to sound unaffected. He paced away from her, struggling to tame his desire for her. She had proven how ruthless she could be where he was concerned. He refused to let her flirtation with carnal delights come at his expense. He would simply forget it had ever happened.

So he told himself, knowing he never would. As long as he lived, he would never forget kissing her.

He hooked his elbow over the top of a crate and crossed his ankles, pretending a nonchalance he didn't feel. "I don't understand what happened just now. Why didn't you invent a lie so the conductor would throw me off the train?"

She shrugged, "Maybe one didn't occur to me."

"Now, that, I don't believe. I may be slow, but I'm finally beginning to understand you, Meryl." He couldn't keep the admiration from his voice. "If you want something badly enough, you find a way to have it, obstacles be damned."

She gave him a thoughtful look. "Hah. If I were that good at getting what I desired, we wouldn't even be engaged in this bet."

He lowered himself to the floor and rested his back against the crate. "I have a feeling your father would eventually have given in. You always did have him wrapped around your little finger."

She paced in front of him. "I don't want to succeed merely because I'm the baby of the family. I'm capable, really I am! Even if you don't think so."

He held up his palm. "Not again, Meryl. Please. I'm exhausted."

She pursed her lips briefly, then exhaled in a rush, the tension draining from her body. Crossing to the crate, she sank down beside him and cradled her knees in her arms. "There's something I don't understand. When I left Omaha, the sheriff—"

"Deputy."

She rolled her eyes. "*Deputy*. Anyway, he was certain of your guilt. Yet you not only convinced him to let you go, you coerced him into helping you catch up with me. How?"

Ah, she wanted insight into his strategy. Again he found himself admiring her quick mind. She never rested, this girl. *Woman,* he silently corrected. "Actually, Meryl, I couldn't have done it without you."

Her brow furrowed. "What do you mean?"

"Your journal. Your own words proved I was innocent."

Her mouth dropped. "You have my journal?" she asked indignantly. "How—"

Joe ignored her and continued with his story. "He didn't want to believe me. Then I remembered that you write everything down."

"You have my journal?" she pressed. "Did you *read* it?"

"I suggested the deputy read your entry for Thanksgiving Day, when we agreed on this crazy, ill-conceived bet. Sure enough, you recounted everything about it in great detail."

"You must have read it," she continued. "You must have. How else would you know what I had written?"

Despite her rising indignation, Joe calmly continued his account. "That convinced him, and he let me go. He was incensed enough with your perversion of justice that he gladly helped me catch up with you. Incredibly clever of him, wasn't it? Using the cattle to delay the train."

She pulled back, her eyes shooting fire. "I can't believe you read my journal. You violated my privacy!"

"That's not all I violated," he said dryly. "Or would have, if we hadn't been interrupted."

His reminder of their intimacy wiped the anger from her. She settled down again, and for several minutes, they sat together in silence. The train's wheels, louder here than in the passenger car, thrummed beneath them, clattering mile after mile on a straight track toward Wyoming.

"Do you hate me, Joe?" Meryl asked into the silence, her voice uncharacteristically small.

Joe sighed. "No. I should. By God, if a man had framed me . . . If anyone else had dared . . ."

"I'm sorry."

Surprised, he gave her a close look. She chewed her lip and avoided his gaze. She actually appeared embarrassed. Her unexpected vulnerability warmed him, and he longed to reach out to her. But if he did, if he so much as touched her, they would end up back where they'd been before the conductor interrupted them.

Or rather, *saved* them, from a terrible mistake.

He knew she didn't love him, and he couldn't begin to define the confusing flux of emotions she engendered in his own heart. He certainly had no right to steal her virtue. Despite her outrageous behavior, Meryl was a lady, born and bred. Moreover, she was the daughter of his employer, a man he longed to impress. Deflowering his youngest daughter in a fit of passion would hardly put him in the man's good graces.

And remaining here with her, alone, was tempting fate. He pushed to his feet. "How about if we make a new deal. No more interference in each other's journey to San Francisco. No more tricks, no more lies. Once we arrive in the city, may the best man win."

Meryl wasted no time springing to her feet, the better to square off against him. She nodded and thrust out her hand. "Agreed."

He hesitated a moment, staring at the finely boned hand she held out. Bracing himself, he slipped his palm into hers. "Then it's a deal."

"Yes. A deal." She made no move to pull back her hand, merely gazed at him across the handshake.

"Very well, then." He squeezed her hand briefly in unspoken acknowledgment, then released her hand.

He stepped back, intending to leave the car. Another matter needed to be settled between them, before things got any more out of hand. "Meryl, we need to stop this."

"The bet?" A flash of fear slid behind her eyes. He knew she worried that without their wager, she would lose all chance at the promotion. That's what really mattered to her, despite her attraction to him.

Strangely, he had begun to care about it less and less the longer their trip lasted. Rather, his thoughts were preoccupied with the contradiction that was Meryl—high-society woman, passionate girl, fearless adventuress. Which was why he needed to keep his distance, until he figured out his intentions toward her.

"Not the bet. *Us.* After what nearly happened here, I think it's best if we avoid each other the rest of the trip. It will be difficult, being on the same train. But if we don't . . ."

"Oh." She rubbed her upper arms, her blue eyes large. "Is that necessary? I know we're competing against each other, but we're both alone, and it's such a long trip."

"I think it's for the best." It would be hard to avoid her, but being near her was asking for trouble.

"So, you won't even talk to me, then? I can't see the harm in talking."

"I won't run from you if I see you coming, Meryl. We've had enough of that." He glanced around the baggage car, scene of their chase—and its passionate aftermath. "We can still be civil to each other. But I won't be seeking you out."

Her face fell and her voice dropped to a strained whisper. "It's because of how I acted with you, isn't it? Like a fallen woman."

"God, no!" He grasped her arms, laying his hands atop hers, and tugged her close. He spoke low, trying to let her know she had done nothing wrong. "Don't ever say that. It's all me. *Me*, Meryl." He kissed her head. He longed to do more, to hold her and comfort her, to let her know it was all right to be vulnerable. But he didn't dare. He released her.

She avoided his gaze. "Very well. That sounds fair," she said, but her voice sounded oddly soft. "I'm going to return to my seat now." Lifting her skirts, she walked regally from the car, leaving him alone.

Twelve

The joyful noise of a dozen voices belting out "Deck the Halls" couldn't lift the gloom that had settled over Meryl.

The passengers in her car had grown more friendly as the miles passed and San Francisco neared. One fellow had begun leading a few of his neighbors in singing carols, and it wasn't long before most of the passengers had joined in. Wrapped presents were tucked under seats and cradled on laps as travelers boarded the train along the route, on their way to stay with friends and family over the holidays.

Their warm camaraderie made Meryl feel lonelier than ever. She missed her home more than she had ever expected. For years she had looked forward to earning her degree and striking out on her own, proving herself worthy to her father. Now she longed for the home fires as she never had before.

From her seat in the coach car, Meryl gazed out at the rolling snowy hills tumbling into the broad Nevada desert. The train had passed through the Rockies to Salt Lake City during the night, winding over and through steep slopes that made the mountains in the East look like little hills. Now the Sierra Nevada Mountains lay ahead.

Over the past two days, she had seen Joe only briefly. His seat was in a different car. After their encounter in the baggage car, he had avoided her. Or perhaps she had avoided him? She hardly knew. She only knew that a deep tension had sprung up between them, a distance and discomfort she had never before felt in his company.

How she hated it! Like using her tongue to probe a sore tooth, she couldn't stop thinking about him, and the change between them. She longed so deeply for his company, her heart ached. He had been out of her life for years while she attended college, yet now she could hardly stand for a day to go by without seeing him.

She had to do something, think of some way to bridge the gap. If she didn't, she would quite simply go mad.

But she couldn't very well seek him out. He had ordered her not to. Did he dislike her? Did he no longer respect her? Did he ever think of her? How she hated not knowing!

She had to end this, now. Grasping her handbag, she headed toward the car exit. She would pass by his seat on the way to the club car. If he was sitting there, she would think of some excuse to engage him in conversation. If not, she would keep looking until she found him.

Once she found him . . . She shook her head. She had no idea what she would say.

She slid open the door at the end and entered

the next passenger car. His seat was empty, so she continued to the club car.

She found him there, relaxing in a leather-upholstered swivel chair, reading a newspaper. At one end of the car, a bartender served drinks at a fully stocked bar. Gentlemen discussed business as smoke from their cigars curled about their heads. Some guests were playing poker.

Despite the decidedly male atmosphere, she wasn't the only woman in the car, and no one paid her mind as she slipped past them toward Joe.

She headed toward an empty chair near his, then slowed, trying to appear as if she hadn't noticed him sitting there until just that moment. "Oh, hello, Joseph. I didn't know you were here."

She smoothed her skirt and sat down.

He lowered his paper and studied her. "Hello, Meryl. Having a good trip?"

"Oh, yes. Marvelous." A steward came to her side and she ordered a bourbon.

Joe arched an eyebrow at her order. "Isn't that a little strong for you?"

"Of course not. *You're* drinking one." In truth, she hated the taste, but had hoped to shock Joe. It had worked, at least a little.

"Do you measure everything you do against what I do?" he asked mildly. Despite his insouciance, his eyes focused on her every move with avid interest.

Heartened that he was secretly thrilled to see her, she countered blithely, "I don't think about you much at all, Joe. Is that the financial section?" Reaching out, she pulled the section of newspaper from his lap and flipped it open to the stock list-ings.

"Don't worry, you're still a wealthy heiress," he said dryly. "I already checked the company's hold-ings."

"That's hardly my only concern. I need to see where other companies stand, to be fully knowl-edgeable about our situation in the marketplace. You ought to know that."

"I suppose your fine degree taught you that?"

"Among other things, such as the adage, 'Keep your friends close. And your enemies closer.'"

His emerald eyes studied her, his paper loose in his fingers. "Is that why you sought me out this morning?" he asked softly. "Because you see me as your enemy?"

She gave him a wry smile. "There you go again, thinking I'm thinking of you, when I'm not think-ing of you at all."

He smiled, that adorable dimple flashing in his cheek. "I see."

"We're in Nevada," she said, her curiosity eating at her. Before abandoning her in Fort Wayne, Joe had told her a story about his past. She still didn't know whether he had been lying. Had he been spin-ning a tale? Or had he truly been confiding in her?

"Yes, we are." He waited for her to continue, ex-pecting that she had a point to make. She did.

"Was your father's mine around here?"

A dark expression crossed his face, and he shook his head. "Southern Nevada." He returned his at-tention to his newspaper.

"Oh."

Silence strung out between them while Meryl struggled to think of something else to say. "So, I should believe you, then? About your father?"

He lowered his paper and rested his hands on it, giving her his full attention. "You thought I was lying?"

"Well, you did have a funny way of winning my trust, didn't you?"

He smiled wryly. "I suppose that's so. But yes. Everything I told you at dinner is the truth, unfortunately."

Her heart ached. He truly did feel shame over his father's poor business dealings. She longed to recapture the emotional closeness they had shared that evening, to learn more of what was in his heart. If only he hadn't asked her to stay away . . . Reaching out, she laid her hand on his. "I'm sorry, Joe."

He stiffened at her touch. "Meryl—"

The train began to slow. Joe took the opportunity to slide his hand from under hers.

Meryl glanced at her lapel watch, and frowned. She didn't remember a stop coming at this point in the journey.

"A water stop," a gentleman across the aisle told her. He pointed out the window behind her.

Meryl turned around. Up ahead, a water tank stood alongside the tracks, at the edge of a deep creek crossed by a trestle bridge. On both sides of the track, thick stands of pine cast shadows across the windows.

The train came to a full stop, steam hissing from the engines.

"We'll only be here a few minutes," the man assured her.

A series of sharp bangs drew her attention to the window again. She wondered if that was a normal sound, but couldn't see what was happening ahead. The tank was out of her line of sight.

Three men passed below her window. The sight shocked her to the core. Despite their recent estrangement, she grasped Joe's arm without hesitation. "Joe. That man has a gun. Look."

Joe glanced up and followed her line of sight. Two men in Union Pacific uniforms were being herded past the window by a rough-looking fellow in worn leather and Levi's. The man held his gun in the air and fired off two more shots. Throwing back his head, he yelled like an Apache, a threatening sound designed to intimidate the passengers.

It worked. The men around her gasped and began talking at once. Screams could be heard from passengers in other cars who also understood what was happening. They were being robbed.

Joe's gaze met hers, the gravity of his expression solidifying her fear. "Stay by my side," he said, his firm tone brooking no argument. "I'll keep you safe."

The concern in his eyes warmed her, but why must he assume that she needed his protection?

A short way down the car, one rotund gentleman pulled a little .22 caliber pistol from his coat. Crossing to the window, he raised the pane.

"Don't be an idiot, they'll kill us all," a white-haired man cried.

Ignoring the warning, the man fired off a shot.

His token resistance was met with a gunshot blast right through the window. The man stumbled back, his face pale with terror, the little gun tumbling to the floor. Shards of shattered glass landed on his suit and struck the floor.

Meryl rushed to his side. Bending down, she encouraged him to reclaim a seat.

"You fool! I tried to warn you," the white-haired man said.

"Hush," Meryl gave him a scathing look. "There's no reason to be mean. He won't do it again. Will you, sir?"

The rotund man shook his head, still unable to speak.

"How many do you think there are?" another fellow asked.

"Don't know," Joe said, trying to look out the window. Meryl wasn't comfortable with how close he was to the window. The robbers had proved they felt no compunction against firing toward them, if not directly at them—yet.

For several endless minutes, silence fell over the passengers. They had no idea what was happening in other parts of the train.

Meryl edged back to Joe's side. "Stop peering out. They might not like it," she whispered, tugging on his arm.

He gave her a curious look, but fell back. "I can't see anything anyway."

"What do you think they're doing?"

"Going after the mail and the safes, probably," Joe said.

"We don't carry mail on this train," the bartender said, rising from behind the bar, where he'd dropped when the window shattered.

"Safes, then. For valuables."

"May not be much of that, either. This is a passenger run, not a mail run."

"You mean the robbers made a mistake?" Meryl asked, her eyes meeting Joe's.

The bartender shrugged. "Could be."

"Then—" Meryl's mind raced through the possible outcomes. "If they're disappointed with what they find—"

"They'll be looking at us," Joe seamlessly finished her thought.

The door at the end slid open, and Meryl braced herself. She recognized the two men she had seen held at gunpoint from the window. They stumbled in, followed by one of the robbers.

"Hands up, everyone. Right now." The robber waved his gun toward them in a broad arc. Hard brown eyes shone from a windburned, beard stubbled face that showed evidence of an unforgiving life in the out-of-doors. He was clad in heavy homespun and leather. He shifted from foot to foot, holding his lanky body tightly, like a gun cocked to fire.

Inexperienced, Meryl drew the conclusion. That could be good—or terribly, terribly bad.

"Git to it, Petey," He stepped aside and a second man entered. Yet this fellow was hardly a man at all. Shorter than Meryl and with a boyish face, he couldn't be more than sixteen.

Petey held open a rucksack and began making the rounds of the passengers as the first robber held them at gunpoint. Not a single gentleman present hesitated in removing rings, tie tacks, cufflinks, and wallets and dropping them into the bag. With nervous twitches, and eyes locked on the robber's six-shooter, the passengers cooperated down to a man.

The boy stopped before Joe and Meryl. From somewhere inside, Meryl found herself resisting, fury pushing aside her fear. These men had no right to frighten everyone so badly, to take things that didn't belong to them. To stop the train from getting to San Francisco.

The two men had reduced confident businessmen into trembling wrecks, and turned Joe into an overprotective bodyguard. Joe hovered by her side, his eyes filled with worry as he glanced at her then back to the robbers. He was more concerned about her than his own safety—yet another sign that he had no faith in her ability to take care of herself.

"Your turn," the leader said, gesturing at Joe with his pistol. Meryl tensed as the silent young robber held out the rucksack.

Joe cast the leader an insolent stare. Still, he didn't resist. With a slow, reluctant movement, he slipped his wallet out of his jacket pocket and dropped it in the bag.

"Now the watch."

Joe unclipped his pocket watch from its fob.

"The chain, too."

His jaw set like rock, Joe slid the chain from his vest and let it slide through his fingers into the sack. From his tense stance, Meryl could feel how much giving in humiliated him.

That knowledge only added to her fury. When the robbers turned to her, she found herself looking into the eyes of the young one. He glanced nervously away, and she realized he was afraid. "You don't have to do this," she murmured.

"Shut up. Take off that bracelet."

The older robber gestured with his gun barrel at her wrist, where the bracelet she had used to have Joe arrested lay.

She began to unclasp it, then hesitated. "No," she said softly.

Joe grasped her elbow. "Meryl . . ."

The leader frowned. "What did you say?"

"I said no." Her voice gained strength. "Surely you are not in the business of stealing from ladies."

The younger robber cast a hesitant look at his companion, and Meryl had the feeling they hadn't discussed any particular code of ethics for their life of crime. The leader considered, while everyone held his breath.

He looked again at the bracelet on her wrist, its facets glinting in the morning sunlight from the window. "Looks like diamonds." His hard eyes met hers. "Take off the bracelet."

Meryl tucked her arms behind her back. "My father gave this to me. It has great sentimental value. I won't let you take it just so you can waste it on drink and cards."

"Meryl," Joe said beside her, his voice filled with worry.

The leader gave her a lopsided grin. He leaned back on his heels and crossed his arms, his pistol dangling from his fingers. "Is that a fact?"

At her side, Joe whispered through clenched teeth, "Give it to him, Meryl."

"Yeah, Meryl, give it to me." He nudged her arm with the gun.

Annoyed that he dared to touch her, Meryl slapped the barrel away, only then realizing what a dangerous stunt she had just pulled. A shiver of fear slid down her spine. Yet she had gone too far to back down now.

The robber scowled darkly, all hints of humor at her resistance gone from his harsh features. He grasped her arm. "Cut out this horse crap and give it to me."

She wrenched her arm away and played her trump card. "My father is a powerful man. If you persist in this foolish stunt, in stealing the possessions of these nice folks, you will be hunted down and held to account. I swear it."

"Damn it, Meryl," Joe said. She didn't risk him a glance.

The robber grabbed her wrist and held it up, peering closely at the bracelet. Meryl cringed at the touch of his callused hand with its dirt encrusted nails.

He whistled low in appreciation. "Who's your pappy, little missy?"

"Mr. Richard Carrington."

Shocked murmurs swept through the car. The robber's eyes brightened, then swept up and down her body. Meryl could almost hear the thoughts clicking into place in his mind like a well-oiled safe. "You don't say," he said slowly, an avaricious smile curling his chapped lips. "Well, I'll be. Can you believe that, Petey? We got us a reg'lar debutante."

"We should be goin', Cal," the young robber mumbled. "We been here long enough."

Cal ignored him. "Daughter of one o' them tycoons back East. You got more than this 'ere trinket, I'm bettin'," he said, finally releasing her wrist. Meryl cradled it against her chest, trying to massage away the imprint of his filthy fingers. "Probably got boxes and boxes of jewels."

"Not *with* me," Meryl said, her chest tightening with renewed fear. What did her parentage matter to this rustic robber?

"Your pappy loves his little girl, don't he?" he asked Meryl, peering closely at her. "And he'd pay a fair price to keep her safe."

A sick feeling churned in Meryl's stomach as the truth sank in. She had made an awful mistake. She shouldn't have ignored Joe's warnings. Fear flooded every fiber of her being, making her feel physically ill as the dread possibilities flashed before her eyes. She opened her mouth to respond, to continue her resistance, but no sound came out.

Cal grinned in triumph. "Petey, I'd say we got a big enough take after all."

"No, Cal. Don't," the boy said ineffectually, panic filling his eyes.

Cal dropped Meryl's wrist, but instead of retreating, he grasped her upper arm with an iron grip. "You're coming with us."

Thirteen

"*No.* She's not going with you."

The words burst from Joe without a thought. His instinct to protect Meryl taking hold, he reached for her to pull her close.

Cal lifted his gun and pressed it to Joe's chest. "Don't touch her. Don't do nothin', or I shoot."

"I'll go with you," Meryl burst out, taking a small step to separate herself from Joe. "Just don't hurt anyone. Please."

"She's a smart girl." The robber gave Joe an assessing look. "Fancy duds. You with her, Slick?"

"Yes. No. Yes, I am," he said, frustrated at his uncertain answer, at how weak it had made him sound. Of course he was with her. From now on, he would do whatever it took to keep her safe. All of the agreements and conditions they had agreed to meant nothing in light of the danger Meryl now faced.

It wasn't supposed to be like this, came the thoroughly useless thought, feeling frustratingly impotent.

The robber peered at him with red-rimmed eyes, his foul breath washing over Joe. "You give her pappy a message from us, hear me? If he wants to see his daughter alive, here's what he has to do. Have ten thousand dollars—"

"Ten thousand!" Petey burst out, his face showing his shock at the amount.

"Make it *fifty* thousand. Fifty thousand dollars and his little girl don't git shot." He slid his hand up her back and grasped her knot of golden hair.

The sight of the bastard's hands touching Meryl infuriated Joe. He took a step toward her, ignoring the gun pressing into his chest.

"Back off, Slick," Cal said, shoving the barrel harder into his chest.

Meryl shot Joe a pleading glance, and he forced himself to remain in place.

Cal continued, "Now listen here. Leave the money at the Red Dog Saloon in Virginia City. If the money's there in three days' time, *she'll* be there," he tugged on Meryl's arm, "safe and sound."

"If you lay one hand on her—" Joe said, his heart thudding heavily in his chest.

"Aw, Slick, now don't you fret," he said, his voice filled with condescension. "We ain't gonna *damage* the girl. Unless she asks for it."

His vague reassurance did nothing to assuage Joe's fear. "Meaning what?"

"She has to be a good little girl, s'all," he smirked. "Do what we say."

"You won't get your money if you hurt her, you hear me?" Joe said through grinding teeth. He balled his hands into fists. "And I'll hunt you down until I find you."

His dark threat seemed to have an effect, for Cal

began to back down. "We want *money*, that's all. We can get *laid* in Virginia City." He slipped a piece of rope from his belt and passed it to his partner. "Tie her hands."

Petey turned Meryl around and began tying her wrists together under Cal's watchful gaze.

Though she stood with rigid determination, Meryl's eyes were wide with fear, her lips white. Joe's stomach churned sickeningly. How could this have happened? How could it have come to this?

He longed to clasp her to him and carry her away, out of danger, away from these unpredictable outlaws.

Her eyes swiveled to his, a spark of defiance in their blue depths. She gave a small, discreet shake of her head. Her trembling lips formed the surprising words, "Don't tell Father."

She couldn't be saying what it seemed. Joe frowned. "Your father will come through," he reassured her. Unless he found a way to rescue her first.

"No," she whispered. She shook her head again, harder, her expression pleading. Understanding dawned on Joe. She feared that after this, her father would always want to keep her close. Her bid for independence would be dashed.

"I can't," he said, his chest aching. He couldn't promise not to contact her father, not when her safety was at risk. That would be foolish under the circumstances. He would have to betray her trust. He had no choice.

Her eyes hardened at his silent refusal, making his heart twist in agony.

Before he could say more to her, Cal shoved Joe
back, forcing him to join the other passengers
near the bar. He watched helplessly as Petey
crouched to bind her ankles. Perhaps if he jumped
Cal while Petey was occupied—

Sensing that trouble could come from this quarter, the robber again aimed his gun straight at Joe's
chest. "Don't even think it," he said grimly.

"It's done, Cal," Petey said.

With his gun still aimed at Joe, Cal retreated,
pushing Petey and Meryl before him. Meryl
dragged her feet so much, Cal finally had to throw
her over his shoulder like a sack of grain.

In that instant, Joe dashed toward him, hoping
to get the jump on him. Too late. With Meryl balanced on his shoulder, Cal spun around and fired
toward him. The bullet whizzed past Joe's ear as he
dived to the floor.

When he looked up again, Meryl was gone.

His arms and legs shaking, Joe reclaimed his
feet, with the help of a couple of the passengers.

"They're taking her into the forest," the rotund
man said from the window. "Must have hidden
their horses in there. This is bad business. Very
bad."

The white-haired man helped Joe to his seat. In
shock, he remained there as around him, people
began to speak about what had occurred. Eventually, the train crew returned to their posts. Before
long the engine growled back to life.

Over and over, Joe replayed in his mind that last
look Meryl had given him. Her angry expression
of betrayal stabbed his heart. She actually believed

he wanted her out of the picture. She actually thought he would put their bet over and above her safety. His fists squeezed in impotent frustration.

"Like hell," he muttered. Somehow, he would find a way to prove her wrong.

Meryl gripped the waist of the young robber named Petey as he led his horse down a rocky incline into a dry creek bed. The bumping and jerking of the horseback ride exhausted her, and the biting wintry chill sent shivers down her spine. The men hadn't given her a chance to put on her cloak before departing the train. Despite the bright sunshine, the December temperature was only around forty-five degrees.

A half-hour after leaving the train, Petey had taken pity on her, and draped a worn Indian blanket about her shoulders. It smelled horsey, but Meryl wasn't complaining.

If she hadn't been trussed like a holiday turkey, she might have considered trying to escape. Besides keeping her wrists bound, the bandit named Cal had tied her waist to Petey's. At least they hadn't thrown her over the horse's back on her stomach.

Out here in the elements, with no idea where she was, she would probably freeze before finding anyone who could help, even with the blanket. She had never seen such a sparsely populated landscape. Her family had traveled frequently to Europe, and south to Florida, and to other important Eastern cities. She had never experienced the dry, desolate deserts of the West, and now she wished she never had.

The sun had reached its zenith by the time they finally halted outside a tumbledown shack tucked against a hillside. A rusting pump outside the shack dripped precious water into a tin bucket. At the side of the shack stood a rough lean-to with a bale of hay for the horses.

Petey waited in the saddle, while Cal dismounted and came over to untie her. Meryl cringed as Cal's hands fumbled at the knot around her waist. She prayed he would continue to look upon her as nothing more than merchandise to be traded for profit. Her heart tightened at the memory of Joe's fierce threats on her behalf. Despite lacking the upper hand, he had managed to scare the man, at least temporarily.

Yet nothing was guaranteed. Cal could decide she wasn't worth the trouble, shoot her, and dispose of her body in some isolated ravine. She wouldn't be found for months, or even years.

Her feet touched the ground and she stumbled. She quickly righted herself, not wanting to appear weak in front of these men. Nevertheless, Petey felt the need to take her elbow and guide her into the shack, the gesture of a gentleman more than a captor. In fact, he seemed almost in awe of her. Meryl pondered this. Perhaps she could make use of this feeling.

She grimaced as Cal tied her up inside, this time to a rickety pine chair. During this brief ordeal, Petey disappeared, probably to tend to the horses. A short time later, he returned with the rucksack.

Cal snatched the sack from Petey and upended it, spilling their take on the floor. Plumes of dust spiraled upward, and Meryl sneezed.

Cal ignored her. His eyes lit up at the collection of loot. A dozen men's wallets, a few pieces of ladies' jewelry, a variety of cufflinks, and money clips with bills attached tumbled across the floor. Cal squatted down and ran his hands through the collection. "Not bad business. Not bad t'all."

"This'll do it, right, Cal?" Petey asked, concern in his voice. "I don't wanna do this again."

"It oughta." Cal began pulling bills from the wallets and riffling through it. "Stupid Comstock. This was a helluva lot easier than digging in the dirt for fool's wages. Shoulda done this years ago."

"You said *one time*. That we wouldn't hafta—"

"It was so damn *easy*," Cal said, ignoring his partner's anxious comments. He gazed at the take in amazement. He pointed at Meryl with his thumb. "Even taking her. She's our big prize. Sure hope they want her back."

"We coulda robbed the other cars instead," Petey continued, worry etched in his round face. "It woulda been safer. They wouldn'ta followed us, then. Now that we got *her*—"

"She's worth more than the few bits we woulda collected," Cal said.

"Yeah, but they'll be comin' for us." He shot her a worried look, as if he thought the law would be knocking down their door any moment. "They'll come lookin' for us, and—"

"And you'll be tried and hanged," Meryl supplied. Her matter-of-fact comment startled both men. The blood washed from Petey's face, while Cal's colored in anger.

"Shut up." Cal jerked to his feet and confronted her, his dark eyes glowering. "Don't say nothin', you hear me? You don't got a say here." He turned back to Petey. "You, too. Keep your mouth shut and do what I say. I know exactly what I'm doin'. Go start a fire. I'm freezing my balls off in here."

Petey put down the gold chain he'd been holding—Joe's watch fob, perhaps?—and crossed to a potbellied stove against the rear wall. Meryl surmised that he was responsible for the household chores.

Meryl studied both men, trying to decide how far she could push Cal without going too far. Her real target would be Petey, the weak one, the follower. Perhaps if Cal left her alone with Petey . . .

Unfortunately, he seemed content to sit on the floor and count his take. Meryl looked around, trying to absorb what had happened to her. And figure out what she might do about it.

Seeing the condition in which these two men lived, she truly began to understand how privileged her own life had been. From what the men had said, Meryl gathered that they were miners put out of work when the Comstock Lode's production began to slow.

This shack of rough-hewn pine boards made a poor home for anyone. She had never been anywhere so rustic. A single window with a cracked pane of glass looked out on the desert. Besides the chair she'd been tied to, there was only one other. An unfinished slab of wood atop two logs served as a table. Their beds were no more than blankets on the floor. A small stack of cans and burlap bags with foodstuffs was piled in the corner, probably organized by Petey.

These men were probably hungry, and cold, and miserable. They had few prospects for employment and little patience. In short, they were desperate. And desperate men could do despicable things.

She wrapped the moth-eaten Indian blanket around her shoulders and fought down another shiver, this time one of fear.

"I need to send a telegram to New York City." His stomach in a knot, his hands clenched on the counter, Joe stood before the ticket agent in the Reno train station.

On the other side of the grille, the agent slid over a sheet of paper, lifted a pen, and dipped it in the inkwell. "To?"

"Mr. Richard Carrington, Six-seventy-five Fifth Avenue."

"From?"

Joe gave him the rest of the information. The agent's pen fell silent as he waited for Joe to dictate the body of the message.

Joe hesitated. How should he word such an awful message? He could think of no way to soften the blow. The thought of breaking his mentor's heart cut him like a knife. And Mrs. Carrington—she would be at her wits' end, tortured by her inability to help from so far away. As their youngest child, Meryl had always been babied, always protected by her large, loving clan, including him.

Until now.

However he worded such a damning message, he would send their world into a tailspin. Yet he had no choice. The law had been notified, of course, as soon as the train pulled into Reno. But without more information, finding Meryl would take a lot longer than three days. Joe had to secure the funds to pay for Meryl's freedom. Mr. Carrington would be able to wire the money immediately, even such a large sum.

"Sir? I have other customers . . ." The agent pointedly looked over Joe's shoulder at the line of half a dozen customers waiting to buy train tickets, send packages, or wire their own messages.

Joe cleared his throat, and braced himself to put the horrible truth into words. "Say this: Meryl kidnapped by train robbers, stop. Send fifty thousand to Western Union office, Virginia City, Nevada, by Wednesday, stop. Threat real, must comply, stop."

The agent looked up from the pad, his eyes widening. "I heard about that," he murmured. "Stole a woman right off the train. Ladies hereabouts are afraid to travel."

Joe's stomach shifted and he feared he would be sick. Meryl, little Meryl, was gone. "Forgive me," he added in a whisper.

The agent hesitated. "You want that added to the message?" he asked, his tone considerably more understanding now.

Joe dug at his eyes with his palms. Such final, damning words. "Please."

"They've started lookin' already," the agent said. "I saw a posse ride out this morning."

"But if they can't find her in time, I need—" Words failed him. When her father learned of her plight, everything would change. Even if Meryl were returned unharmed, she would never forgive Joe for telling Mr. Carrington. Her distraught father would be on the next train west. He would take her back to New York, and she would never again be trusted out in the world, on her own.

Assuming she was returned alive. Assuming he hadn't failed her and her family completely.

His chest tightened and moisture pooled in his eyes. He blinked it back. He had to keep a clear head, work fast and smart. The race he and Meryl had engaged in was nothing compared to the ticking timeline that now pursued him.

The agent nodded. "I'll send it right off." He picked up the paper and turned toward the telegraph machine.

"No." Joe snatched the paper from his hand. With luck, he wouldn't have to involve her father, or put her family through such agony. He had another option, even though it meant draining his own account. "I want to wire my bank in New York."

Fourteen

The glow from the potbellied stove, the only light in the shack, drew Meryl's gaze. It gave her something to focus on in the wee hours of the morning, in the chill silence of the shack. Something besides her predicament.

With her bound hands, she tightened the Indian blanket around her. On the floor, her two captors slept in their bedrolls. Cal had taken his pistol to bed with him, and threatened to use it on her should she try to escape.

The back of the chair dug into Meryl's shoulder blades. To her dismay, the men had deemed it safest to keep her tied to the chair overnight so they could both sleep. A rope bound her to the chair at her waist, while her wrists were tied together before her. She had tugged at the ropes, naturally, but made no progress in loosening her bonds.

As night had descended on the tiny cabin, terror unfurled deep in her stomach. She was alone with two strange men, rough men, in the wilds of the Nevada desert. She tried not to dwell on her situation for fear she would break down entirely. Once that happened, she might as well give up.

Instead, she gazed at the fire's glow, and thought of Joe.

What was he doing now? Probably sleeping in a hotel room in Virginia City. She had no doubt he was waiting there for her; also no doubt he had ignored her plea and wired her father for the funds to free her.

She knew better than to ascribe romantic feelings to his concern. Joe had too much honor to desert her. *Besides, he cares something for me. Even if he doesn't have romantic feelings for me.* She had seen it in his eyes when she was in danger, seen it in his barely leashed fury when her captors took her.

His kisses . . . How she had relished his kisses. Even now, memory of their indiscretion set her pulse pounding. But she had been foolish before where Joe's heart was concerned.

She remembered the first time she had imagined kissing Joe. It seemed so long ago, that Christmas Day when he had brought a visitor to the Carrington home.

Miss Angelina Beaudace. A redheaded debutante from Boston, visiting friends—and Joe—in New York. She was a Radcliffe girl; he was on break from his first year at M.I.T. Meryl had been fifteen, and given permission to wear a grown-up gown for the very first time.

Not that she filled it out very well. She was a late bloomer, her mother had assured her. Still, the contrast between herself and Miss Beaudace was obvious even to her.

Miss Beaudace was polished, sophisticated, and well-endowed. Joe seemed exceedingly proud that he had caught the attention of such an aristocratic lady. Where the Carringtons were considered new money—and had lots of it—Miss Beaudace was from old money. Her family name provided entrée into the loftiest realms of New York and Boston society.

Why that should matter to Joe, Meryl couldn't fathom. He had always been a part of *their* social circle, and *they* were certainly good enough. They entertained the Astors and the Vanderbilts, for goodness' sake! Unless he was actually *attracted* to Miss Beaudace.

During the visit in the parlor, while Mr. Carrington discussed Joe's education and plans with him, Joe hardly ever glanced Meryl's way. To Meryl's consternation, this bothered her more than she cared to admit. She didn't understand her feelings, and didn't welcome them.

All of the insults she longed to hurl at Joe clogged in her throat. Despite his lanky boyishness, Joe was acting like an adult now—wearing a three-piece suit, shaking father's hand, and asking his pretty friend if she needed sugar for her tea. So Meryl sat in the corner, despite her lovely lady's gown, feeling like a little girl and—for the first time in her life—unable to think of anything smart to say, or anything to contribute to the exceedingly dull conversation.

After awhile, she escaped the family gathering and retreated to the music room on the third floor. There, despite her gown, she curled up on the window seat and hugged her knees, fighting the strange feelings of unrest brewing inside her.

"Hey, Pest."

Joe's voice startled her and she jerked to her feet, a curious thrill shooting through her. "Joe. What are you— I thought you'd be gone by now."

"Trying to rush me out the door? Don't fret. We're about to leave. Miss Beaudace wants to visit a cousin of hers . . ."

Meryl had no interest in Miss Beaudace's cousin. "Well, goodbye, then," she said, turning back to the window.

Silence came from behind her, and she thought he had left. Until he spoke. "Do you always have to be so rude?"

Her back to him, she shrugged. "I don't think I'm rude. Just honest."

"Honest that you don't want me here? I told you I would be leaving soon. But I have something I thought you might like."

Warily, she turned around. "What?"

He held out a little white box with a ribbon tied around it. "It's a present. For Christmas." He stepped over to her and held it out.

Meryl stared down at it, delighted and shocked. Joe and she had never exchanged gifts before. "You— That's for me?" Gingerly, she took the box from his hand.

"That's what I said."

She looked up at him from under lowered lashes. "Are you sure? I can't imagine why . . ."

An annoyed look flashed across his face. "I can

take it back." He reached for the box, but she snatched it to her nearly flat chest.

He lowered his hand, and she studied the box, peering at it closely. She shook it, but heard nothing.

"Aren't you going to open it?" he asked in exasperation. "I don't have all day."

"It's a lump of coal, isn't it? Wrapped in tissue paper so it doesn't rattle. Or a dead spider. Or maybe—"

He grasped her hands, securing them around the box. "Meryl, look at me."

Slowly, she lifted her eyes to his.

"It's not a trick this time. Just open it."

Carefully, she untied the ribbon, while he shifted impatiently from foot to foot. Finally free, she let the ribbon drop to the floor and slowly— ever so slowly in case a snake jumped out at her—lifted the lid.

Something inside caught the light in the room. She dropped the box lid and stared in amazement at the slender gold pendant within. "Oh, it really isn't a snake," she said in amazement. "I still don't understand why . . ."

He shrugged, looking almost embarrassed. "It just reminded me of you. Or your hair, or something." Lifting the necklace from the box, he held it up. "I'll put it on you, if you like."

Meryl didn't trust herself to answer. She presented her back to him, and watched as the pendant appeared at her throat. His warm hands slipped behind her neck, sending an unexpected tingle down her spine.

In delight, she fingered the pendant, a tiny pearl set in gold. It was a grown-up gift, her first from a boy. His generosity stunned her, and she was unsure what to make of it. She knew that men who gave women gifts were courting them. Did he want to court her? Did he secretly love her? How should she treat him now? What if he tried to kiss her!

"Thank you," she murmured, conscious that his hands remained on her shoulders for the briefest of moments.

"I've been looking all over for you, Joseph. I'm tired of entertaining your friends alone."

The intrusive female voice broke the spell. Meryl turned around and glared at the redheaded Miss Angelina Beaudace.

"I hope I'm not *intruding*," Miss Beaudace said. The way she stressed the word *intruding* made it sound like a joke. The curve of her lips made the situation seem even more ridiculous.

"No, I'm ready to go," Joe said lightly. He gave Meryl a brotherly pat on the shoulder. "Go show your mother and sisters. I bet they'll be impressed."

With a final wink, he left her there and followed Miss Beaudace out the door. As they exited, she heard Miss Beaudace complain, "Why are you spending time with her? She's just a little girl."

"Then there's no need to be jealous, is there?"

Meryl's heart dropped to her feet. *No need to be jealous.* Not of her. She was only fifteen, and Joe had probably given her the gift on a whim, to placate her, to keep her from making a scene. Or to impress her family.

She sank onto the window seat, feeling lost and

insignificant, Joe's gift cold against her throat. Why had he bothered? She remained nothing to him but a silly little girl. She would always be nothing but a pest to Joseph Hammond.

Evening had fallen on Virginia City. All day Joe had visited saloons and gaming parlors looking for anyone who might know a Cal or Petey who matched the descriptions of the men from the train. He had learned only that they both used to work the Comstock Lode as miners.

Until a bartender told him he had seen Cal coming to the bordello.

Joe's first stop in town had been a visit to the town marshal, who had already heard the account from the Reno sheriff. He had agreed to send a deputy out on a cursory search of the countryside, but not until daybreak. Without more details on the bandits' whereabouts, he told Joe, the search would no doubt be fruitless. The landscape was too vast, the weather too bitter.

Despite Joe's entreaties, he received only one other concession from the marshal. The lawman promised to alert his deputies to be on the watch for anything suspicious. Then he reassured Joe that if Meryl didn't turn up before the robbers' deadline, they would pull an ambush when the two men rode into town.

That plan sounded good on the surface. But Meryl might be with the robbers. Joe could envision a shootout if the bandits resisted arrest. He didn't want to risk Meryl getting hurt if the situation turned ugly.

Yet the alternative—leaving her the captive of a pair of ruthless men for three full days—wasn't to be borne.

Which left him in a terrible position, with a critical need for information. This bordello was a starting place. With any luck, it would lead straight to Meryl. He pushed through the door.

Compared to the snow-swept boardwalk, entering the bordello felt like stepping into another world. Joe looked around the reception room at walls papered in garish red and gold. The half-dozen sofas and chaises longues in the parlor of the old house were upholstered in clashing colors and fabrics, from deep burgundy leather to sea-green velvet. Resting upon them were a few ladies of the evening waiting for customers.

Joe shook fresh snow off his coat and wiped his slush-drenched boots on the mat inside the door.

"My goodness, a man who knows to wipe his feet. You look awfully cold. We can warm you up nice and good."

Joe looked up from the elaborate, faded design in the worn carpet. An aging lady-of-the-evening stood before him, her generous breasts barely squeezed into a cloth-of-silver gown. She slipped her arm in his and encouraged him to enter the parlor.

"I appreciate it, ma'am," he said. Joe guessed she was the bordello's madam. Her gray-streaked hair, corpulent frame, and careworn face told of a hard life. He'd seen more than his share of such women in Mexico, Europe, and parts of New York for that matter.

"You ain't local, with that accent," she commented conversationally.

"No, I'm not."

"Abby's available. Or Georgina, my Negress, if you'd like an exotic one." She gestured to a bone-thin brunette and a Negro woman in turn, both of whom looked bored while they sucked on their cigarillos.

"I need to see the proprietor."

She dropped his arm and stepped back, her eyes narrowing with suspicion. "You the law? We got no trouble with the law hereabouts. They leave us alone."

He shook his head. "No. It's personal."

She relaxed only a little. After considering a moment, she gave a single nod. "Then come this way." She led him toward a small front room and closed the door. "Hurry up now, I don't have all night."

"I need information on one of your clients. He robbed a train this morning with another man."

Lines gathered between her brows. "I'd be out of business in no time if I blabbed about my clientele."

"I figured as much." The frustration in his gut nearly choked him. The last thing he needed right now was a madam touting her "ethics." It was easy enough to test them.

Sliding his hand into his pocket, he extracted a wad of cash. As he hoped, the madam's eyes brightened with avaricious delight.

Joe began riffling through the bills. "Cal is his

name. Used to work the Comstock. Mean son of a bitch with brown hair and squinty eyes. Looks to be thirty, but he's probably only twenty-five. He has a brother or a companion, round face, maybe sixteen or seventeen. The kid doesn't talk much. *His* name is Petey." He flattened a twenty-dollar bill on the desktop with his palm.

She reached out to take the money, but he dragged the bill back before she could touch it.

Her eyes lifted to his, glinting with a hint of respect. "I seem to recall a fellow that might be your Cal." Her eyes flicked to the bill, then back to his face, her lips curved in a knowing smirk. "Then again, we have so many customers coming through here. Virginia City's a busy place."

Joe peeled off a second bill and added it to the first. "Tell me everything you know about him. I'm trying to find him, and his companion."

"Not his brother. But you're right that they're both miners with the Comstock. Or, they were, before the lode started drying up. So, they've taken to thieving, have they?"

"And kidnapping. I don't think they're expert at either." A fact greatly in his favor. With any luck, they had failed to cover their tracks. With luck, and this woman's help.

"Kidnapping." Her expression shifted from greed to genuine interest. "Who?"

Joe hesitated. He felt as responsible for Meryl as a husband would. Even if she hated the idea of being taken care of, especially by him. Besides, the lie felt marginally sufficient to express his outrage. "My wife."

Fifteen

"He's my husband. I ran away from my father to marry him, so he disowned me. So, you see, it's pointless to try to extort money from him. You might as well let me go." Meryl finished her tale with a silent prayer that she sounded convincing.

Unfortunately, Cal wasn't buying her story. "That's not how it sounded on the train," he observed with a smirk.

Despite his command the day before that she remain quiet, she had gradually worked her way into the conversation. Perhaps the men enjoyed the distraction. She hoped the better they knew her, the less inclined they would be to harm her. And, if they began taking her for granted, they might relax their guard, allowing her to escape.

A kerosene lantern on the rickety table flickered, softening the shadows. At night, the shack's rough edges seemed softer, her surroundings less decrepit.

As the sun set on her second night as a captive, Cal began polishing his pistol. Petey—who had taken the role of cook and cleaner—had stepped out for a few minutes, leaving a thin stew simmering on the potbellied stove.

"I didn't tell you the truth because I was scared," Meryl said.

"And you ain't scared now?" Cal looked down the barrel of his pistol. "You oughta be." Frankly, she admitted to herself, she was terrified, her every nerve on edge. Yet she refused to let them see it. Over and over, she reminded herself that things could be worse. Much worse.

"He won't pay you," she said again. "No one will pay you for me, so you might as well release me. I promise I won't tell anyone you took me."

"How about that husband of yours?"

"My poor husband is penniless. Why do you think my parents disowned me?"

"Because you talk too much?" Cal shook his head. "Damned annoying female." Setting his gun aside—unfortunately, out of her reach on a table across the room—he stood up and began to pace. "Where in the hell is Petey? I need to get to town."

A loud bang at the door drew his attention. Petey came in backward, hunched over, dragging a scraggly tree. Its trunk dripped sap on the pine flooring.

"What the hell is *that*?"

Petey avoided his contemptuous gaze. "A Christmas tree," he mumbled.

"Christmas tree. My, my." He slowly approached Petey, then bent to speak right into his face. "Ain't that sweet. Ya think the James brothers have themselves a Christmas tree? Ya think they give a good goddamn about Christmas?"

"I *like* Christmas," Meryl said, more to interrupt Cal's building tirade than to share her feelings.

Cal snorted. "See, Petey? You're a sissy, just like a woman." Grabbing his coat off a hook he shrugged into it. "I'm goin' to town. I'm fed up with sittin' around this dump."

A look of panic crossed Petey's face. "But what about me? Cain't we just tie her up and leave her?"

"And risk fifty thousand walkin' out the door? You *crazy?*" Stepping toward Petey, he slapped him across the skull, hard. "Don't be a dolt. Now, do a good job watchin' the lady and maybe I'll bring you back something nice, like a peppermint stick from the general store."

Meryl doubted the general store was his destination. More like saloons and bordellos.

He left the shack, the cracked door closing behind him with a rattle. Meryl listened closely, hoping to determine in which direction he would ride off, thus learning where "town" was. Unfortunately, with the soft snow outside and the scrape of the tree as Petey dragged it to the far corner, she couldn't hear well enough.

Knowing the direction wouldn't help if she couldn't undo her bonds, of course. Under the blanket, she bent her wrists yet again, testing the limits of the rope, hoping somehow they would miraculously loosen and give her a chance to escape. She had been bound for so long, her hands constantly tingled. The muscles in her neck and back were so stiff, pain shot through her whenever she shifted position. The more she struggled at her bonds, the more raw her wrists became.

Petey pounded a pair of crossed boards into the tree's base, then righted it. The four-foot tree—little more than a sapling—sat off-kilter, its trunk crooked. Nevertheless, Petey stood back and admired it, a hint of pride in his round face.

A lump formed in Meryl's throat. He seemed so pleased at such a simple thing. Odd that the Christmas spirit could affect even outlaws. "Your tree is a wonderful idea. How are you going to decorate it?"

Petey turned to her. He shrugged. "Don't rightly know, ma'am. Maybe popcorn."

"I can help you decorate it. If you untie me, I can—"

He shook his head. "Cain't do that, ma'am. Cal would have my hide." The boy avoided her gaze as he busied himself melting a slab of lard in a skillet on the potbellied stove. He was clearly nervous over his involvement in her kidnapping, but he was more afraid of his partner's wrath.

"You seem like a nice fellow, Peter," she said, intentionally avoiding the diminutive of his name. "Why do you let him tell you what to do?"

He ducked his head, his face coloring. "Everyone calls me Petey."

"Petey is a little boy's name, and you're hardly a boy. Which is why I wonder why you let Cal tell you what to do."

"He's smarter than me."

"I don't know about that. You're certainly better looking."

Petey's blush intensified, giving Meryl a strong indication of his youth and inexperience. Naturally outgoing, she had never had difficulty speaking to all types of people, young men included. She had to use whatever advantages she might have to get herself out of this situation. And with Cal gone, she might not have another chance.

He didn't reply. Opening a small burlap bag, he scooped out a handful of corn and dropped it into the skillet.

"I adore Christmas," Meryl said to his back. She was determined to keep talking, to engage the young man in conversation, to make her plight real to him. By doing so, he might let his guard down around her. "My mother made sure our entire house was decorated, with pine boughs, swags of holly . . . And the tree," she said, a faraway tone in her voice. "So lovely. Mothers are so good at making Christmas special. Well, at least mine is."

"Mine was, too," Petey said, still minding the skillet as the kernels began snapping into fluffy popcorn.

"Did your mother put candles on your tree? Mine did. I have four sisters, and every year we each make an ornament. Last year I made a cloth heart with lace and a sprig of baby's breath. This year . . . Well, this year," she gave a soft laugh. "I guess I won't be home this year, seeing as I'm here."

He turned around. "We ain't keeping you that long. We're gonna give you back, I swear it. Cal said so."

She sighed deeply. "I suppose, if he's telling the truth. I'm just so afraid . . ." She filled her voice with the secret terror that plagued her.

Petey looked away, embarrassment flickering in

his eyes. "Don't do that, ma'am. Did your mother
. . . Does she cook Christmas dinner?"

"Oh, yes." Well, Mrs. Carrington supervised the
servants who cooked the meal. "We have all the
fixin's—turkey and plum pudding and cider . . .
What about your mother, Petey? Are you going to
spend Christmas with her?"

"I don't got a mother, ma'am. She done died."

Her voice softened. "I'm so sorry. It was rude of
me to ask."

"Naw. I like thinking about her." Lifting the skillet from the stove, he dumped the freshly cooked
popcorn onto the table. Pulling some thread and
a needle from a wooden box, he sat down and
began to create a garland from the popped kernels.

"That looks like fun," Meryl said. "I wish I could
help, but . . ." She lifted her bound wrists from
under the blanket and held them up.

"Well," he glanced up at her. "I suppose if you
stay put, with that rope keeping you in the chair,
it'd be okay." He knelt before her and untied the
rope binding her wrists.

In a few minutes, her hands were gloriously free.
Meryl massaged her wrists, shocked by her victory.
She longed to rip the rope from her waist and dash
out the door. But she counseled herself to be pa-
tient. She would be a fool to jump the gun.

Instead, she behaved like a proper guest. With
the room lit by a single lantern, a strange intimacy
fell between captor and captive as they spent the
evening hours stringing popcorn and reminiscing
about Christmases past.

While their gentle conversation succeeded in lowering Petey's guard, it began to have an effect upon Meryl as well. Her eyes grew misty as she watched Petey drape their creation around the humble little tree. It wasn't a very elaborate tree, and it lacked a star on top. Yet it sparked memories of Christmases past, happier Christmases she had shared with her family—and Joe.

In the quiet of the shack, the years slid away. She remembered one Christmas when she was only five. Joe had been there, helping to decorate the tree. Because her father was at work, the eight-year-old Joe had volunteered to play the man of the house and put the star on top. Naturally, she had objected. He was merely a visitor, after all. *She* wanted to put on the star.

They had argued about it, until their mother commanded that they leave it until her father returned from the office.

That's when Joe had pulled her aside. Taking her hand, he had led her to the tree and given her the star. Then, climbing on a footstool, he had lifted her up. Even so, she had to stretch and stretch, and still she could barely reach the top branch. Just when she managed to slide the star in place, Joe lost his balance. Together, they fell against the tree, knocking it over and shattering dozens of glass ornaments.

Meryl smiled at the memory. Thank goodness her mother had found their folly amusing. And Meryl had never forgotten that Joe could actually be kind, even to a pest like her.

She squeezed her eyes shut to fight back fresh

tears. She had never believed it was possible to miss someone as badly as she missed Joe. His teasing smile, that dimple flashing in his cheek; his eyes—sometimes as ferocious as a storm, sometimes as cool as a still mountain lake; and his patience with her, a girl who had done her best over the years to be a thorn in his side.

Petey's voice broke her reverie. He stood back and looked at their creation. "Well, that's it. It's time to turn in. You need to . . . um . . . go out?"

Occasional breaks to visit the outhouse were the only chance she had to stretch her legs. Petey would escort her outside and wait for her by the door, an embarrassing situation for them both. This time, she shook her head.

Soon, Petey had curled into his bedroll on the floor and silence had fallen in the darkened cabin. Hope flared in her chest. She barely dared to breath, to risk drawing attention to herself.

She rubbed her hands along her sore arms. Petey had forgotten. Her hands remained unbound.

She waited until a soft snore issued from his bedroll. Her hands shaking, she began untying the rope at her waist.

The whinny of a horse outside startled her, and her fingers stilled. Cal had returned.

Frustration struck her with such force, tears sprang to her eyes. As fast as she could, she loosely retied the rope at her waist and tightened the blanket about her, then tucked her unbound wrists beneath the cloth. Closing her eyes, she pretended to sleep, and prayed.

* * *

At the top of a rise, Joe reined in his horse beside Deputy Yarnell's and scanned the quiet valley. The first rays of the morning sun were just striking the hillside above a broken-down shack.

"There's the shack," the deputy said, his voice sending out a puff of mist into the still morning air. "If the whore wasn't mistaken, that'd be where Petey and Cal are hiding."

Joe slipped his palm around the butt of the Derringer he had purchased the day before in a general store. He had never shot a fellow man, but he wouldn't hesitate to use it. Unsure how long the search would take, he had also purchased sturdy boots and a sheepskin coat to wear. To his surprise, the shack was much closer to town than he had expected.

"There's smoke," the deputy said.

Joe squinted at the shack. A thin gray curl spiraled from a metal pipe in the roof. Hope sprawled in his chest. "Then they're in there."

"Somebody is. Let's go see who." Yarnell kicked the flanks of his horse and led the way through low sagebrush into the valley.

They were halfway down the hill when the door of the shack slammed open. A man sprinted out, yelling at the top of his lungs. Lifting a pistol, he fired it toward the north, opposite from the way Joe and Yarnell had come.

"Where are you, damn it to hell? I'm coming for you, you little bitch!" He dashed around the side of the shack into a lean-to.

"That's him," Joe said, his heart pounding. They had found them. In his excitement, he lurched his horse forward.

Yarnell grabbed his reins and brought him up short. "Let's see what he's up to."

Joe's impatience nearly made him challenge the man. He itched to gallop down there and lay into the bastard.

Perhaps the deputy had a better idea. He pulled his rifle from his saddle, set it on his shoulder, and cocked it.

Less than a minute later, Cal reappeared on a horse, galloping away from the shack in the direction he had fired his gun.

"Now." Yarnell spurred his horse on a path to intercept the bandit.

Joe drew his Derringer and followed. But he found it difficult to tear his gaze from the shack. If Meryl was in there . . . He longed to race down there, snatch her out of the shack, and spirit her to safety. Get her as far away from this hellhole as possible.

The deputy intersected the bandit's route thirty feet ahead of him. He reined in and lifted his rifle. "Drop your gun." Joe pulled up at his side, his own gun at the ready.

Cal jerked his horse to a stop, its hooves dancing backward several steps. Joe expected him to do as the deputy said. Only a fool would face down two guns.

Cal was, apparently, a fool. Whipping his pistol up, he fired off a shot. It struck the deputy. He cried out and reared back. Then Cal turned his gun on Joe.

Joe didn't hesitate. This wasn't like hunting grouse, he thought briefly. The target was much closer, and larger, and armed. The Derringer bucked in his hand, the shot echoing off the surrounding hills.

The confrontation happened so fast, it took a moment for Joe to absorb it all. A strange look crossed Cal's face. Then he began to pitch forward, remarkably slowly, finally tumbling head-first off his horse.

Joe swung off his horse and hurried to Yarnell's side. Yarnell gingerly dismounted, his hand on his shoulder. "He winged me," he said, sounding surprisingly casual considering he could have ended up dead.

Yarnell approached the bandit with care, his rifle held at the ready despite his injured shoulder. He gave the bandit a nudge, then knelt and rolled him over. Cal's sightless eyes stared up into the gradually brightening morning.

"You killed him," Yarnell said calmly. He looked up at Joe. "Thanks."

The lifeless body made Joe feel odd. In the hours since Meryl's disappearance, he had entertained more than one fantasy of bloody revenge against this man. While he had supervised armed guards to defend the Mexico railroad construction, he personally had never killed a man—until now.

He ought to feel worse. All he could think about was Meryl, and that this man would never hurt her again. He was so close to saving her. Turning his back on the bandit, he jogged toward the shack.

"Hammond, hold up!" Yarnell called behind him.

Joe ignored him. He was certain he could take Petey if the kid was foolish enough to make a move. He wouldn't hesitate to shoot him, too. Vaguely, he wondered when he had become so bloodthirsty.

He stepped into the shack. Petey was sitting on the floor. He threw up his hands. "Don't shoot me. Please don't shoot me."

Joe stared down at him. Such a pathetic excuse for a hardened criminal. "Where is she?"

"She—she ran off. She took a horse and rode off."

"When? Which way?"

Petey thrust out a shaking hand and pointed in the direction his partner had begun riding. North, away from Virginia City, but toward the railroad where she had been taken.

"When?"

Petey looked at him with wide, terrified eyes. "Don't shoot me."

Joe grabbed the front of his shirt and dragged him to his knees. "When did she leave?"

"I don't know. Before dawn sometime. Cal—" His nervous eyes shifted toward the door. "Is Cal—"

"He's dead," Joe said. "And you will be too, if you aren't telling me the truth."

Tears sprang to Petey's eyes. "I am, I swear it!"

Joe's fist tightened, fury welling up. The bastards had dared to take her, dared to threaten her. "Did you hurt her? Did you do anything—"

Petey shook his head furiously. "No! Nothing! Please. She helped me decorate my tree."

Joe glanced at the sad little tree in the corner, draped with a popcorn garland and ornaments cut from tin cans. The thought of Meryl throwing her considerable abilities into such a project struck him as strangely touching and sad.

"She helped me. She helped me." Petey's voice fell to a low murmur. Joe released him and stepped back to find Yarnell at his side.

He holstered his Derringer. "She ran off. I'm going to get her."

He half expected Yarnell to protest, to tell him to wait or some other such nonsense. Instead, he gave a slow nod. "I'll deal with him." He nodded toward Petey. "And the other one."

Joe didn't wait a second longer. Now nothing stood between Meryl and him—if he would be able to find her.

Sixteen

Meryl clasped the Indian blanket tightly around her shoulders with one ice-cold hand. She had been riding for more than an hour. That length of time would have been a cakewalk if she was in a proper riding habit, on a mount with an English saddle, on a warm summer day.

Now she felt awkward and cold and more uncomfortable than she ever had. For two days she had been tied to that hard chair. She had never felt so exhausted, so on the verge of collapse. Every bone in her body ached with fatigue. Her muscles screamed with every step of the horse's hooves.

Any moment she expected to hear Cal's horse behind her, galloping in pursuit. Her nag—Petey's, rather—had slowed to a walk to pick its way over the rocky, icy ground. She didn't even know if she was headed in the right direction—whatever "right" meant.

When she had slipped from her captors, she headed back the way they had first brought her to the shack. At first the terrain had seemed familiar. Now, in the early morning light, she wasn't certain she had ever come this way. And even if she found her way to the railroad tracks, she would have many miles to travel before reaching Reno.

Her only other hope was finding a ranch or farm, or any sign of habitation in this cold, bright wasteland.

Fatigue weighing her down, she briefly closed her eyes. Her horse slowed, yet she hardly noticed. Sleep lured her, soft and warm, a haven from the fear that hounded her. She found it impossible to resist. Closing her eyes again, she began to drift away.

A sharp sound startled her and she jerked awake. She had fallen asleep! Tightening her hands on the reins, she urged her horse forward. From the increased brightness of the morning, she guessed she had dozed for at least twenty minutes.

Behind her came another sound—rocks sliding upon each other. She looked over her shoulder and saw the silhouette of a horse and rider coming over the hill behind her. Terror struck in her heart, snapping her wide awake. What a fool she'd been, sabotaging her own escape by drifting off to sleep.

Kicking hard at her horse's flanks, she urged it to a gallop.

Hooves pounded behind her, drawing closer. Terror welled in her throat.

"Stop! Meryl, hold up!"

She didn't slow. The wind whistling in her ears, and the panic in her chest, made it hard for her to focus on anything but escape.

The man called out again, closer this time. Close enough for her to hear his voice.

"Meryl! Meryl, it's Joe!"

"Joe," she whispered. Afraid to believe it, she risked a glance over her shoulder, bracing herself for disappointment.

He was only thirty yards back, close enough for her to make out the shape of his face, see his honey-gold hair touched by the sunrise. He was still missing the hat he had lost when jumping onto the train.

Her heart lurched and she pulled hard on her horse's reins, then swung around.

"You were going the wrong way," he called as he came closer. The sight of his wry smile warmed her heart.

"You found me," she said, stating the obvious. "You found me."

He dismounted. Stepping beside her, he held up his hands and caught her as she slid to the ground. "Yes, I found you," he said, smiling down at her.

She threw her arms around his shoulders and hugged him, hard. The tears that had pressed against her eyes since her capture finally released. Despite her desire to appear strong, she buried her face against his sheepskin coat and sobbed. She was used to being strong, to being safe and in control of her world. Her captors had stripped that from her, and only now, now that she was again free, did she realize what she had lost.

He rubbed her back and shoulders, trying to ease the sobs that wracked her body. "It will be all right. Everything will be all right," he murmured. His soothing words fell on her like liquid honey.

Sucking in a breath, she gripped his lapels, refusing to release him. The thick fabric under her hands felt strange. "This coat. I don't recognize this coat," she said, finding that simple fact easier to focus on than the emotions that flooded her.

"I bought it for . . . By God, your wrists." He lifted her hands in his and studied the raw skin encircling her wrists. "Bastards."

She tightened her fists and tried to pull them away. "Not Petey. He's just a boy, a confused boy. I hope— He's not—"

"Only the other one is dead."

"You killed him?"

By his silence, and the look on his face, she knew he had. Her Joe, her childhood friend, her sophisticated gentleman, had been brought to murder? Because of her.

She wanted to tell him—had to tell him—something, something that longed to burst from her heart. But though she opened her mouth, she couldn't give voice to the confused flood of sentiments she felt at that moment. She was so tired, so very tired. All she knew for certain was that she wanted to be away, far away from there.

"Can we— Can we go now?" she asked, sounding like a little girl.

He bent and dropped a gentle kiss on her forehead. "Let's go."

During the ride back to town, Joe found it difficult to tear his eyes from Meryl. She looked positively exhausted, her clothing wrinkled, her face wan and tired. Dark circles had appeared under her cerulean eyes, making them appear even larger and more vulnerable. Her golden hair hung in a long braid down her back. She no longer looked like the pert, neatly turned out heiress from the East.

The welts on her wrists infuriated him. If he hadn't already killed Cal, he would enjoy repeating the experience. Used to thinking of himself as a cultured gentleman, his bloodthirsty reaction shocked him.

After leaving the horses at the town livery for the marshal, he escorted Meryl to the International Hotel, and up to the suite he had rented. She said almost nothing to him. She seemed so unlike the lively, determined girl he had raced from New York. He prayed that her lack of spirit stemmed from exhaustion, and that she wouldn't bear lifetime scars from her appalling misadventure.

She drifted into the room like a wraith. Her gaze fell on the large four-poster bed covered by a thick down comforter, and she let the worn Indian blanket drop from her shoulders. "A bed. I love beds."

"You should sleep. I don't imagine you slept much in that shack. Or are you hungry?"

"Last night I stayed awake so I could escape. But I *do* need a bath. Is there . . ." She looked around.

He crossed to the bathroom and opened the door. "Right in here. I'll draw it for you."

Leaving her in the room, he knelt by the claw-foot tub and adjusted the taps. He enjoyed doing this simple, homey task for her. Teasing her had always been enjoyable, he now admitted, because she gave as good as she got. Now, after her frightening experience, that spark of antagonism had been subsumed by a tenderness that surprised him. For the first time in their lives, Meryl was allowing him to see the vulnerable woman underneath the bravado.

He half expected her to have fallen asleep on the bed by the time the bath was ready. Instead, he found her sitting on the edge, staring at nothing. His heart snagged. She seemed so childlike, so lost.

He stood before her and held out his hand. "Your bath awaits, madam," he said lightly, thinking he might tease her out of her melancholy.

She slid her delicate hand into his and allowed him to help her to her feet. She entered the bathroom and he almost followed her in, he was so anxious over her. Then he caught himself, and let the door close behind her.

His own room lay through a connecting door. He swung it open and entered. The International, Virginia City's finest hotel, catered to the well-to-do. The city itself was in an unlikely spot for visitors, clinging precariously to the mountainside in the Sierra Nevada foothills. The explanation was simple—the town of thirty thousand rested atop the largest, most profitable mine between Denver and San Francisco.

Joe had traveled a U-shaped route from Reno to reach Virginia City. The Comstock Lode—silver entwined with gold—had turned the mining town into the West's first industrialized city. The rich strike not only caused the town to spring up almost overnight, it funded the Civil War and brought statehood to Nevada.

The boom brought prospectors, speculators, prostitutes, and businessmen, and all those who followed in their wake. The result was an opulent town boasting respectable hotels, restaurants, and newspapers, alongside disreputable saloons, brothels, and opium dens. Prospectors who had become instant millionaires from the Comstock Lode had constructed elaborate mansions. Fancy emporiums selling imported furniture and fashions from Europe stood alongside unpretentious country stores. And simple inns competed with fine hotels for business.

Joe hadn't once considered renting a room in any but the finest establishment in town. After emptying his bank account for her ransom, he had plenty of cash on hand to see to Meryl's needs. After what she had suffered, he vowed to make things right.

Her needs took precedence over every other concern, her happiness became his goal. He had no idea when this compulsion to care for her had begun, certainly long before now. Perhaps it had been part of him all his life. Even as a boy, he had watched out for her, though she probably didn't realize it. He would never allow any of his pranks to endanger her. Since childhood, his compassion for her had lain dormant, waiting for him to recognize how much this girl—this woman—meant to him. Now, there was no going back.

He stared at her closed bathroom door. From inside, the sound of splashing water reached him. Did that make him a fool, to feel for her as he did? If she knew his feelings, would she welcome them? Or would she try to push him away?

For now, it didn't matter. After her ordeal, he knew he would stay by her side as long as she let him.

Seventeen

Meryl left the bathroom wrapped in a towel, hoping to find clean clothing to wear. To her relief, she saw that Joe had arranged for her trunk to be delivered to her room. She would no longer have to wear the tan and gray traveling suit she'd been living in since Omaha, the clothing she had been kidnapped in. In fact, she decided, she would never wear it again.

Opening the trunk, she pulled out a nightgown of French cotton and slid it over her body. On top of that, she donned her cornflower-blue silk robe. She ran her palms along the smooth fabric. She had never noticed before how heavenly high-quality fabrics could feel. She had taken them for granted, along with almost everything else in her privileged world.

She took her silver-handled brush and comb from her small valise—again put in the room by Joe—and crossed to the walnut bureau. Her reflection in the carved bureau mirror seemed utterly strange to her. Who was this woman staring back at her, her eyes shadowed and sad? Why couldn't she let go of what had happened, and become again the assured, self-confident girl she had always been?

"Who are you?" she whispered. "What has changed?" Why did she no longer know herself? She had a hunch that the change wasn't only because of her kidnapping. Something else had changed within her, something she couldn't define.

A soft rap drew her attention to a door connecting to another suite. "Meryl, are you finished?"

Without giving a thought to the proprieties, Meryl strode to the door and opened it. Seeing Joe standing there, a warm smile on his face, filled her with relief and pleasure. At that moment, there was no one else she would rather see than this man. Her friend, her rescuer. "I didn't know you were . . . I didn't realize you were right next door. That's . . . nice." Above all, she didn't want to be alone.

"Convenient, isn't it?" He closed the door behind him, his green eyes filled with concern as he studied her. "Feel better?"

"A little." She struggled to adopt a nonchalant attitude, to act normal. With Joe, normal had always meant lighthearted teasing and practical jokes. "I've never gone so long without washing my hair. It was almost as bad as when you put glue in my shampoo."

Her attempt to lighten the mood failed miserably. Instead of drawing a smile from him, he remained somber, studying her. She sighed, and gave in, dropping all pretense that she wasn't utterly vulnerable. She only had the strength to be who she was at that moment—a traumatized woman trying to feel normal again.

She turned back to the mirror and began trying to work out the tangles with her comb.

Moving beside her, he urged the brush and comb from her hands. "I'm not playing tricks on you now, Meryl. Let me do that for you. Come, sit over here." Taking her hand, he guided her to sit on the edge of the bed.

She didn't resist, despite a tendril of awareness that such attention might be dangerous in some undefined way. She had been raised to be wary of intimacy with bachelors, yet she felt so close to Joe, she couldn't imagine playing coy or acting stand-offish with him. Nor did she have the strength but to submit to his care.

He also seemed unconcerned with social formalities, for he climbed onto the bed behind her. Lifting her hair in his hands, he laid it behind her shoulders and smoothed it down with his palms.

Meryl sat perfectly still, her little niggle of awareness blossoming into full-blown realization that she had become completely susceptible to his charms. He had only to touch her and she began to melt inside. She recalled the hours she had spent in that shack daydreaming, reliving their intimate kisses, dreaming of kisses to come. If he ever again invited such attentions from her, she would revel in it.

He began working the comb through her waist-long locks, carefully resolving the tangles. "Tell me if I pull too hard," he murmured into her ear.

Meryl responded with a wordless peep that sounded nothing like her. She couldn't bring herself to talk, not if she hoped to make any sense.

Joe's fingers worked such delicious magic on her, she could scarcely breathe. Tingles wended their way from her scalp down her spine. She never wanted him to stop touching her.

"You're holding yourself so stiffly. Are you sore?" Setting the comb aside, he began massaging her shoulders. Meryl winced as his thumbs found remarkably tender places. Yet the discomfort felt so good, she wanted to cry.

She swallowed and forced herself to reply, attempting to infuse her tone with normalcy despite the pleasure radiating from his touch. "The hard seat on the train, and then the chair in the shack—"

"Chair?"

"The wooden chair they tied me to. It dug into me."

Grasping her shoulders, he turned her to face him, a dark, angry look on his face. "They tied you to a *chair?*"

His barely concealed rage made her feel alarmingly vulnerable. With an effort, she fought the urge to give in to her emotions, to let the tears fall. "What did you expect?" she shot back, her voice quavering. "A suite like this one?"

He shook his head and sighed deeply. "Never this." He resumed the massage, to her satisfaction. It felt too good to come to an end so soon.

"It should never have happened," he continued.

"I'm perfectly aware of that," she said with mild annoyance. "If I had known what they would do, I would never have challenged them. I should have been more circumspect. I don't blame you one bit if you point out my egregious error of judgment."

"Don't blame yourself, Meryl. You can't predict what men like that will do for a few dollars."

"Do you think I wanted my father to learn how utterly incompetent I am? I can't even travel across the country by myself without jeopardizing my own safety."

"You were doing fine," he replied.

"You're lying."

"Besides, you weren't alone."

"Do you think that will matter to my father? He'll never trust me again, not with anything important. Not with anything *un*important, for that matter. My foolish boldness ended my future prospects with the company. That must please you."

He continued rubbing her shoulders, his large hands sending delicious thrills down her spine. "He doesn't know."

"What?" she glanced at him over her shoulder, uncertain she had heard right.

His eyes met hers, and she knew he was telling the truth. "I never told him." He said it as if it were a completely reasonable statement.

"You—you never told him." Joe Hammond wasn't usually a careless man. Had he really relied on his ability to find her before the deadline set by the robbers? A chill swept through her at the risk he had taken. "But, if you hadn't found me, then—"

He resumed the massage, no longer meeting

her gaze. "I didn't say I hadn't prepared the ransom, only that your father wasn't involved."

"How?" She turned around and confronted him. Laying her fingers on his jaw, she forced him to meet her gaze, and read the truth in his eyes. A tremor of shock raced through her. "Joe, you didn't." Yet she could see by the look in his eyes that she was right. "You were going to use your own money! I know your father left you a small trust, but goodness, Joe, fifty thousand dollars! That's nothing to my father, but to you—"

She faltered as the obvious explanation occurred to her, dashing her sudden joy. "You promised Father you would keep me safe. You couldn't let him see how you had failed. You were worried about your future."

"No. Not because of that."

"Yet this situation only benefits you," she said, feeling desolate. She had been living in a fatigue-induced daydream far too long. She was finding it difficult to separate what she wanted from what *was*. "All of the decisions you have made work in your favor, including coming for me."

"And I'm that calculating," he said dryly. He climbed off the bed, his expression unreadable. "I'll let you get some rest."

"Wait." She grasped his hand, desperate to keep him there. He may annoy her sometimes. She may not trust his motives. But she hated the idea of being alone, at least this night.

He had done so much for her already, regardless of his reasons. But she wanted to ask him for one more favor, if she dared. "I don't want to be alone."

He looked down at her, waiting for more from her.

Gathering her courage, she gave voice to her longing. "Would you stay with me for awhile? Would you hold me, like you did that night on the train?" She exhaled. She had said it.

For an endless time, he continued looking at her, his expression a cipher. Then he slowly lifted his hand and cupped her cheek. His thumb traced her cheekbone. "Meryl. I don't think—"

She grasped his hand against her cheek. "Don't make me beg, Joe."

"Begging would never suit you, Meryl. Very well. I am a little tired after everything that happened." She realized he hadn't slept either, possibly since she had been kidnapped.

Behind his rationalization, she could hear the unspoken thought. As long as they slept, and nothing more, there could be no harm in it. He helped her climb into bed, settled the covers around her, and closed the heavy drapes against the advancing morning sun.

His silence continued while he undressed. She fought the fatigue weighing down her eyelids and watched him shed his trousers and shirt. Clad in only his underthings, he came around the bed and slid in beside her.

For a tense moment, they lay as if a wall separated them. She turned onto her side, her back to him, then slid closer, until her backside touched some part of him—his leg? His hip? No matter. For he responded. Rolling against her, he wrapped his arms around her, cradling her in his strong embrace as if he had every right to hold her with such intimacy.

She exhaled in a rush as his heat filled her, and she began to relax. She settled against him, willingly giving herself up to his strong, protective embrace. For the first time in forever, she felt at peace.

Joe woke up with an ache in his groin so fierce, he thought he might die from it. His hips pressed against Meryl's bottom. He increased the pressure, just a tad, desperate for release from the sweet torment she provoked in him.

Visions of seducing her heated his blood. She was so warm and sweet and alluring cradled in his arms. She belonged here, he decided. Petite and soft and sweetly shaped . . . He leaned closer and breathed deeply of her. Her skin smelled of French-milled soap, her hair of sweet lilacs. Her tousled mane caught a bar of late afternoon light escaping from behind the draperies. The light gilded her, making the shell of her ear appear almost translucent in its delicacy.

What would she think if she knew how aroused he became when he touched her? He was so tempted to find out. To seduce her. If he slid his hands upward, he could cradle her small, firm breasts in his hands. He imagined her soft moans of pleasure as he caressed her, introducing her to the carnal delights that men and women could share.

Giving her a massage had been delicious torment, but lying beside her now was physically painful. She appeared to be sleeping solidly, but the ache in his groin was so fierce, he shifted away. Any moment she could awaken and notice his indiscreet body, sparking fresh annoyance toward him.

Annoyance . . . Their earlier conversation tumbled through his mind, succeeding in damping his lust. Releasing her, he rolled onto his back and stared at the bed's satin canopy, visible in the late afternoon light that slid through the edges of the drapes. She didn't even notice, she was so dead to the world.

She doesn't trust me.

The truth stung, but he couldn't deny her mistrust. She believed his desire to keep her safe was motivated by personal gain. She actually entertained the idea that he had rescued her merely to remain in her father's good stead. How could she think that of him? Why?

A lifetime of experience, that's why. For years, she had been accustomed to various humiliations at his hand—discovering ink on her backside or frogs in her picnic basket, or a dozen other little humiliations he had subjected her to over the years. She could think of him in no other way.

No, that wasn't quite true, not anymore. Things had changed. They had both grown up. He felt so close to her, so grateful to discover the spirited, feisty woman she had become.

She needed him. She relied on him. She wanted him here, beside her. He reveled in that realization, as unexpected as it was exciting.

I'm falling in love with her. His chest began to ache as the truth sank in. Desperate longing filled him to draw her near, to kiss her again, to make sweet love to her.

To make her mine. He longed to keep her with him, to build something from their shared experiences, to win her love.

He sighed at his foolish, romantic notion and tried to think realistically, using the clear-headed reasoning that had always served him in business dealings. Engaging Meryl in a love affair—which society would consider tawdry regardless of their emotions—would hardly encourage her to trust him.

No, Meryl Carrington should never be bedded like some tart off the street. She was his boss's daughter, for one thing. A longtime family friend, for another. There was only one way he should ever be allowed such intimate access to her, despite her willingness to sleep beside him and draw comfort from his embrace.

And there were other obstacles. They were still at odds in this contest for the San Francisco contract. It meant so much to her to prove herself. How could he possibly win both her and the contract? How could his success do anything other than push her away again?

Only one answer made sense. Conviction filled him. Of course. It was obvious. It was such a perfect answer, he was amazed he hadn't seen it before. It would solve everything—their ill-begotten competition, his longing to bed her, her obvious need for him, even if she wouldn't admit it.

His idea involved a bit of risk, but no more than he had already taken. He was used to fighting for what he wanted. He would be a fool to hesitate now.

Meryl was sleeping so deeply, she didn't even stir when he slid from the bed. He had something important to do.

Eighteen

A light touch on Meryl's cheek drew her from sleep. She opened her eyes to find a man's face silhouetted against a darkened window.

She started, her eyes flying open, a lance of terror shooting through her.

"Shhh, it's me, sweetheart."

Joe. She sighed in relief. She recognized his tender smile now, the dimple winking in his cheek. She recalled Joe putting her to bed, then lying down beside her. Now he was kneeling before her, tickling her cheek with his handkerchief. The Virginia City hotel room. She was far away from her captors and could rest easy, knowing he would watch out for her.

Sweetheart. Vaguely, she wondered about the term of endearment he had used, but her muddled thoughts couldn't work it out properly. Her surroundings, the nighttime view out the window, disoriented her, and she struggled to come more fully awake.

"About time you woke up," he said. "You've been asleep for a long time."

"How long?" she murmured.

"Twelve hours, give or take. You might have stayed asleep another twelve hours, but I couldn't wait any longer."

She didn't understand his meaning, but her thoughts were just beginning to clear. One thought in particular filled her head. "I dreamt you left. For San Francisco."

His eyes darkened and his smile faded. "You can't be serious. By God, you are serious."

"Mmm," she affirmed. Of course she was serious. Now that she was out of danger, nothing should prevent him from winning their bet.

"After what you've been through, you really think I would leave you here?" he said incredulously.

"Our bet still holds," she said, sitting up. She realized her breasts hung free, in a rather sheer nightgown. She drew her knees to her chest. "My robe. Where is my robe?"

"Here." He took it from a wing chair and handed it to her. That's when she realized he had transformed himself back into a nattily dressed gentleman. He looked ready to go to church. Gone was the shadow of a beard, the heavy sheepskin coat. He wore a freshly pressed tweed suit with a striped vest of gray and cream. A neat, off-center part tamed his freshly barbered hair, which had been smoothed back with a touch of pomade.

What had he dressed for? He said he wasn't going to San Francisco. Besides, it was evening. Perhaps he planned to attend a business meeting or dinner. Whatever was up his sleeve, she intended to find out.

She shrugged on her robe and hurried to the bathroom. If he was going to be ready, then so was she—for whatever came. Unfortunately, her clothes were in the main room.

When she came out, she found Joe standing in the center of the room, looking uncomfortable. Perhaps she should have asked him to leave before attending to her personal toilet. Yet, strangely, she didn't really mind that he had remained. It enabled her to keep an eye on him, at least.

Why had she invited him to sleep with her? What was wrong with her? This was Joe, the man she was competing against. Her enemy, for all intents and purposes. And what had she done? Acted like a silly, foolish woman. Begged him to stay. Allowed him to see her vulnerability, her weakness, her tears.

Yes, she was grateful he had rescued her. How could she not be? Yet it frustrated her that she had needed a man to rescue her. Worse, that man had been Joe. He had never respected her when they were children. Now he surely saw her as a weak, needy female.

And she had only made it worse. Exhausted, recovering from fear and uncertainty, she had lost her sense, *in his arms!* She had clung to him, begged him to stay, allowed him all manner of indiscreet familiarities a woman should allow only her husband. Yes, she had kissed him on the train. But that had been a foolish mistake, as well. She had to begin thinking straight, remembering why she had come out west. Remembering why Joe was really with her.

The best she could now was repair the damage. Perhaps it wasn't too late to set him straight, to prove herself capable, to remind him she had a goal she wasn't about to forgo. She had worked so hard on that proposal for Westgate's purchase. She was so close to San Francisco, too close to give in. Certainly not for him, even if he made her feel unusual feminine longings, feelings that muddled her mind and made her lose her sense of purpose.

She refused to let him get the better of her. Resolving to be firm, she spoke bluntly. "You don't have to be in attendance upon me." She released her hair from under the collar of her robe and let it cascade down her back. "I'm quite capable of taking care of myself."

His deep, indulgent chuckle sounded patronizing to Meryl. "I'm well aware of that, Meryl. I'll leave you alone, but first . . ." He glanced away, then back at her. "First, there's something I need to discuss with you."

She didn't like the serious sound of his voice. She eyed him warily as he stepped closer and grasped her hand. She wanted to pull her hand away, but feared that would show too clearly how his touch sent her pulse racing, how vulnerable she was to his charms.

He led her toward the pair of wingback chairs before the fireplace. Joe must have started the mellow blaze while she slept. "Sit here, please," he said, pointing to one of the chairs.

She complied, and he took the chair across from her. She stared closely at him, seeking some indication of the nature of his thoughts. "You contacted Mr. Philbottom, and he's not selling."

"No," he said with a touch of ruefulness. "That's not it."

Something else, then. It had to be about their agreement, or he wouldn't have such a serious expression. "He already sold the company to Vanderbilt, or Forbes, or Harriman," she realized with dread. "I *knew* Harriman had his eye on it. We took too long getting to San Francisco!"

Again he shook his head. "This isn't about the railroad purchase, Meryl. But, to ease your mind, I did wire him that we'd be coming soon, and—"

"Soon? Why not today?" She lurched to her feet. They were sitting around in Virginia City when there was business to conduct.

"Sit down, Meryl. It's Saturday. He's not expecting us until Monday."

"Oh." She sagged back into the chair, uncomfortable that Joe had gotten so much groundwork laid ahead of her. Yet he had said "us." "What do you mean, *us?*" she asked suspiciously. "Did you tell him we were *both* meeting with him? We never agreed—"

He held up his hand to interrupt. "I merely said that a representative of Atlantic-Southern would be arriving to discuss the purchase with him, not specifically who."

She shifted, amazed once again by his consideration for her. Even with something that meant so much to him. Every time she tried to ascribe shady motives to Joe, he proved himself a man of sterling character—and made her feel awful for suspecting the worst. "Oh. Well. That was kind of you, considering."

He arched a brow. "Considering what? That I'm an untrustworthy cad?"

She sighed. "No, that you and I are competing, in case you've forgotten, which I am quite certain you have not."

"No, I haven't. But this isn't about that. It's about something much more important."

She crossed her arms, feeling suddenly on edge. What could he possibly be talking about? "Go ahead."

"Meryl, I've been thinking," he began, sounding thoughtful. "No, not just thinking. Making a decision. A critical decision."

He paused a moment, glanced out the window, sucked in a breath, looked at her, exhaled, then finally began speaking again. "It seems to me we get along well. That is, when we're not trying to thwart each other's efforts to succeed. When we're not in direct competition. It's the competition that causes the problems."

He leaned forward, his hands clasped between his knees. "I've thought of a solution, and it makes absolute sense. It's one of the best ideas I have ever had, if I do say so myself." He gave his dimpled smile, and she tried hard not to let it affect her, not to be taken in by his charm. He was up to something, and she was damned if she would allow him to snatch the upper hand.

"I've taken into account our history, our mutual experiences. Your family and mine, our shared childhoods, our expectations, and even our ambitions."

What was he leading up to? She gazed at him

warily, but didn't ask, deciding it was smarter not to interrupt his discourse. His obvious struggle for words might reveal something about his plans or motives, something she could later use to her advantage. Yes, he had been a gentleman—until now. But until their bet ended, she would be a fool to trust him. Even if she secretly longed to.

"I know you've thought me a boor and a savage and a general louse for—well, forever. But I do hope you have seen equally strong evidence that I'm no longer a child. I've grown up, Meryl, just as you have. I'm a man—"

"I'm well aware of that," she said, fighting her embarrassment. Goodness, was he ever a man—strong, handsome, with a touch that set her on fire. She could hardly look upon him any other way.

"Right. And I see *you*, Meryl. Not as a child, but as a lady. As a woman." His voice grew gruff on the last word, sending a shiver down her spine. Warily, she studied his intense eyes.

The raw need reflected in their emerald depths stunned and excited her. He wanted her, and he was letting her see it. "An attractive, desirable woman," he added in a low tone that set her pulse pounding.

He could be so distracting! She had to focus on the business at hand, and stop imagining silly girlish fantasies. She straightened her spine and tried to return a businesslike tone to their encounter. "What are you trying to say, Joe? You're going round and round. Haven't you learned yet the importance of arriving at the station before the train leaves?"

"Damn it, Meryl." He slapped his knee. "Do you have to be so antagonistic?"

She threw out her hand. "I'm not being antagonistic, I'm merely trying to get to the point, whatever that may be!"

"Fine! I'll tell you the point." Shoving his hand in his jacket pocket, he withdrew a small box. "This is the point."

He snapped the box open, and in the lamplight, Meryl caught the glimmer of a crystalline jewel inside. It couldn't be . . .

To her shock, he dropped to one knee before her. His eyes met hers, and she froze at the serious look in them. She couldn't believe he really meant what she thought, until the words left his mouth.

"Marry me."

Nineteen

"What?" Meryl said, stunned beyond coherent thought. Inside the little box rested an expensive diamond ring, its facets winking at her in the golden firelight.

Joe took her hand. "I want you to marry me."

Delight flared in Meryl as she realized the meaning of his question. Joe wanted to marry her. *Marry her!*

Her excitement stunned her almost as much as his unexpected proposal. This isn't what she truly wanted, was it? So why did the idea thrill her to the depths of her being? And Joe—What could he possibly be thinking?

"Why?" she finally asked, struggling to adjust to this new definition of their relationship, to the world of possibilities opening before her.

"I've explained the reasons, Meryl," he said with excruciating calmness. "Because it makes so much sense, for both of us."

"How—how long have you wanted to—marry me?" Had he been in love with her for years, perhaps? Teasing her because he was too afraid to really show her how she felt?

"I realized it this morning." His gaze slid toward the rumpled bed, where he had lain beside her as if he belonged there. Perhaps he believed he did, that by allowing him such liberties, they had stepped so far beyond the bounds of propriety, he had no choice but to do the "honorable thing."

Trying to hide the sinking feeling in her stomach, she adopted a matter-of-fact tone. "You haven't damaged my honor, if that's your concern. Even though we were, or rather, you were . . . *with* me . . . That is, you're like a brother to me."

His lips tightened. "Oh, you think so?" Leaning closer, he slipped his hand behind her neck and urged her closer.

He kissed her lightly, tenderly exploring the curve of her lips with his. The tip of his tongue danced along the soft contours, as if he enjoyed touching her like this so much, he would willingly spend a lifetime at it. His reverent attentions made her ache with a wealth of unexpressed emotion. She opened herself to his attentions, reveling in the sweet, sensuous feelings flowing through her.

She threaded her fingers through the silken hair at the nape of his neck. The heady, masculine scent of his hair pomade filled her nostrils. He smelled so clean and delicious, she wanted to bask in his attentions.

He withdrew the delightful ecstasy of his mouth. A crooked smile drifted over his lips. "Do you see now? Perfect sense."

She gazed into his eyes. For one long minute, she allowed herself to drift in the fantasy.

Until she realized he had said nothing about

love. Her heart tumbling to her feet, she pushed back in the chair. "You're doing it again. Taking advantage of my weakness for you. I'm not going to succumb to your dubious charms, Joe. You should give it up. It's not going to happen."

"Then why do I feel *I'm* the one succumbing?" he asked dryly.

"I admit kissing you is . . ." She struggled for an appropriate word.

"Pleasurable," he supplied.

"Pleasurable," she agreed, feeling her face heat. "But that's hardly a reason to wed."

He shrugged. "It is if one wishes to consummate such passion."

"*That's* why you want to marry me?" Shoving against his chest, she sprang to her feet. "I hardly think that's sufficient reason—"

He rose to stand beside her. "I told you the reasons. We've known each other all our lives! We get along—to a point," he said, prevaricating. "Think how much stronger we would be as a couple, rather than as antagonists."

"This is all well and good, but it's hardly enough to base a marriage on." She looked at him closely, searching for signs of love, something to remove her growing doubts. All she saw was the same Joe she had always known.

"I think I know what this is about." Her suspicions dispersed the sensuous fog that had enfolded her, clarifying the truth in her heart. "You're afraid I'll win our bet, and this is a way to divert me. Make me start thinking about wedding gowns and reception guests, and all that blather, instead of proving to you that I am your equal."

He extended his hand toward her, but she stepped back, putting needed distance between them. "Meryl, I'm not trying to sabotage you. But you must admit that things would be easier if we—"

"Easier for you, you mean. Easier in so many ways." A sinking feeling filled her. He didn't believe she could succeed without a man. Joe, of all people, didn't believe in her. That truth stung worse than anyone else's doubts ever could.

His smiled vanished, replaced by a scowl. "Yes, Meryl, having you by my side would benefit me as well."

The nature of those benefits crystallized in her mind, and she realized how right she had been not to trust his motives. "If you married me, you would become my father's son-in-law! You know he would want you to succeed in the company, because of me. What better way to ensure your own success than by marrying me!"

His lips parted in disbelief. "By God, I can't believe it. After everything we've been through together, you still think the worst of me. Damn it, Meryl, I want to marry you because I care for you, can't you see that?"

She grasped her robe close at the neck. "Well, that helps, I'm sure. It helps that you wouldn't be stuck with someone you thoroughly disliked for a wife."

Stepping close, he settled his hands on her shoulders. Despite her mistrust of his motives, she swayed toward him. "I thought my honorable intentions, my proposal, would prove to you that you ought to trust me."

The intimate rumble of his words, the intensity of his gaze, spoke to the weakest part of her. Her eyes grew heavy, and once again, she slid under his spell.

He continued in a murmur, "Trust what I feel for you. What you feel for me."

She struggled to fight him, at least with her words. "And what, pray tell, is that?"

"This." Her drew her even closer. Her heart thrummed with languid heat as she anticipated another of his earth-shattering kisses. Instead, his lips landed on her neck, then slid to her collarbone, sending delicious shivers throughout her body. He whispered against her skin, "You feel it, too. You feel it, just as I do."

His lips danced along the sensitive place between her neck and collarbone. She closed her eyes and tilted her head back, inviting his explorations.

"I want you, Meryl, so badly," he said, his voice a murmur of desperate need. "I want *us*."

"Want," she murmured, her lips against the tweed of his jacket. Firelight danced along his hair, imbuing his honeyed locks with a golden sheen.

His hands drifted up her silk-clad arms and he cradled her face, drawing her gaze to meet his. A victorious smile lit up his face. "I'm so glad you've let me in, Meryl. You've let me see the real Meryl, the vulnerable woman who needs a man—"

"Needs?" The word doused the passion from her more thoroughly than ice-cold water. Meryl tore herself from his embrace. She wrapped her arms about herself and stared at him, her chin high. "I don't need you, Joe. Yes, you rescued me from a dire situation, perhaps even saved my life. But that's not the same as needing you in my life every day, as one might a husband."

His eyes darkened. "You don't feel the need when I'm kissing you? The hunger that threatens to consume your common sense?"

Oh, she felt it, all right. "That's not the point. Passion needn't entail a lifetime commitment. I am free to desire a man without losing my heart to him."

He looked at her skeptically. "Is that so?"

She paced away from him, toward the bed. "Yes."

"Very well. If you're so unaffected, if you're so completely in control of your heart, come back here and prove it."

Pulling in a breath, she turned around. He looked so confident standing by the fire, shoulders broad, feet spread. So attractive and sophisticated in his well-tailored suit. Part of her longed to rush into his arms, to be done with the struggle, to submit. Yet she recognized that once again she and Joe were engaged in a war of wills, in another wager, this time for life.

If she gave in now, under his terms, she would never be happy, even as his wife.

A fire built within her to prove herself, to prove to him that she could experience passion without the ring. Of course she could. All she needed to do was follow her secret, illicit longings.

She took a hesitant step forward to close the ten-foot distance between them. He merely watched her advance—waiting to call her bluff, no doubt.

She paused after a single step, overwhelmed by her lack of experience in matters of a carnal nature. What would one of those dance-hall girls in Mexico do? Mrs. Yves-Kendall—how would she begin to seduce a man?

Perhaps she didn't have to do anything. Men were the natural aggressors. Her role was to issue an invitation, to demonstrate that she was ready and willing. Once she did, he would probably be too concerned with propriety to take her up on her offer, and that would be the end of this nonsense about needing a husband.

Despite telling herself it was nonsense, her hands trembled as she loosened the knot in the belt of her robe. She let the silk slide from her shoulders and puddle on the carpet, leaving her in only her nightgown. With its high neckline, her maidenly modesty remained protected. But her breasts hung free, pressing against the thin fabric.

Joe's relentless stare grew more intense, focused on the area of her chest. Yet he didn't back down. Instead, he crossed his arms and leaned back on one foot.

The expectant gesture annoyed Meryl. She could see the disbelief in his eyes, the certainty that she would turn and flee from his manly presence.

He was about to learn just what kind of woman he was dealing with. Her fingers trembling worse than ever, she began to undo the topmost button at her neck.

This time, he visibly stiffened. But instead of bolting, he had the audacity to smirk at her. He slipped off his tweed jacket and laid it over the arm of the wingback chair behind him.

Annoyed, she glared at him with defiance while undoing a second button. In response, he unfastened all four buttons of his vest and shrugged it off. He tossed it atop his jacket.

That left him in his trousers, shirt, and braces. He was still fully clothed, she thought with disgust. He hadn't risked a thing.

In rapid succession, she undid the pearl buttons of her nightgown down to mid-sternum. He snapped his suspenders from his shoulders and had his shirt off before she paused, leaving him in his undershirt.

For a moment, his physique distracted her. Her eyes played over his arms, the rippling muscles sculpted by the glow from the fireplace behind him.

He dropped his shirt over the rest of his clothes, then his eyes met hers, silently mocking her.

Narrowing her eyes in defiance, she undid two more buttons. The fabric of her gown fell back to expose the rise of her breasts. She swallowed hard. *This is no more than he would see should I be wearing a ball gown,* she reminded herself. Yet the nightgown felt far more intimate.

Joe must have seen her nervousness. "Meryl," he said softly. "You don't have to do this."

Finally, she was rattling his composure. Any moment he would back down. Now was not the time to lose her resolve. Yet a part of her felt disappointed that their game would end so soon. His body fascinated her, and she wanted to see more of it.

She freed a few more buttons. "That's right, Joe, I don't have to. I *want* to." Her gown fell open, revealing her skin all the way to her navel. She had never displayed so much cleavage to a man.

The heat in his eyes told her he enjoyed the sight. Her breasts tingled, her nipples tensing into tight knots that pressed against the thin cloth.

Joe licked his lips.

Meryl was afraid to move, for fear the fabric would drop open even further, exposing her breasts. She had never thought she would go even this far, but she was prepared to go further, if necessary. She waited, tense and ready, her eyes playing up and down his body.

Finally, he reacted. But instead of leaving the room, he grasped the edge of his undershirt and whipped it over his head.

"Oh," Meryl gasped despite herself. He was gorgeous. Lean and hard, without an ounce of useless flesh. He reminded her of paintings by the Old Masters she had studied in art class. Some of those pictures of nude men had made her feel warm and sensual just looking at them. But this man was real. Sandy hair dusted the hard planes of his chest, trailed down his flat stomach, and disappeared into his trousers.

"Your move."

His taunt snapped her from her trance, replacing her admiration with annoyance. He had seen her desire for him on her face, plain as day. Perhaps she could repay the favor. Reaching up, she tugged her gown down one shoulder, exposing most of her breast.

Joe shifted and swallowed hard. "Meryl," he said, his voice rough. Now he would leave, she thought, waiting expectantly. Right now.

Yet he remained standing there, gazing at her as a hungry man would a king's feast. His blatant desire delighted and excited her. How far could she push him before he broke? He was on the verge of breaking. She could feel it. She had the upper hand. For despite her fascination with his body, he seemed positively mesmerized by hers.

Having power over him was a heady, intoxicating feeling, one she wasn't going to give up without a fight. Drawing in a breath, she slowly exhaled, and let her gown puddle at her feet.

Her knickers, her last remaining item of clothing, hid so little. She was doing the unspeakable—letting a man gaze upon her nude legs, her nude breasts.

And gaze he did. Joe's breathing sounded harsh in the quiet of the room. "Damn it, Meryl," he swore. This was it. Even though he was half undressed himself, she had exposed what no man but a husband should see. He would dash back to his own room, and never again would he assume she needed to marry to enjoy her sensual nature. Never again assume she needed *him*.

Then he moved. To her shock, instead of turning tail, he headed straight for her. In three confident strides, he had reached her and pulled her into his arms.

There was nothing gentle about his kiss this time. His lips possessed hers, demanding, hot, almost harsh in his expression of need. The hard planes of his chest smashed her bare breasts, exciting her beyond bearing.

She could have resisted. Could have been the one to flee, to give up, to surrender.

And let him win? Out of the question. She gave in, but to quite a different battle, the battle against her own carnal desires. She wrapped her arms around his neck and opened her mouth to his questing tongue.

At her bold gesture, he still did not retreat. He plundered her lips and her mouth, holding nothing back. His palm sought out her breasts, stroking and caressing each in turn. His intimate caresses turned her knees to jelly. If he hadn't been supporting her, she would have tumbled to the floor.

His palm skimmed along her bottom. Grasping her rump, he snugged her up against his hips.

She began to lean into him, the fire inside her building to a fever pitch that erased all semblance of modesty. She wanted to be closer to him, *needed* to be closer. *No, not need. I don't need him,* she reminded herself, even as she hooked her leg around his waist in an effort to draw him harder against her.

Her enthusiastic reaction threw him off balance. He stumbled backward. He barely managed to bring them to the bed before he lost his balance. He fell squarely on his back with Meryl sprawled atop him. Her thighs burned where their hips joined. Her nipples scraping against his chest pounded a sensual beat in her blood.

Her eyes met his. A languid smile spread over his lips. "I knew we would eventually end up like this."

"Oh, did you?" she responded, shocked by how breathless her voice sounded. "How could you possibly know such a thing?"

"You've been in love with me since you were a little girl—following me around, trying to capture my attention. Well, darling, you have it now."

Despite the fact that his contention had more than a hint of truth, his smug confidence grated, firing her blood with a mixture of anger and passion. She was positioned atop him, which gave her an advantage—or ought to.

Shifting her position, she locked her knees around his hips and grasped his arms, pressing them down beside his head. He had pinned her like this once when she was eleven, after she had slipped spiders down his back. Their chase in the park had ended with him pinning her down.

Even then she had felt something strange inside at the intimate contact. She suspected he had, too, for he had released her after only a moment, his face turning a light shade of pink.

She glared into the handsome face of the grown man he had become, but found no embarrassment there.

"You've finally caught me, Meryl. And, trust me, you have my full attention." His gaze drifted to her swaying breasts, then returned to her face. A smile teased his lips and his eyes sparkled. "So, what exactly do you intend to do to me? Whatever it is, I promise I won't mind."

Twenty

Sitting astride Joe, Meryl stared down at him and chewed her lip. Even prone beneath her, half-naked, he exuded confidence and power. She had to take the upper hand. She could hardly do so physically—she would have to do so with words.

"I intend to force you to admit I don't need you," she said, desperate to sound strong, determined not to let him into her heart even if she shared her body with him. "I have never needed you, and I never will."

"Is that so?" Bracing his hands on her upper back, he drew her breasts toward his mouth. When he spoke again, his hot breath tingled the sensitive flesh of her left nipple. "Poor Meryl, so confused. I'll show you what it means to need."

She watched in fascination as he slid his lips over her breast's rosy, swollen peak. The audacious contact sent an intense wave of pleasure through her, and she gasped.

With his warm, wet tongue, he rolled her tender flesh against the roof of his mouth, sending bolts of pleasure through her.

Weakness overtaking her, she curved her back

and dropped to her elbows, digging her fingers into his thick hair, her face pressed to the pillow. His lips tugged at her swollen flesh, the tip of his tongue dancing over her aching flesh. Meryl wriggled, heat building in the center of her womanhood. Her movements drew an animalistic growl from Joe. Her eyes drifted closed, and she began to float away, toward heaven.

Finally, the delicious torment ended. He broke contact. The room air felt cool on her moist flesh. To her astonishment, she actually whimpered, her longing was so intense.

He brushed back the golden locks that had tumbled past her shoulders to tickle his chest, then stroked her cheek with the back of his hand, his green eyes heavy-lidded with arousal. "That's just a taste, sweetheart."

"It doesn't mean I need you." She sucked in a breath, which caused her breasts to lift, the nipples so swollen, they nearly brushed his face.

Crinkles of amusement formed at the corners of his eyes. His tongue darted out, stroking one of her nipples and causing her to gasp.

He dropped his head back on the pillow. "You expect me to believe you, when you react to me this way?"

"I don't need you," she repeated, willing it to be so. Doubt flickered in his eyes, until she added, "But I do want you."

In one smooth motion, he rolled her onto her back. How unfair that he had the advantage of a man's experience in such matters. She had only her instincts to guide her, to prove to him that she could enjoy this, could take pleasure in him, without giving her life to him.

Yet for now, her instincts seemed to be doing an excellent job. She gave herself up to her longing to touch Joe, to stroke his hair, to feel the firmness of his arms beneath her palms.

With a gentle tug, he pulled free the satin bow at the waist of her knickers. He slipped his fingers beneath the drawstring waist, loosening it enough to slide his palm over her hips and pushed the cloth down.

She aided his efforts and kicked her final garment away. She had gone too far to back out now, yet she didn't care.

He left her then, but only for a moment. Meryl watched him shed his trousers and drawers, leaving him nude. In the firelight, she studied his long, lean body as he stretched beside her.

So beautiful. A golden god, she thought, the description so apt, it brought tears to her eyes.

He pulled her into his arms and slid his leg over hers possessively. His touch warmed her from head to toe, their bodies entwining like two halves of a broken whole.

His lips met hers in a deep, sensuous kiss. He stroked her hip, her thigh, the inside of her knee. The swollen shaft of his manhood pressed hard and hot against her femininity.

"So right," he murmured against her lips, his fingers tangling in the soft curls at the apex of her thighs. "So perfect, and so right."

She understood the sentiment. He stroked her body—her legs, her back, her stomach—anticipating what she wanted to feel before she realized it. Everything was so fresh and new, yet they caressed and kissed in perfect understanding, as if they had been intimate for years.

He slid his fingers against her womanhood, stroking skin so sensitive, a deep, low burning built inside her that she was desperate to quench. Yet she feared releasing herself to the pleasure. "I have heard it will hurt," she murmured into his neck.

"Only the first time. The first of many," he whispered back, his lips tracing the curve of her neck as his fingers slid inside her moist recesses, preparing the way.

He guided her knees higher, replacing his fingers with the tip of his manhood. Rising on his arms, he gazed down at her. "Relax," he urged.

Because of her contrary nature—at least where Joe was concerned—his request made her grow tense. She pressed her knees against his abdomen, keeping him from coming nearer.

He cupped her face. "Please, Meryl. Trust me, just this once."

She bit her lip. "That doesn't help."

His eyes glowed with an understanding only he could share. Of everyone in her life, he alone understood her contrary nature. "You aren't woman enough for a man like me," he taunted. His fingers again stroked her, sending waves of pleasure through her. "You would rather be with a meek, mild fellow you can boss around."

His taunt worked. Passionate fire consumed her worry, leaving only the heat of desire. "Try me."

Locking her legs around his hips, she opened herself to him.

He could not have escaped if he tried. With a groan, he entered her in a long, slow stroke.

A shudder of pain passed through her, but began to fade almost immediately as he slowly moved inside her. She gripped his shoulders, desperate to cling to something secure as wave after wave of pleasure threatened to sweep her into oblivion. Closing her eyes, she fell into the sensation, until nothing of her remained but that which she shared with Joe.

Meryl lay in Joe's embrace, gazing at the satin canopy stretching above them. Never had she imagined the consuming power of passion, of becoming one with a man. In some fundamental way, she felt changed. The man responsible for the change continued to hold her, now that their passion was spent.

Joe . . . She had done it. She had slept with Joe. Things would never again be the same between them.

Her reasons for allowing such intimacy—allowing, she scoffed at herself; more like reveling in—paled now that the deed was done. What had she proven, exactly? Unless he still believed—

"Things are different now," he said, echoing her thoughts. He rose onto his elbow and gazed down at her. Twining a lock of her hair about his fingers, he stroked it with his thumb. "Ever since Thanksgiving, I've been thinking of you differently. You really took me aback when I saw you at dinner, in your gown, all grown up." He tapped her nose and smiled. "You've always been cute, Meryl. Now you're gorgeous."

She smoothed back a lock of hair that had fallen over his forehead and smiled. "It's funny, but I had the same reaction toward you."

"I knew it. I had a feeling we would end up this way." Lifting her hand, he kissed her palm. "You've made me so happy, Meryl."

"Joe," she said, wondering at his happiness and, to her dismay, envying it.

"Wait. I think it's time." He released her and shoved off the bed. She laid her head on her pillow, watching his lithe movements as he crossed the room.

"Time for what?"

He crouched down, then returned to the bed and sat on the edge. "For this."

He lifted her left hand and slid the diamond engagement ring on her third finger.

Meryl sat up and scrambled for the sheet, pulling it against her with her right hand while the left hung in the air, the stone weighing it down.

Joe clasped both her hands in his. "Let's marry as soon as possible. Our families won't mind, we've known each other for so long. How about a Christmas ceremony? If I negotiate the Westgate deal right away, we can return home."

"I?" she echoed, unease filling her.

"There ought to be just enough time for you to plan whatever you need for a small ceremony, but then, that's a woman's purview. As long as it's quick, I'll be happy."

"Christmas is only three weeks away," she murmured, the only coherent thought she managed to voice. He had given so much thought to the future—their future.

"What can I say? I'm anxious to make you mine. After all, we've been courting all our lives."

Meryl pulled her hands away and wrapped the sheet more tightly around her. "No," she whispered.

His smile faltered, but only for a moment. "Very well, I can wait until spring, if you insist. Will that give you enough time?"

"No."

"Then summer—"

Meryl pressed her fingers to his lips, silencing him. "No. I won't marry you, Joe. You forget how we ended up like this."

A muscle flexed in his jaw. "You can't be serious. You mean those silly things you said about passion—"

Her shoulders straightened. She should have known he would try to twist the facts. "I proved it, haven't I? I still don't need you." The words sounded harsh even to her ears.

The disappointment in his eyes was so raw, she had to tear her gaze from his. *He has said nothing about loving me,* she reminded herself fiercely. *Even if he had, I wouldn't have to* need *him.*

"Meryl, now is not the time to play games," he said with a scoffing laugh. "Haven't we done enough of that? After what we shared . . ."

His words died as Meryl pulled off the ring and held it out to him. "You've decided exactly what that is, for yourself. But to assume that I want to marry you, after I already told you no, just because—"

He made no move to take the ring, pretended he didn't even see it. "Just because what? Say it, Meryl."

Pulling in a steadying breath, she forced herself to define their blissful, glorious lovemaking with the harshest, most unsentimental word she could think of. "Because we . . . copulated," she said, knowing her cold choice of expression would hurt him almost as much as it hurt her to say it.

Joe jerked to his feet. His steely glare froze her through, obliterating the last traces of warmth from their lovemaking. "I always thought I knew you, Meryl. I thought you understood me better than any other person I have ever met. Apparently, I was wrong."

"You knew what you were doing," she said, desperate to put forth her argument, not to allow him to paint her as the villain. "You expected to trap me after you bedded me. You believed I would give in to preserve my reputation. You're just that desperate to marry the boss's daughter."

"My goodness, how well you know me," he said with a scornful laugh. "I should be so calculating. Perhaps then I would have recognized what kind of person you really are."

Meryl pulled her knees to her chest. His words stung more than she ever would have imagined words could.

He snatched his trousers from the floor, then gathered the clothing he had left by the fireplace, shed in the throes of passion. He headed for the connecting door.

Meryl moved onto her knees and gripped the bedpost. "Joe, don't—"

He spun back to face her. "No, Meryl. *You* don't."

"Your ring." She held it out to him on her palm. It burned where it touched her, taunting her with its false future.

"Consider it payment for an adequate *copulation*." The door slammed behind him.

Meryl sagged back on her heels, her stomach tight with misery. How awful that their friendship should end like this. How dreadfully things had turned out. She should never have allowed him so close.

She had done the right thing, she reassured herself. She would show him she could stand on her own. She didn't need him. She would never need him. Tomorrow, she would catch the first train for San Francisco, and prove how little she needed Joseph Hammond.

Even if she wanted him.

Twenty-one

Meryl shifted in the straight-backed chair, trying to find a more comfortable position. For almost three hours, she had been waiting in this anteroom outside the office of Mr. Avery Philbottom. At his small desk nearby, a gentleman secretary kept darting curious glances at her while he typed on his Underwood machine.

The aging office on Powell Street had seen better days. Dust lay thick in the corners, and a strip of wallpaper hung loose near the ceiling. A sense of desperation hung about the place, a dullness and lack of activity that presaged a business sliding into financial ruin. Considering the look of the place, Westgate Railroad wasn't in a strong position from which to negotiate.

Her nerves on edge, she rehearsed the upcoming conversation over and over, desperate to succeed. She glanced toward the door for the hundredth time, but it remained closed, the office silent except for the tick of a wall clock and the tap of the secretary's typewriter keys. Any moment Joe might appear—even though he hadn't been on her train. Any moment he might sweep in and steal her thunder.

Logically, she knew there was little chance he could catch up to her. Still, she fretted as the wall clock ticked off each minute. She had been waiting here for so long, it wasn't entirely inconceivable that he had already arrived in the city on a later train. She almost wished he *would* arrive, so she could stop thinking about him. About *them*.

The previous morning, as the Virginia City station clock had ticked closer to the moment of departure, she had braced for the inevitable confrontation. She had expected he would arrive in a rush, just in time to catch the train and laugh at her.

But he hadn't. She was clearly in the lead in their competition, bringing her closer to victory. His lack of competitive spirit confused her. He couldn't be giving up. This victory meant as much to him as to her. She remembered his story about making a success of himself, of proving himself to her father while disproving his own father's legacy.

She wouldn't even entertain the notion that he no longer wanted to compete with her. Or, rather, against her. Refused to consider that her rejection had dispirited him so badly he lost the taste for the hunt, the chase. He was her antagonist—he always had been. She had to see him that way. It was the only view that made their final, awful confrontation bearable.

Meryl smoothed her skirt. She had donned a dove gray suit with few frills, except for a modest lace jabot at her neck. She didn't want to appear fussy. After all, this was a business call, not a social call. The satchel at her feet held the handwritten acquisition proposal she had meticulously drafted, proof of her serious-minded intentions.

The secretary rose, collected a sheaf of papers, and entered Mr. Philbottom's office. A moment later, he returned. "Mr. Philbottom is ready to see you now," he announced, holding the door open for her.

Finally inside the office, Meryl glanced around. To her surprise, the office was small and cluttered. Railroad maps hung crookedly on the walls, along with fading photographs of iron horses being inaugurated before their maiden runs.

Nor was Mr. Philbottom the dapper railroad tycoon she had anticipated. His generous stomach sagged over the waistband of his wrinkled trousers, and a napkin hung from his collar. She had the feeling she had interrupted his lunch, though it was well past two.

He pulled out the napkin and rose when she entered, his eyes almost impertinent in their assessment of her. "Miss Carrington! So good to see you. Your father— He is doing well, I pray?"

"Yes, thank you." With confidence, she extended her gloved hand to the gentleman who might change her future.

He took her hand and bent over it, then offered her a seat in a chair across from his messy desk.

As he reclaimed his seat, he gave her a pleasant smile. Meryl began to relax, certain that such a warm welcome heralded a smooth, uncomplicated negotiation. She had prepared for this meeting; she knew Westgate Railroad's weaknesses and strengths, its market value, its relative importance among all the lines in the region. She knew the main stops—and most of the minor ones—on the vast network of tracks that crisscrossed California, Nevada, and Oregon. Even better, she knew how to save the ailing railroad. If Mr. Philbottom had any business sense or ambition, he could turn Westgate Railroad around.

After studying reports she had been given to file, she knew exactly what this company needed. It was crying out for reorganization. Its railcars needed to be upgraded to make its service competitive. The schedules needed to be restructured to improve connections to other lines in the region. She intended to address each of these problems, given the authority. All it took was convincing Mr. Philbottom to sell at a decent price.

"And the rest of your family? They are also doing well? Please, have a bite to eat. I have fresh coffee and sandwiches." He gestured to a cart laden with cookies and sandwiches with more heft than her family cook had ever made.

Meryl lifted her hand. "Nothing for me, thank you." She adjusted her purse on her lap and turned back the veil over her face. Mr. Philbottom seemed so cordial and respectful. Relief filled Meryl at how well their meeting had begun. At this rate, she would have the negotiation concluded within the hour.

"Very well." He glanced at a clock on the wall behind his desk. "I have a meeting in twenty minutes, but we can visit until then."

A visit? Did he not understand the nature of her

purpose here? Meryl sat near the edge of the chair, her spine straight. "I'm here as a representative of my father. As you know, he is interested in acquiring Westgate Railroad."

"Ah, your father. He's quite bullish about railroading, isn't he? Built himself a real empire."

"That's one way of putting it. He would like to bring Westgate Railroad into the Atlantic-Southern family."

He arched a thick brow. "Family? What an odd way of putting it. A womanly way to put it, wouldn't you say? I would much rather hear about *your* family. Tell me, dear, what brings you to the City by the Bay?"

Frustration tightened in her chest. "As I've explained, I'm here to negotiate the sale terms of Westgate Railroad. Didn't you receive a telegram to let you know I would be arriving today? Or, rather, someone would?"

"Yes, from a Mr. Hammond. But he didn't mention Carrington was sending his daughter to do his work for him. A very odd situation."

"Not that odd. My father trusts me—"

"I'm sure he does, dear," he said patronizingly. "Speaking of family, my daughter is giving a soirée next week. I'm sure she would love it if you attended. We don't see many New York socialites hereabouts."

"Perhaps. What I mean by family is allowing Westgate to continue with the same employees, for the most part, after the purchase. We would hate to put people out of work. Even you, Mr. Philbottom. We would like to find a place for you, if you prefer to remain."

"Well, that's dandy of you. That would be up to the board and the new president, now, wouldn't it? Not the owner's daughter. Can't see how you're in a position to be making promises."

His condescending attitude grated on her nerves. "Yes, I *am* making promises. I'm here on behalf of my father, who has granted me the authority—"

He shifted in his chair, his eyes no longer meeting hers. "This isn't really something you and I should be discussing."

"Am I wrong that you are looking for a buyer?"

"Well, yes, I am, but—"

"And you respect my father. So what remains is to determine a fair price. I know Westgate has lost money over the past two years. My father is expert at reviving failing railroads, and some of that expected profit will be taken into account in setting a sales price. In fact, I've worked out a proposed purchase price and terms, a proposal I would like you to take to Westgate's board of directors." Sliding a bound report from her satchel, she placed it on the desk in front of him atop the loose piles already there.

He didn't lift a finger to touch her tidy, freshly bound paperwork. He looked at her in disbelief. Finally, an embarrassed smile flitted across his face. "Miss Carrington," he said. "You aren't really interested in these financial matters. The thing is—" He leaned forward and spoke in a conspiratorial tone, "I would rather discuss this business with someone a tad more qualified than a young socialite. In fact, if I believed for a moment that your father really sent you, I would find it insulting. There *are* other buyers interested in Westgate."

Meryl gripped her purse, fighting the urge to snap at him. She had to be nice to this fellow, despite his presumptions, despite his veiled threats of finding someone better with whom to conduct business. No mention of his condescending attitude had appeared in the reports she'd read. Of course it hadn't. The reports had been written by men. "Sir," she began, trying on a smile. "I understand I may be a little different from most of the gentleman with whom you conduct business."

"That's the thing, dearie. They're business*men*. You are a lady, and a young one at that. If you don't mind, I would much prefer we stick to general topics—the weather, for instance. Foggy morning we had." He gestured with a pudgy thumb toward the dusty window behind him. Beyond, an overcast sky hung low over the bay at the base of the hill. Ferries clogged the waters between the shores.

"I didn't notice," she said flatly.

"Ah, have you found a hotel yet?" he asked, looking like a man who had thought of a conversational lifeline. "If not, may I recommend the Palace? A fine establishment. It has six elevators. And its glass-covered lobby—carriages drive right inside."

"Yes, I am staying there," she said coldly. The man had returned to his congenial tone, but only because they were again engaging in small talk. And he was trying to get rid of her.

"Well, good then." He rubbed his hands together and rose to his feet. "I hope you enjoy your stay in San Francisco. If you like, Harold can call you a cab."

"Mr. Philbottom, if you will just look over the proposal—"

His expression darkened. "Excuse me," he said coldly. "As I said, I have other appointments."

Meryl had overstayed her welcome. Worse, she was on the verge of queering the negotiation entirely, merely to make a point. She couldn't do that to her father or his company. She stood up. "Very well. Another representative should be arriving shortly. I expect you will treat *him* with greater respect and consideration than you have shown me."

Holding her head high, she marched through the anteroom, past the frowning secretary, and out the main door—right into Joseph Hammond.

Twenty-two

Joe looked at Meryl in shock. She should have been long gone by now. She arrived early enough to complete the negotiation without any interference from him.

Fresh pain filled him at the sight of her, looking pert and pretty in the gaslights along the corridor walls. How he longed to pull her into his arms again. Or grab her and shake sense into her! "Miss Carrington," he said stiffly. "So, you're the first to arrive after all."

"You came sooner than I anticipated," she said, her voice cool. Yet she wouldn't meet his gaze.

"I slept in," he said dryly. "I had forgotten how determined you could be, to my obvious folly. Ah, well, a fellow has to try." Despite wanting to be the one to bring Westgate into the company fold, he was actually glad their ill-begotten wager had finally ended. Perhaps now they could somehow find their way back to becoming friends. Someday.

"So, you've succeeded. I hope you're happy now, Meryl. Congratulations." He thrust out his hand.

She gazed up at him. The raw emotion on her

face struck him like a physical blow, obliterating his anger. Beneath her veil, her blue eyes were wide, her skin flushed.

He lowered his hand. "Meryl. Are you well?'

She tore her gaze from his and pushed past him toward the stairs. "Don't be ridiculous."

He ought to let her go. God knows things had ended badly enough when they last parted. But he couldn't help himself.He grasped her arm and halted her progress. "Damn it, Meryl. Talk to me."

"Everything is marvelous, Joe. Simply marvelous."

"Have you—You *did* succeed . . ." He gestured back toward the Westgate Railroad office.

"I succeeded, in something," she said, her words more bitter than any he had ever heard from her. She pulled her arm from his grasp and continued toward the stairs.

He watched her leave. He had no right to ask her to trust him, and no reason to expect things between them would improve. Being here, at Westgate Railroad, was all that really mattered to her. All that had ever mattered. No matter how he might feel, he couldn't force her to love him.

Let her go, he told himself, knowing the phrase was far from taking hold in his heart.

The clang of a passing cable car startled Meryl, yanking her from her reverie and back into the world's winter chill. Activity surrounded her, from the horse-drawn carriages and omnibuses passing in the street to businessmen seeking restaurants for a late lunch to shoppers hurrying by, their arms laden with Christmas packages. Elaborate displays in storefront windows drew crowds fascinated by mechanical toys and carousels.

She passed a street corner where a man in a Salvation Army uniform rang a bell beside a large kettle. Meryl dug a handful of bills from her satchel and dropped them in the kettle, not concerned with how much she was donating. She could only think of Joe, of her failure, of her sense of utter and complete loss of anything that mattered in her world.

The weight of failure was too heavy to bear. She had failed not only herself, but her father. Perhaps Joe would succeed—he probably would succeed. She had hung all her hopes on this success. She had even ruined her friendship with Joe, in favor of her ambition.

No, that's not true, she told herself. *He wanted to marry you, but not because he loved you. The competition meant even more to him than to you.* He would return to New York the victor; she would return empty-handed. After such a stunning failure, her father would see no reason to give her a position of responsibility within the company, and she would have no evidence to prove she was worthy of his trust.

Perhaps her father and Joe had been right all along. She was only qualified to be a wife and mother. She shouldn't even have bothered studying at college. A finishing school like those her sisters attended would have suited just as well.

All her effort, all her research and plans, had been for naught. Yet, she admitted, she could have tried harder with Mr. Philbottom. She could have presented stronger arguments, played it tough, not backed down so easily. She had simply lacked the will to fight.

The cheerful sound of voices raised in a familiar Christmas carol snagged her attention. The singing, while not without its flat notes here and there, drew her with its exuberance.

Following the singing, she climbed the steps into a church. Standing in the vestibule, she watched the choir rehearse. About a dozen men and women stood in a group near the altar. Their rendition of "See Amid the Winter's Snow" ended. A fellow serving as their director stood up from a front pew, applauding. The choir members laughed and began chatting.

Meryl took a seat in a back pew to listen to the music, a reminder of Christmases past, of cheerful and warm family gatherings.

Those gatherings had always involved Joe. He hadn't been there every day. She hadn't seen him for four years while he was in Mexico and she at college. But she had always assumed he would be a part of her life, always be there. He had been part of the fabric of her life for so long, not having him left her feeling unraveled. He meant more to her than she had ever imagined.

Now, they had gone so far beyond their former relationship, they could never return to how they had once been. She had lost her friend forever.

The choir began the slow notes of "O Little Town of Bethlehem." The moving melody brought moisture to Meryl's eyes, bringing back memories of

Christmas seasons past, when she had gone caroling with her sisters—and Joe. Her chest ached with all the lost promises of youth. She had never imagined things changing so much. Never imagined losing him, just as she had discovered him anew.

The only good thing about this trip had been Joe, she realized—finding him again, discovering how much she cared for him, their friendship blossoming into something deeper—at least for her.

I love him. A tear rolled down her cheek as the truth settled into her heart. Yet she had pushed him away so hard, he would never forgive her. She would never forgive herself.

He wanted to marry me. What a fool she had been. Her stubbornness and blindness had cost her that chance at happiness. Even if Joe didn't love her, her love for him might have been enough for both of them.

Now she would never know.

Joe had met men like Mr. Philbottom before. He had the tired, hungry look of a creature beaten down, one willing to find an easy out in a battle he no longer relished fighting.

He sized him up within a few minutes of entering his cluttered office. The man greeted him warmly. "So you work for Mr. Carrington, do you? I was hoping he would send a qualified fellow. I know it's a great distance, but the least I had hoped was a businessman of my ilk."

"Yes, sir, I'm here about the purchase you previously discussed with my employer. Though I may be treading ground already covered by another—"

"You mean the girl, Carrington's daughter. Pretty little thing, isn't she? She was just here. She came thinking I would do business with her. When you arrived, I knew she'd been—well, confused, is the best way I can put it. Thinking men's business somehow involved her. Strange ideas women have these days, like those feminist upstarts trying to give women the vote. Ridiculous stuff."

Clearly Meryl had failed. Joe couldn't find it in him to rejoice. He steered the conversation back to Meryl, trying to find out what had transpired. "So, Miss Carrington. What did you tell her?"

"What do you think?" A scoffing laugh erupted from his barrel chest. "I only do business with men, of course. This deal is very important to me."

"I understand that. Of course it is."

"Set me up for life, it will. I don't need some bossy female mucking up the works." He patted a bound report on his desk. "This proposal is excellent. I should have no trouble selling it to the board."

Report? Joe picked it up and began to scan it. Meryl's neat script covered the pages in smooth outline form. As he began to absorb the document she had written, shock settled in his chest, making it hard to breathe.

By God, he knew she was clever. He had expected anything she wrote to be neat and organized, as this proposal was. But this proposal showed a keen understanding of business, of both companies' strengths and weaknesses. Even better, like a seasoned business manager, she had identified and addressed every possible objection the Westgate board might have. With everything so clearly spelled out, the board would be foolish to bypass Atlantic-Southern's offer to buy them out.

"Girl tried to pass off this work as hers," Mr. Philbottom said. "I take it you were the author of it?"

He swallowed hard. Despite the pain she had dealt him, pride for her swelled in his chest. He lifted his gaze to Philbottom's. "Actually, Miss Carrington wrote it. I expect she told you this."

His mouth opened and hung there, like a fish out of water. He said slowly, "She did? Well . . ."

"Yet you assumed this work wasn't hers." Joe let the report fall closed and returned it to the desktop. "Why?"

Mr. Philbottom looked at him in disbelief, a wry smile on his face. "A fancy girl like that? Do you have to ask?"

Joe sighed. No, he didn't. He understood the assumptions—had made them himself about Meryl, about all women. But he knew now she deserved a place. A shot, a chance.

A chance he had never been keen on giving her. Was it any wonder she hadn't accepted his proposal of marriage? He had never fully believed in her, not as she deserved to have a man believe in her.

"In any case, I'm happy with what I've read," Mr. Philbottom rubbed his hands together and picked up a fountain pen. "I'm ready to sign a letter of

agreement, and I can virtually guarantee the board
will agree with me."

Mr. Philbottom was practically salivating over the
proposal. Indeed, it was generous, but Joe knew
with the proper investment of time and energy, the
projected income would far exceed this initial expense.

In fact, with the West continuing to grow, Westgate Division might become Atlantic-Southern's
crown jewel.

And he could be its president.

Mr. Philbottom scrawled his name on the top
page of the proposal, then pushed it toward Joe.
"Here you go." He held out the fountain pen.

Joe reached for it, then stopped and gave Mr.
Philbottom a hard look. "You're happy with the
new position she has carved out for you?"

Philbottom looked flustered. "Of course. It's
quite generous. Other buyers would probably toss
me out on my ear without a by-your-leave."

Joe nodded. He was satisfied that, even after the
change in ownership, Philbottom wouldn't attempt to block a change in management. "Then
you won't mind if I add another small requirement
to the deal."

Twenty-three

A tiny snowflake landed on the windowpane. For a brief moment, it displayed its intricate crystalline shape. A moment later, the snowflake had melted, leaving behind only a drop on the glass, and a memory.

Mesmerized, Meryl watched the snow fall, gradually growing heavier as dusk descended on Christmas Eve. Most of her sisters and their families had already arrived.

Their joy in each other had affected her more than she could have imagined. Hot tears had threatened, so she had retreated from the boisterous gathering downstairs to this window seat in the quiet of the music room.

"Honey? I'm thinking of baking some cookies. Gingersnaps or lady fingers. Would you like to help?"

Meryl turned from the window. Clara stood just inside the door, an apron tied at her waist. Despite the cook's large staff, Clara enjoyed taking part in the Christmas preparations too much to leave them to the servants.

Meryl smiled, though it felt forced and unnatural. "Not right now. Perhaps later."

Stepping closer, Clara sat down on the window seat beside her. "Christmastime is such a gay season. It's wonderful for bringing everyone together. Hannah and Lily, you and I, Father and Mother. The only one missing is Pauline." Their middle sister, living in India with her nobleman husband, had the farthest to travel.

"She might still make it."

"Oh, I hope so. Family is the best part of Christmas, don't you think? Remember when we were children, huddling under the covers, waiting for Father Christmas to bring us presents? It was years before I knew the truth of it," Clara said.

"I remember. I think I'm the one who ruined it for you."

"You were always the skeptic. But sometimes it's nice to believe."

Meryl grasped Clara's hand where it rested in her lap and gave it a squeeze. "I can't—" Her throat squeezed tight. She had to look away, or risk breaking down entirely. "That is, I don't think I would do your cookies any good."

Clara smiled softly. "Well, let me know if you change your mind. I'd love to have your help, even if you usually eat most of the dough." Standing, she left her alone.

After she left, Meryl found she was too restless to remain here, studying snowflakes. She rose and followed her sister.

On the second floor landing, the high-pitched laughter of her nieces and nephews echoed down the hall from the nursery at the end. Hannah and Lily had traveled from London with their nannies to mind their children. It sounded like the three oldest were playing a game of blind man's bluff.

Meryl envied their carefree enjoyment of a simple party game. She considered joining them, but knew she would only damp the children's spirits.

She continued down the stairs to the parlor floor. The cheerful voices of her older sisters and their husbands reached her from the large blue parlor, where the Christmas tree had been erected. Clara and the servants had spent the most time decorating the huge room. Boughs of fir and holly were draped along the mantel, and the family's crèche rested on a table along with pine-cone candles and cinnamon-scented potpourri.

Instead of joining them, Meryl turned in the other direction and crossed through a much smaller parlor toward the dining room, where her mother and Clara were overseeing the setting of the table. Her sister's words brought Meryl up short.

"Everyone is concerned about her." She hadn't realized she had been so transparent. She leaned against the wall by the door.

"If only Joseph would arrive," her mother said. "He could lift her spirits. He always could. They've always been so close."

She heard the clatter of cups being set down. "I don't know if Meryl sees it that way," Clara said. "She has always talked about him as if he were her enemy."

Her mother's rich laugh followed that com-

ment. "Enemy, ha! That's why she trailed him all
these years? Gone out of her way to tease him?
That's not the behavior of a girl toward a boy she
dislikes."

"I know," Clara said with a sigh. "I can't remember a single family outing where they weren't
spending most of their time together—even if it
was plotting some kind of torment for each other."

Meryl couldn't listen to any more talk about Joe.
No more fresh reminders of what she had thrown
away.

Perhaps she was spending too much time alone.
She needed to be with the others, be with her family, and stop thinking about him. If only her father
would come home from the office. Then she could
finally tell him her decision, and lift at least part of
the weight that rested on her chest.

She headed back down the hallway, then into
the blue parlor, the largest in the house. In the
corner, a fifteen-foot-tall fir glowed with candles
and handmade ornaments, many of which she had
made with meticulous care over the years.

She and her sisters had teased each other during their ornament making sessions. Bookish
Hannah's were always a little jarring, with clashing
colors. The stylish Lily had made the loveliest pas-
tel floral creations. Pauline, the adventurer, had
patience only for the sparsest of ornamentation—
a bit of lace, a few beads, and she was through.
With her warm heart, Clara had spent more time
advising the rest of them than making her own.
And Meryl's—hers had been as near to perfect as
she could make them, always copying a previously

existing pattern, desperate to prove she could do it "right."

Whatever right might mean.

"Meryl, come in!" Lily waved her into the room. She was sitting on a sofa beside her dapper husband, Alexander Drake, a high-ranking officer in the British Foreign Service.

"Oh, yes," said her sister Hannah, who sat beside her husband Benjamin. "We can always use more hands. Ben, I need more almonds."

The five adults were assembling baskets of treats for the needy, a task organized by Clara's husband, Stone. The two of them owned and managed the respected Carrington Charitable Homes in the city for homeless families, built as a testament to their father's civic pride and Clara and Stone's love. Meryl envied them their sense of purpose in life.

"Here. Take my place. I'm going to see what trouble Clara's baking in the kitchen." Stone rose and gestured to the wingback chair he'd been sitting in. "Your job is to make sure these four don't leave anything out of any basket, or put two of the same thing in one."

"Thank you." Meryl settled in, and immediately saw room for improvement in the general confusion. They were reaching across each other for items, and taking more time than they should filling each basket. "I hate to be intrusive, but this would work much more efficiently if we passed the baskets to each other, each of us putting in one or two specific items."

The four looked at her, then at each other. "Oh, that sounds smart," Hannah said.

"But you're almost finished, so it wouldn't make sense to change your methods now," Meryl said, sitting back with a sigh. It didn't really matter; the two couples were having a gay time of it despite the disorganization.

"Would you like to put together a basket?" Lily held out an empty one to her. Meryl shook her head. "If you don't mind, I'd like to watch. It's rather . . . entertaining."

The two couples began to laugh. Meryl envied the spirited fun her sisters took in their husbands' company, teasing each other while working together. She had once believed she might have that—with Joe.

"Do you realize that in two years it will be the turn of the century?" Alex said in his crisp British accent. All of her brothers-in-law were British. *And I fell in love with the boy next door,* she mused. Despite knowing it wasn't healthy, all of her thoughts returned to Joe.

"We'll have to throw a ball, the biggest party yet!" Lily said.

"Actually, that's not true," Benjamin said in his quiet, matter-of-fact tone. No doubt he had some complex rationale for his statement. The earl was always engaged in some scientific pursuit or other, along with his wife Hannah.

"Excuse me?" Alex said.

"The twentieth century won't begin until January first of the year nineteen-oh-one."

"That doesn't make sense," Hannah said.

"It most certainly does, my dear," he said, looking at his wife with affection. "Remember your basic math. The year nineteen hundred is the one-hundredth year of our current century."

Hannah smiled at him. "I believe you're right. My husband. He's so brilliant." She tucked her hand in his.

"Wait a minute," Alex protested, not ready to give in.

"But nineteen hundred will look so much nicer on the invitations," Lily added.

A good-natured argument ensued among all four of them. Stone, Clara, and her mother arrived in the middle of it, Clara taking Benjamin's side and Stone and Mrs. Carrington taking Alex's.

"Well, Meryl, it seems you're the tie-breaker," Alex said. "Which is the true start of the century?"

"Wait! We have to determine what's at stake," Lily said. "I propose the loser has to give something nice to his wife."

"I agree," Hannah said, nodding her dark-haired head. "If you lose, darling, you must buy me that new telescope I've been admiring." Leaning over, she kissed her husband on the cheek.

"I can't see why you need it," Benjamin said, but there was a teasing tone to his voice. Meryl had a hunch she might be receiving the telescope for Christmas.

"And if Alex loses," Lily said, "We're going to host all of you in London to celebrate the start of the New Year."

"It's not for two years, dear," Alex said. "Can you wait that long?"

"I didn't mean in the year nineteen hundred,

silly. I meant next month." There was never a bad time for a ball or a party in Lily and Alex's world.

Clara looked thoughtful. "The twentieth century. What will it bring?"

Stone said, "Our lives have already changed so much in the past few years. Men are so clever these days, like that Edison fellow inventing electricity."

"He didn't exactly invent it," Benjamin said. "He discovered how to tap a natural force. Like the recent discovery of radio waves."

"And X-rays," Hannah added.

"Telephones. Surely *they're* not a natural phenomenon," Lily said, teasing her brother-in-law. "I *adore* them."

"The motor car," her husband said with a grin. "I adore *them.*"

Lily laughed. "He thinks he's getting one for Christmas."

"You mean I'm not?" Alex looked crestfallen. Lily merely laughed.

"The vote for women," Meryl added in a soft voice. The others looked at her curiously. "It's just a matter of time before American men will get smart about it."

"Wait! Meryl, you haven't yet said when the new century starts," Hannah said. "Which date is it?"

"Well," she began, not wanting to commit to either date. She found it difficult to care either way. Regardless of the enthusiasm expressed by the others, she could only see a bleak future devoid of purpose. Devoid of Joe.

The doorbell rang, saving her from having to choose sides. Even though she knew their butler,

Edgar, would answer it, Meryl leapt to her feet. "I'll go see who it is," she volunteered, then hurried from the room.

Anxiety coiled inside her. Joe . . . What if their visitor was Joe? She had been afraid to ask anyone whether he intended to come. He rarely missed at least a short visit over Christmas. This year, his mother was in Europe and he was alone. He *had* to come. Even if he despised her, she hated to think he would be spending Christmas Eve alone.

I should have invited him, she thought as she walked down the foyer toward the front door. *I should have swallowed my pride and asked him to come.*

Before she reached the door, Edgar swung it open. Pauline and her husband Nate stood on the stoop, presents in their arms. Their Indian maid trailed behind them, her sari, under a cloak, even more colorful than the gifts she carried.

Joe wasn't coming. As much as Meryl loved seeing her sister, disappointment stabbed her. She shoved it aside and hurried to greet Pauline.

As soon as the three newcomers had given their outerwear to Edgar, Meryl saw that her sister was with child. "Pauline, you never said."

"I was afraid Mother would insist I not travel, but I wasn't about to miss Christmas."

"I'm so glad you're here. It's wonderful news about the baby. You look so beautiful." Meryl gave her a hug, tears pressing against her eyes. She was such an emotional wreck, she feared she would break down altogether. Through sheer force of will, she pulled herself together and smiled at them both. "You look wonderful. Both of you. And so happy."

"Finding the right man makes that easy," Pauline said lightly. "Don't look so sad, Meryl. I'm sure there's a man out there for you. You won't be left out forever."

Pauline's astuteness surprised Meryl. Perhaps part of her sadness was due to being the last remaining unwed sister. Still, if Joe hadn't broken her heart, she wouldn't have minded remaining single, at least for a while. "The others are in the blue room," she said.

"All of them? Hannah and Lily, too?"

"All but Father. He has yet to come home from the office."

"Wonderful! Everyone together again. I love Christmas." Their arms linked, Pauline and Nate headed down the hall, their Indian maid following.

Instead of accompanying them, Meryl hung back. She wasn't ready for yet another joyful reunion. Her spirit was exhausted, and at that moment all she wanted was to lie down. She was thinking of the best excuse to give her mother for retreating to her room, at least until dinnertime, when her father's voice intruded.

"There she is. Meryl, I would like a word with you."

Her father stepped through the front door. Again Edgar appeared and took his hat, umbrella, and snow-dusted coat. They shared their usual chitchat about his day. After a few minutes, Edgar left him alone with her.

Meryl sighed in relief. She had been longing to tell her father the decision she had made. His desire to talk with her would provide the perfect opportunity. "Shall we go to your office?" she asked.

"Yes, let's."

They entered Mr. Carrington's office, down the hall from the blue parlor. The staff had already lit a fire here, as they did every night before he came home. In its light, the surrounding mahogany paneling glowed with warmth.

Mr. Carrington lowered himself into his favorite chair by the fireplace. Meryl sat across from him in a matching leather-upholstered chair of forest green.

"It sounds like they all are enjoying themselves," he remarked, nodding in the general direction of the blue parlor. The noise level had increased sharply with Pauline and Nate's arrival—and their surprise announcement.

"Yes, they are," Meryl said.

He studied her closely. "Yet you aren't."

"I'm—I'm fine, Father."

"Pumpkin, you're lying to yourself. I'm not quite sure why you're so melancholy, considering your efforts in San Francisco were such a success."

"They were?" Of course they were. Joe could talk a stone into weeping.

"The purchase of Westgate was made final today, in fact. You realize Joe finished all but the last bit of paperwork last week, and returned to New York?"

"Yes, I heard." Everyone in the company heard,

and she—even filing papers in Mr. Smithson's office—had been no exception.

"I invited him to come celebrate with us tonight. *Insisted* he come, as a matter of fact." He studied her closely as he said this.

Meryl tried desperately to hide her reaction, the burst of glee she felt at this news followed by near desperation at how she might avoid him. She darted her gaze away, then steeled herself with purpose and looked straight at her father. "You *will* make him president, won't you? He has earned it."

Her father's eyes widened in surprise. "But, Pumpkin, isn't that the position you wanted?"

"I haven't earned it. I don't know what Joe told you. Or didn't tell you. But I failed. We did travel there together, but not as colleagues. We were adversaries. We had an agreement—whoever could secure the Westgate purchase would be named president. That person is Joe, not I. In fact, when I tried, I failed miserably. Mr. Philbottom wouldn't even give me the time of day." She chewed her lip, then shook her head. "No, I take that back, he would give me that. Wanted me to attend his daughter's soirée. He had no other use for me or my proposal."

"You're wrong, Pumpkin." Leaning forward, he clasped her hands between his large ones. "That proposal you wrote is exactly what the Westgate board agreed to, with only one small change."

"They did? I—I didn't know. I assumed Joe—"

"Joe told me he had never read such a well-researched and presented proposal. He was quite impressed."

Meryl felt a flicker of pride that he thought so well of her work. "Perhaps so, but he is the one who negotiated the deal. He is the one who secured the Westgate board's agreement, not I. I was ineffectual. Worse than that, I could have ruined everything merely by being there, and being a woman."

Now was the time, she told herself. The time to put an end to a silly girlhood dream and accept the reality of who and what she was. "In fact, father, that is why I am no longer interested in the position, or in any position with Atlantic-Southern. I am leaving the company. I've come to realize that I'm not cut out for business."

"Not cut out—" Her father looked at her, a stunned expression on his face. "I can't believe I'm hearing this. After your studies, after all of your dreams. I know you imagined being my successor one day. I have to admit it would be unconventional, but hardly unheard of. Besides, you're my *daughter*. I would be proud to have you follow in my footsteps."

This time, Meryl lost her battle to keep her tears in check. For so long she had dreamed of hearing those words pass her father's lips. Now that it was happening, she could hardly believe it. Still, it changed nothing. Without the heart for the business, she would only bring the company to ruin. "Father, I can't," she said through trembling lips. "I just can't. I'm sorry, but it's no longer in me."

"There, there." Her father pulled out a handkerchief and began dabbing at her cheeks, just as he had when she was a little girl. "Pumpkin, tell me. What has changed?"

Me. Him. Everything. "I can't—I can't say."

He tucked the damp handkerchief into her palm and she began to blot her own tears. A confident tone filled his voice. "I think you may change your mind. In fact—" He leaned close and lowered his voice.

Before he said two words, Pauline burst into the office. "Meryl, Father. Joe is here."

Twenty-four

Meryl trailed behind her father to the blue room, her stomach in knots. In lively spirits, her family stood about, drinking eggnog and swapping tales with Pauline, Nate, and now Joe.

Meryl hesitated inside the doorway. From this vantage point, she feasted her gaze on the man she secretly loved. He looked so good—even more delicious than marzipan.

His well-tailored suit enhanced his lean, well-built physique. A flash of heat filled her as she recalled how that body appeared *sans* clothing. Considering the emotional distance between them now, she could hardly believe their illicit union had really happened. Except for the ring which now hung on a chain around her neck inside her blouse. The weight of it was a constant reminder of what she had thrown away.

Joe glanced past his hosts toward the door, then looked again. His words died mid-sentence. "Meryl." He took a step toward her.

"Meryl, don't just stand there. Come over here," Clara said. "You remember Joe, don't you?" she asked, a smile playing on her lips. "The fellow you ran off with on Thanksgiving Day?"

"I swear, I thought they'd eloped," her mother said. "Until Meryl returned without him. To think she actually traveled to the other side of the country just to prove a point about women in business!"

Meryl only half heard the discussion. Her gaze was snagged by Joe's. He wouldn't look away from her, and she couldn't bring herself to stop gazing at him. She realized then that she no longer cared if they knew, if all of them knew, that she loved this man.

"Joe. You came." The muted words slid from her throat.

"I did, yes. I was hoping . . ."

Resolve filled her. "I need to talk to you. Come." Reaching out, she grasped his hand and began to pull him toward the doorway.

He followed willingly enough, to her relief. She wouldn't have blamed him if he had dug in his heels and refused to have anything to do with her. But there were things she needed to say to him. Lacking direction in the rest of her life, she was sure at least of her need to speak to him.

She led him down the hall to the conservatory at the back of the house. Here, despite the light snow falling outside, greenhouse plants grew in verdant abundance.

She led him to a stone bench and sat beside him. That's when she realized he held something in his hand, a long narrow box. "You should have given your gift to my mother," she said.

"It's not for your parents. It's for you."

A burst of warmth filled her heart, a memory of a long-ago Christmas when she'd been fifteen—and first realized she loved him. Just like the day he'd given her that pendant, she found it hard to understand why he would single her out for his favor. "Me? Why?"

He glanced at his feet, but then returned his gaze to meet hers. "Why not open it and see?" He held it out to her.

Reluctantly, she accepted it. "This wasn't necessary," she said, feeling unbalanced by this unexpected kindness. "I can't imagine why you would be giving me gifts, after everything that happened—everything I did."

His grave expression unsettled her. "Open it and see."

Meryl could see that he wasn't going to talk to her until she dealt with the gift, so she removed the red ribbon and opened the box. Inside, nestled in a bed of tissue paper, was a triangle-shaped piece of polished walnut. It was the size and shape of nameplates businessmen put on their desks. She lifted it from the paper and read,

"MERYL CARRINGTON, PRESIDENT, WESTGATE DIVISION."

Meryl burst into tears. While his belief in her filled her with joy, another side of her ached that he had given her such an impersonal gift. His acknowledgment that she was his equal in business left her with one certainty—he had given up any romantic thoughts of her.

"I have no doubt that you will prove yourself a worthy successor to your father," Joe said, his voice tight. "Because of that, I'm leaving Atlantic-Southern."

"What?" Meryl whipped her gaze to his, the nameplate forgotten.

"I've accepted an offer to serve as vice president of a steel company in Pittsburgh."

"Pittsburgh! But—"

"It makes sense, Meryl. Who knows? Maybe we'll work together someday. I can supply the steel to your ever-expanding railroad empire."

"No. No, you can't."

He frowned. "I don't see why—"

"You don't understand. I just asked father to name *you* president of the Westgate Division. This is a kind gesture, Joe," she said lifting the nameplate. "But we both know it's a lie."

He rose unsteadily to his feet. Turning to face her, he crossed his arms. "I swear, Meryl, the day I understand you is the day my troubles vanish. Isn't this what you wanted all along?" He gestured toward the nameplate.

"I did, yes, but that doesn't mean I have earned it. You're the one who successfully negotiated the sale. You know you are. All I did was write a paper—"

He threw up his hands. "By God, Meryl, you're a business genius, don't you see that? I couldn't have done better if I had spent weeks at the task, and even then I would have left out something important that would have had to have been addressed."

Frustration filled her. "What good is that if I can't follow through in the negotiations? No good, that's what."

"You can hire people to do that for you."

"And you can hire people to write proposals for you." Her cool gaze met his, and his jaw tightened. "So, we're at an impasse. You're not taking the job, and neither am I."

"It's too late. You have to take it."

"What do you mean?"

"When I met with Mr. Philbottom, I had that requirement added to the agreement. You're to be named president or the deal is off."

"But Father said the purchase was finished today!"

"And we both assumed you would be ecstatic having finally gotten what you wanted all along."

She swallowed hard. "So, I'm to move to San Francisco. And you're moving to Pittsburgh." She hadn't realized the prospect of being apart from Joe could hurt worse than it already did. But now she knew the truth. He wasn't bothered at all by leaving her. He even arranged it!

Disappointment stabbed at her, a sharp pain in her heart. To her dismay, she realized that, deep in her heart, she had pinned far too much hope on this Christmastime meeting. She had secretly hoped Joe would take one look at her, forgive her for everything, and want her back. She had actually imagined he might still care for her. "So, I'm to be president." The words should thrill her. But her future felt so empty without Joe in her life.

"Yes. I would have thought you would be happy about it."

"Is this what you want?" She peered closely at

him, desperate to find some indication he still felt
something for her.

Moisture filled his eyes. "I want you to be happy.
I hope now, Meryl, you will be." Stepping back, he
straightened his jacket. "I won't overstay my welcome. I know my being here is bound to make you
uncomfortable. Even if it doesn't affect you, it's
hard for me to . . ." His words died, and a trace of
pain flitted across his face.

"To what?" That flash of pain set her nerves on
edge. Meryl longed to know what he was thinking,
about her. About them.

"To see you. Goodbye, Meryl. I hope your career
gives you every happiness." Turning away, he
pushed through the conservatory door and into
the hall.

Meryl stared at the nameplate in her hand, the
first step in her dream of inheriting the company.
Her first success.

Yet she felt so utterly miserable. "No."

Just as with Mr. Philbottom, she hadn't really
tried to convince Joe to take her back. She was giving in so easily. Yet perhaps it wasn't too late to
negotiate with him, if she hurried.

Jumping to her feet, she pushed through the
door and dashed after him.

He was nowhere to be seen. Meryl hurried past
the blue parlor toward the front door, then came
up short when she heard his voice coming from
the blue parlor. *Of course. He was saying goodbye to
her family.*

She heard Clara protest that he was leaving too

soon, a sentiment echoed by her mother. Meryl didn't wait for him to escape them.

She swept through the open doorway and crossed to where he stood near the Christmas tree. Stopping squarely before him, she announced, "You're not leaving, Joe. Not like this."

"Meryl, I can't stay. Not with . . ." He hesitated, glancing at her family, who watched with interest. "Everything."

"Wait." She pressed her hand against his chest, freezing him in place. "I want to show you something." Lifting her hands, she undid the topmost button on her blouse. His eyes widened. Reaching inside her collar, she grasped the chain around her neck and withdrew it. The engagement ring dangled there, its facets glinting in the light from the Christmas tree.

Behind her, her mother gasped. Meryl slid the ring from the chain.

Joe frowned. "I told you to keep it," he muttered.

"He asked you to marry him?" Pauline asked. "I knew it! I knew you would end up together."

Meryl ignored her boisterous sister. All she saw was Joe, standing before her, her one chance at happiness. Now wasn't the time for pride. "I made a mistake, Joe. An awful mistake. I was afraid you didn't believe I could do it. So I pulled away from you, when I should have trusted you. Now . . ." Her eyes explored his. Seeing the warmth emanating from them, she found the strength to continue. "Now, Joseph, I realize the truth. Being with you doesn't diminish me. It makes me a better person.

I love you and I want to be with you, more than anything in the world. Even if you don't love me back."

His eyes widened in disbelief. His stunned expression melted into one of joy. "Don't love you? Meryl, I've always loved you. It just took a very interesting train journey for me to realize it."

Joy filled Meryl's heart, making her believe anything might be possible. Anything at all. "Are you still willing to marry me? Because I want to marry you. More than anything. Please say yes."

"She's asking *him* to marry *her*," her mother whispered so everyone could hear. "I've never seen the like."

He didn't hesitate to answer, his reply short yet firm. "Yes." Lifting her hand, he extracted the ring and slipped it on her finger.

Then, to Meryl's overwhelming delight, he pulled her into the comfort and pleasure of his embrace. Meryl—who prided herself on never crying—once again found tears on her cheeks as she buried her face against his shoulder. "I've been absolutely miserable without you around to pester me," she choked out. Her family laughed.

"So have I." Joe pulled back and lifted her chin. "I love you, Meryl. Even when you're driving me crazy. There's still one problem, though."

Please, no more obstacles. Not now, she silently pleaded. Yet whatever he wanted, whatever requirement he had, she felt ready to comply. "What is that?"

"Who is going to be president of the Westgate Division?"

Did it even matter anymore? Yet her father was relying on her. On them. The answer came then, clear as day. "I propose a merger. We're best when we work together. We'll run the company together."

He smiled broadly. "Again you have identified a problem and determined a sensible solution. You have a deal." He extended his hand, but instead of shaking it, Meryl threw her arms around his neck and kissed him full on the lips.

The kiss felt like coming home. She belonged with this man as she never could with another. And he belonged with her.

The sound of applause pulled Meryl from her joyful haze. Forcing herself to separate from Joe, she glanced around at their avid audience, a blush tingeing her cheeks.

"I knew that mistletoe would work eventually," Clara said, her eyes sliding to a spot above their heads. Meryl craned her neck. Sure enough, in her flurry of decorating, Clara had suspended mistletoe from the ceiling—and not just above her head. Sprigs of it had been hung every five feet. "Clara, you've gone overboard."

"Not at all. I was praying it would work its magic, and it did."

"I'll say." Meryl smiled up at her husband-to-be and future business partner. "But how did you know magic needed to be worked?"

Clara shrugged, as if the answer was obvious. "The way you've been dragging your tail, I knew you were suffering from a wounded heart. And I knew it had to be Joe."

She had been that transparent? "How?"

"For once, you never talked about him. Besides, you've always been infatuated with him."

"I knew it!" Joe said, smiling victoriously.

Meryl gave him a mock frown. "Don't start thinking too highly of yourself, mister."

In response, he leaned close and whispered an intimacy in her ear that made her blush to the roots of her hair.

"I can't believe it! I simply cannot believe it!" Her mother's exclamation drew the eyes of everyone in the room. Mrs. Carrington grasped her husband's hand. "She's the last one, Richard. And she'll be well married, even if I had almost nothing to do with it this time."

Meryl's sisters exchanged glances. Despite their mother's planning and plotting, virtually none of them had ended up with a man chosen by their mother.

"Yes, dear, she couldn't have done better if you had chosen the young man," her father agreed with a smile. He crossed to Joe and slapped him on the back. "Welcome to the family, son. Though it feels as if you are already a part of us."

After a round of excited congratulations, Mrs. Carrington gasped. Again everyone looked at the heart and soul of the family. "Mother, what is it?" Meryl asked, terrified that some unforeseen obstacle might yet prevent her dreams from coming true.

"Merely that it struck me," her mother said, her voice sounding small and lost. She looked up at them with large eyes. "With all five of my daughters married, however shall I spend my time?"

Historical Romance from
Jo Ann Ferguson